Praise for *Death and the Girl Next Door*

"Only Darynda Jones could make the Angel of Death crush-worthy! Wickedly sharp with brilliant wit, *Death and the Girl Next Door* will leave you craving more!"   —Lara Chapman, author of *Flawless*

"Outrageously funny, sinfully sexy, with a cast of characters that steals your heart from the very first page . . . I loved this book!"
—Inara Scott, author of the Delcroix Academy series

"Snapping with sarcasm and a pitch-perfect voice, *Death and the Girl Next Door* brings Darynda Jones's signature humor and supernatural sass to Riley High. Trust me, there's nothing grim about this reaper!"   —Roxanne St. Claire, *New York Times* bestselling author of *Don't You Wish*

"*Death and the Girl Next Door* is unputdownable. Darynda Jones breathes fresh life into the Young Adult genre with exciting twists to legends we only think we understand and edgy, compelling characters you can't help but care about."
—Gwen Hayes, author of *Falling Under*

"*Death and the Girl Next Door* delivers a smokin' hot story and a guy to die for. Darynda Jones gives one candy-smacking, awesome read that won't let you go until the end."
—Shea Berkley, author of *The Marked Son*

"I loved this book. *Death and the Girl Next Door* is equal parts funny, thrilling, and hot. Teens will fall hard for the hero, an original and exciting take on the Angel of Death."
—Maureen McGowan, author of the Twisted Tales series

death and the girl next door

death and the girl next door

DARYNDA JONES

 ST. MARTIN'S GRIFFIN ✹ NEW YORK

DEATH AND THE GIRL NEXT DOOR. Copyright © 2012 by Darynda Jones. All rights reserved. Printed in the United States of America. For information, address St. Martin's Press, 175 Fifth Avenue, New York, N.Y. 10010.

www.stmartins.com

Design by Anna Gorovoy

Library of Congress Cataloging-in-Publication Data

Jones, Darynda.
    Death and the girl next door / Darynda Jones. — 1st ed.
        p. cm.
    ISBN 978-0-312-62520-7 (pbk.)
    ISBN 978-1-250-01722-2 (e-book)
    1. Teenage girls—Fiction.   2. Orphans—Fiction.   3. Stalking—
Fiction.   4. Paranormal romance stories, American.   I. Title.
    PS3610.O6236D43 2012
    813'.6—dc23

                                                    2012026408

First Edition: October 2012

10   9   8   7   6   5   4   3   2   1

For my gorgeous nieces and nephews:

Maxwell Scott (Mad Max)
Ashlee Duarte (Ashee Pot Pie)
Sydnee Scott (Master of the Universe)
Mitchell Scott (the Terminator)
Stephen Duarte (Stevie D)
Alex Eakins (Alexander the Great)
ZiZi Eakins (the Zi Guy)
and Rhia Eakins (the Two-Foot Tornado),

whose parents are paying for their raising
with a steep variable interest rate.
And surcharges.

ACKNOWLEDGMENTS

First and foremost, I must thank my *uh-mazing* agent, Alexandra Machinist, who proves that nuclear powerhouses can come in tiny packages. And to my *spectacular* editor, Jen Enderlin. Thank you so much for taking a chance on this series!

Thank you to everyone at St. Martin's Press who helped with this project. And to Eli Torres, copy editor extraordinaire, I hereby promise to curb my use of the word *glare* from this moment forward. And my use of the word *moment*.

Thank you to Nikki Hyatt for sitting next to me with a cattle prod while I wrote the first version of this book so many years ago. Your skill with torturous objects is awe-inspiring. Thanks for the nudges.

Thank you to my early readers: Nikki, Tammy, Kit, Dan Dan, Kiki, DD, Liz, Sienna, and Ashlee, aka my Ashee Pot Pie.

Thank you to Ashlee and Sydnee, who are nieces, yes, but from two different families, for the use of their names. So, not twins as this book would suggest, but gorgeous girls all the way. And to Lorelei King for letting me steal her name as well. Hope you're getting along okay without it. Thanks for breathing life into my characters.

Thank you to my family for being so enthusiastic about my writing. You make my world go 'round.

Thank you to my incredible assistant, Danielle "Dan Dan" Swopes. You are the bomb.

Thank you *soooo* much to the fantastic authors who offered their valuable time to read this work and give quotes: P. C. Cast, Roxanne St. Clair, Shea Berkley, Gwen Hayes, Tera Lynn Childs, Inara Scott, Maureen McGowan, Lara Chapman, and Rachel Hawthorne/Lorraine Heath. Thank you, thank you, thank you!

Thank you to Liz Bemis and the talented team at Bemis Promotions for all the great work.

And a very special thank-you goes out to Sienna Condy for literally naming this book! I loved the title the moment I heard it. It's cute, clever, and captivating. Much like you.

A gigantic thank-you to my chapter mates, the LERA-lites, my agency siblings whom I've grown up with, my St. Martin's sisters-in-arms, and the lovely ladies of the Ruby Slippered Sisterhood. Astonishing creatures, one and all.

And last but never ever least, a huge, heartfelt thank-you to you, the reader, without whom none of this would be possible. Thank you for making my dreams come true.

death and the girl next door

TRAITOR

The small town of Riley's Switch, New Mexico, had only one coffeehouse, so that's where I sat with my two best friends, knowing beyond a shadow of a doubt that only two of us would make it out of there alive. Though I did tend to exaggerate.

The fresh scent of pine from the surrounding mountains, which mingled with the rich aroma of coffee, lingered forgotten. In its place was a tense silence. It thickened the air around us. Emotions soared and rage simmered as I glowered at the traitor sitting across from me, waiting for him to flinch, to cower under my scrutiny. I would make his life a living heck if it were the last thing I did. Mostly because I wasn't allowed to use the word *Hell*, being the granddaughter of a pastor and all. Otherwise, Casey Niyol Blue-Spider, aka *the Glitch*, would be toast.

"I swear, Lorelei," he said, caving at last as a telling bead of sweat trickled down his temple, "I didn't take it." He shifted nervously in his seat and scanned the Java Loft, most likely to see if anyone was paying attention to the unscrupulous activities going on right under their noses. Since we were the only patrons in the place, probably not. "And even if I did, and I'm not saying I did," he added, jabbing an index finger toward me, "who the heck cares?"

I lowered my voice, controlled the tone and inflection of every word, every syllable, striving to make myself sound menacing. I took up a mere five feet of vertical air space, so menacing was not always easy for me to accomplish. Slipping into a cryptic grin, I said, "You realize the minute I touch your hand, I'll know the truth."

His gaze darted to the hand he'd wrapped around his whipped almond toffee cappuccino with nonfat milk, and he jerked it back out of my reach. His hand. Not the whipped almond toffee cappuccino with nonfat milk.

My best friend Brooklyn leaned in to me and whispered, "You know he accidentally deleted seventeen songs off your classic rock playlist, right? And he used your toothbrush once without asking." She glared at him, the contempt in her eyes undeniable. "I say make the traitor squirm."

Glitch's jaw tightened, and I could sense his inevitable defeat like a dog senses fear.

"Tag-teaming?" he asked, indignant. "Isn't that a little unsportsmanlike?"

"Not for a couple of heartless dames like us," Brooklyn said.

I turned to her with a smile. "Oh, my god, I love it when you talk pulp-fiction detective."

"I know, right?" she said, her dark skin and brown eyes a picture of joy.

Brooke and I met when we threw down in the third grade. By the end of my first and only catfight, I had a few missing hairs, a broken fingernail, and a new best friend. And we were practically twins. If not for the fact that she had long sable hair, chestnut skin, and light brown eyes, and I had curly auburn hair, pasty white skin, and eyes the bizarre color of chimney smoke, people would never be able to tell us apart. Probably because we were both exactly five feet tall. Not a centimeter more. Not a centimeter less. It was eerie.

In choreographed unison, we refocused on the slimeball sitting across from us.

"Spill," she said.

"Okay, sheesh." He pushed back his cappuccino and folded his arms over his chest, a defensive gesture that only added fuel to my suspicions. "I admit it. I had a copy of the test beforehand, but I didn't steal it."

"I knew you cheated." I reached across the table and whacked him on the arm. Thankfully, Glitch wasn't much bigger than either of us, so the punch quite possibly registered somewhere deep in the scary depths of his boy mind. Or that was my hope, anyway. "You blew the curve, Glitch."

Guilt washed over him. I could tell by the thin line of his lips, the chin tucked in shame.

"You're such a wiener," Brooklyn said. "I really needed those extra points."

"And where on planet Earth did you get a copy of the test?" I had to admit, I was more than a little astonished. And a tad jealous.

He shook his head. "No way. I'm not giving up my source. And besides, you both got B's. It's not like you failed the stupid thing."

Brooklyn reached over, curled a fist into his T-shirt, and pulled him forward until their noses were mere inches apart. "Clearly you do not understand the innate intricacies and often illogical drives of an A freak." She let go, disgusted. "I hate your guts."

"No, you don't." He took a swig of his cappuccino, unconcerned.

Like Brooklyn, Glitch was a bona fide child of two nations, with dark, coppery skin from his Native American father and hazel green eyes, compliments of his Irish-American mother. And thanks to a compromise between the two, he had the coolest name on earth: Casey Niyol Blue-Spider. The mix of ethnicities gave him a rich, enigmatic attraction. Though he hardly needed to, he kept his short black hair spiked with blond highlights in an attempt to make himself seem wild and unpredictable, which was always good for a laugh. Glitch was about as wild and unpredictable as a carrot stick. Though he did have an unnatural fear of turtles that was interesting.

"You're just intimidated by my manly physique."

Brooke snorted. "This coming from a boy who's barely tall enough to get on the roller coaster at the state fair without a permission slip from his parents."

His grin took on an evil luster. "Least I get on, short pants."

"Oh yeah? Well, at least I wasn't voted most likely to acquire gainful employment as Santa's elf."

"Guys, guys," I said, holding up my hands for a cease-fire. "We can't fling short jokes at each other when we're all short. It's just not effective."

"That's true," Brooklyn said in disappointment.

"No, it's not. I am three, count them, three"—he held up three fingers for us to count—"inches taller than the likes of you two. I can't believe I'm willing to be seen in public with either of you."

"Glitch," Brooklyn said, a warning edge in her voice, "I will stab you in the face if you ever speak to me again."

He squinted at her, completely unmoved, then turned to me and asked, "So, did your grandmother get her computer running?"

"No. You're just going to have to stop by sometime and fix it."

"Cool." He smiled in anticipation. "What's for dinner tonight?"

I knew he'd do that. Brooke had already invited herself over, claiming she needed to upload her assignment because the Internet at her house was down. Glitch would come over, fix my grandmother's computer in about ten minutes, and then my two best friends would spend the rest of the evening keeping me company.

It was the same every year. For a week before until a week after the anniversary of my parents' disappearance, they spent almost every waking moment with me, watching over me, seeing to my every need. They were amazing. I'm not sure what they thought I would do if left alone—I'd never been particularly suicidal—but they were the dearest friends a girl could ask for. The air seemed to turn dreary this time of year, thick and heavy, so having them around did help. And I totally loved being waited on hand and foot, so naturally I milked it for all it was worth.

The bell jingled, announcing a new customer before I could answer Glitch, but I was busy prying my fingers apart anyway. I'd spilled mocha cappuccino over them—*hot* mocha cappuccino—when I tried to add a sprinkle of cinnamon earlier, and few things were more disturbing than sticky fingers. Forest fires, perhaps. And people who claimed to have been abducted by aliens.

"I have to wash my hands before we go."

"Okay." Brooklyn rummaged through her bag and pulled out her phone for a quick check as I scooted out of the booth, grateful for the excuse. For some reason, the fact that my parents had been gone almost ten years exactly, like some kind of milestone anniversary, had me more melancholy than usual. "I'll keep an eye on the traitor," Brooke continued, "until we can decide what to do with him."

"Do you need ideas?" Glitch asked, turning feisty. "I know lots of things you could do to me."

"Do any of them involve piano wire and a razor blade?"

I laughed to myself and headed toward the back of our favorite and pretty much only hangout. It sat a mere block from our alma mater, Riley High, and we practically lived in our corner booth. I ducked past the snack counter and into a very dark back hall. Judging by the boxes lining the narrow passage, I'd be taking my life into my hands if I risked a journey to the little *señorita*'s room without illumination, so I ran my hand along a paneled wall. Where would I be if I were a light switch? Just as the tips of my fingers found the switch, a silhouette stepped out of the shadows and brushed past me. I startled with a gasp.

"Excuse me," I said, placing a hand over my heart.

"Sorry." The guy paused slightly before continuing on his way, and in that instant, I saw the makings of utter perfection: a long arm with shadowy curves that dipped around the fluid lines of muscle; a tall, wide shoulder; dark hair that curled playfully over an ear and led to a strong, masculine jaw. Something inside me lurched, craving a closer look at his face, but he walked by too fast and the hall was too dark for me to catch anything else.

After a couple of seconds, I realized my hand had brushed against his arm. It was enough to send a vision crashing into me, like the flash of a nuclear bomb, bright and unforgiving. Tamping down my surprise—I hadn't had a vision in a very long time—I pressed shaking fingers to my forehead to wait out the familiar storm, to see what treasures would wash ashore in the aftermath.

Yet the things I saw were unreal, impossible, and certainly not of this world: A desolate landscape lay before me with scorched clouds and a roiling, violet sky. The air was stagnant and so impossibly thick, breathing it took effort. Then I heard the clanging of metal. I turned to watch in horror as a being, a boy of no more than sixteen or seventeen, fierce and somehow not quite human, struggled with a dark, monstrous beast. The boy's arms corded as tendon and muscle strained against the weight of the sword he wielded. He slashed again and again, but the monster was fast, with razorlike talons and sharp, gleaming teeth, and the boy knew what those teeth felt like when they sank into flesh, knew the blinding pain that accompanied defeat. But he also knew the power he himself wielded, the raw strength that saturated every molecule of his body.

Another herculean effort landed a thrust in the monster's shoulder and continued through its thick chest. The monster sank under the boy's sword with a guttural scream. The boy looked on while the beast writhed in pain, watched it grow still as the life drained out of it, and somewhere in the back of the boy's mind, he allowed himself to register the burning of his lungs as he struggled to fill them with air.

Blood trickled between his fingers, down the length of his blade, and dripped to the powdery earth beneath his feet. I followed the trail of blood up to three huge gashes across his chest. Evidently three of the monster's claws had met their mark, laying the flesh of its enemy open. I gasped and covered my mouth with both hands as the boy spun toward me, sword at the ready. Squinting against the low sun, I could almost make out his features, but the vision evaporated before I got the chance. A heartbeat later, I was back in the dark hallway, gasping for air, one palm pressed against my temple, the other against the wall for balance.

I squeezed my eyes shut, fought the memory of the vision, the fear that summoned the taste of bile in the back of my throat, the feel of blood dripping down the boy's arm.

Ever since I could remember, I had a tendency to see random flashes of inconsequential situations in my head, which, by definition, could point to any number of debilitating diseases. I wasn't psychic or anything. I couldn't conjure visions whenever I wanted. Images just seemed to crystallize in my mind out of nowhere, and at the most inopportune times too, shimmering like reflections off water. Sometimes they were just flashes of nonsense, glimpses of the impossible, like a rip in the afternoon sky that let night seep through. Nothing ever came of those.

But sometimes the visions either had been or would be, as though I could see into both the past and the future. Like the one time I accidentally saw into the past after touching my grandfather's hand. He had been a thousand miles away, and I caught a glimpse of the first time he laid eyes on Grandma. She'd tucked a strand of hair behind her ear as she walked to class with her friends, only to have the wind toss it back across her face. She laughed and tried again, and I felt the tug of interest in Grandpa the minute it hit him.

The ability rocked, I admit. But never in my life had I seen anything with so much punch, so much texture.

I hurried to the bathroom and splashed cold water on my face. Clearly that had been one of those flashes of nonsense. But it seemed so real. I could feel the weight of the air, the depletion of the boy's energy as he fought, his limbs shaking from exertion and from adrenaline as it pumped through his powerful body.

I blinked and forced myself back to the present, forced myself to calm. Stepping back into the hall, I glanced around in search of the dark-headed boy, to no avail. Disappointment washed over me. For one thing, I wanted a better look. For another, I wanted a better look. The first was for obvious girl reasons. Those arms. That jaw. Who could blame me? The second was because of what I'd just seen. Surely my vision was metaphorical in some way. Scorched clouds in violet skies didn't exist. And thankfully, neither did that beast.

I must've been in the restroom longer than I'd thought. Brooke and Glitch were waiting for me outside. But I couldn't get those images out of my head. I'd never seen anything like them in my life.

As I grabbed my backpack with a shaking hand, I sensed someone watching. I turned to see Cameron Lusk sitting in a booth, his shoulder-length blond hair visible even in the shadowy corner. Though we lived in a small town and Cameron and I were in the same sophomore class, we hadn't spoken in forever. He was more the loner type, scowling at anyone who tried to communicate with him. But still, he was right there. It would be rude of me not to acknowledge his surly existence.

"Hey, Cameron," I said as I fished a tip out of my bag and turned back to our table.

"Your friends already left a tip," the barista said from behind the counter. "See you tomorrow." She grinned at me, knowing I'd be back. If I remembered correctly, she'd graduated a couple of years earlier and had gone off to college in Albuquerque. Must not have worked out, since she was now a barista in a small-town coffee shop. Or it worked out perfectly, and she'd gone to college to become a barista in a small-town coffee shop. Hard to imagine, but okay.

"See ya," I said before glancing at Cameron again. He took the whole brooding thing way too seriously. The glare he'd graced me with could have frozen heck itself. "See you tomorrow, Cameron."

He lifted a finger in acknowledgment. I felt oddly honored.

"What took you so long?" Brooklyn asked as I stepped into the late-afternoon sun. New Mexico was nothing if not sunny, even where we lived in the Manzano Mountains.

"Did you see that boy?" I asked, scanning the street.

"Cameron?" Brooklyn asked. If the distaste wasn't clear in her tone, the wrinkling of her nose would have said it all.

"No, a dark-haired boy, tall and really, really muscular."

Brooklyn jumped to attention and joined me in the search, turning every which way. "What boy? I didn't see a boy. Especially not a tall, dark, and muscular one."

Glitch peered in through the coffee shop window. "I didn't see anyone either. Maybe you imagined him."

"I had a vision," I said breathlessly, and two sets of eyes widened on me. I knew we'd spend the rest of the evening talking about what I'd seen. If my vision was even remotely authentic, something very dreadful was about to happen to that boy.

SUPERNOVA

Three days later, I found myself struggling against both melancholy and euphoria. But if I'd known my day was going to suck like a turbo-powered Hoover, I totally would've faked the flu and stayed home. Or chicken pox. Or malaria. Instead, I'd walked to school like it was any other day. Like my heart wasn't breaking. Like my head wasn't reeling and my feet weren't weighted down by the sudden and tragic onset of clinical depression, making each breath a trial, each step a struggle. I totally needed a car.

I walked along Main Street, past trees and small businesses geared more toward tourists than locals, until my high school

came into sight. Riley High was the latest and greatest achieve-
ment of the Riley's Switch Board of Education. It was sparkling
and new with stone arches that would've looked more at home
in an architectural magazine than in a small New Mexico town.
Heavy plate-glass windows lined the front with arched pillars at
the entrance. The whole thing was topped off with a scarlet dome,
like a castle tucked into the mountainside. Several outbuildings
encircled the school, including the gym, the agricultural and
construction shops, and the cafeteria. I had to admit, when I
started here my freshman year, the place intimidated me more
than a little. But I adjusted quickly when I realized how much
the boys had grown over the summer. High school was a grand
place to be.

I spotted Brooklyn in the sea of students rushing to class and
zigzagged toward her. Hugging my notebook to my chest, I took
turns dodging a group of wrestlers practicing their chosen profession in the hallway and barely escaping with my life when a line-
backer decided to plunge through the crush of bodies.

Who knew high school could be so dangerous?

Brooklyn was busy dialing the combination on her locker.
She glanced at me between spins. "Hey, you."

"Hey." I leaned against the wall of bright red lockers and
asked, "Do you remember what today is?"

She stopped midspin, her dark visage puckering in soft admonishment. "Of course I do. How could I not?"

I shrugged and glanced down. It was weird. I figured the tenth
anniversary of my parents' disappearance would be excruciating.
Like if I'd broken a leg or gotten a really bad paper cut. Instead,
the pain in my chest was more like a whisper bouncing off the
walls of an empty cavern. I just woke up and they were still gone.
Like they had been every other morning for the last ten years.

At first their absence had seemed like a dream, but the depth of despair my grandparents fell into convinced me they were really gone. And everyone asked me questions. What happened? What were we doing there? What did I see? Nothing, I would tell them. Again and again, nothing. I didn't understand why they were asking me questions I couldn't possibly have the answers to, but they said I'd been with my parents when they disappeared. The police found me unconscious beside our car at the old Pueblo ruins outside of Riley's Switch. I didn't remember being there. I just remembered waking up in the hospital days later, my body so heavy, I could barely move, my lungs so thick, I could barely breathe. And no one had any explanation as to why.

Then came the questions. Over and over until my grandparents, in their state of utter bereavement, ordered the authorities to stop and took me home to grieve. I found out later that the entire town had helped look for my parents. Search parties scouted for days, hunted for clues. Even the FBI showed up, but nothing was ever found. Not a single shred of evidence. As cliché as it sounded, they literally vanished without a trace.

The official report stated that my parents had wandered off and lost their way back. But they would never have done that. They would never have left me. And yet, because there was no evidence of foul play, the investigation lasted only a couple of weeks.

And I, the only one who could offer any explanation, could remember nothing. The guilt of that fact weighed on me more and more every year, like a jagged boulder in my chest that grew with each passing moment.

I'd never told anyone about the guilt except for Brooke.

Her eyes filled with sympathy. "Why didn't you stay home?"

"And wallow in a deep pit of despair alone when I could force you to wallow with me? No, thank you."

She nodded. "That's a good point. I'm pretty good at wallowing."

"And," I said, withdrawing inside myself just a little, "I have something awful to confess."

"Yeah?" Intrigue scooted her closer. "How awful?"

I hugged my notebook tighter and said, "I keep thinking about that boy from the Java Loft. For three days, that boy and that vision."

A knowing smile softened her face. "And you feel guilty?"

"Absolutely. Don't you think I should?"

"No."

"I mean, here I am, practically orphaned ten years to the day, and my mind keeps replaying that vision over and over in my head. I've never seen anything like it. Or felt anything like it, for that matter. He was so fierce, so desperate, and yet somehow not quite human." I took in a deep breath and refocused on Brooke. "But to think about that on today of all days."

She put a hand on my arm. "Lor, I'm certain your parents wouldn't want you wallowing for their sake."

"I know, but—"

"No buts. I can't even begin to imagine what it's like to have your gift, to see the things you've seen and feel the things you've felt. I understand where you're coming from, but if you really loved me, you'd describe that boy in much more detail and include pertinent information like chest measurements and white blood cell count."

I grinned playfully and leaned in closer. "Well, I did try my hand at drawing him."

Her smile widened. "And?"

After a quick scan of the area to make sure no one was looking, I eased my notebook forward to reveal my latest masterpiece.

Her stare locked on to the image I'd drawn. The boy from the vision. She inhaled a soft breath. "Oh, my."

"I know." I'd caught only a fraction of his face during the fight. Dark eyes one instant. A strong jaw the next. Lashes, thick and impossibly long. So I didn't really have that much to go on, but I drew what I remembered.

"Is the boy in your vision the same one from the hall?"

"Probably," I answered. "At least that's how it usually works. But how could that even be possible?"

"Beats the heck outta me."

"Maybe my vision was a metaphor for something he has to face in his life. Something awful."

"Like finals?"

"Exactly. Only, you know, more life-threatening."

A slow nod confirmed her agreement. "Maybe. I know one thing: He's absolutely gorgeous." She leveled an approving eye on me. "You are getting seriously good at this stuff. You should sell your drawings on eBay and pay for a trip to the casinos. Put those skills to good use."

Brooklyn knew my glimpses into the Twilight Zone didn't really work that way. I wasn't psychic like that. I just saw things every so often when I touched people. There were no guarantees that what I saw actually happened, or ever would.

"I only use my powers for good," I said, offering her a teasing scowl.

She threw me a doubtful look. "What about that time the creature whose name shall not be spoken aloud backed her car into Principal Davis's SUV? You saw that two days before it happened."

"Oh, right, well, most of the time. But this vision was different. So much emotion. So much turmoil."

"So much hot guy flesh," Brooke added.

I studied the picture and realized I did focus on the guy's muscles a bit, but that was mostly what I saw.

"So you didn't see his whole face?" she asked, commenting on the fact that I'd only drawn his dark eyes with long lashes and the barest sliver of his pout.

"No." I sighed in frustration. "I got bits and pieces. It was like a puzzle I couldn't quite solve."

"And you're not very good at puzzles."

"True." I fixed a contrite look on her as she analyzed the picture. "Sorry I called you so late last night."

"Are you kidding? I would've been upset if you hadn't called me. Being stalked sucks," she said, referring to the fact that for the last three days, ever since I'd seen him in the Java Loft, Cameron Lusk had been following me. Just out of the blue. For no comprehensible reason whatsoever. Every time I turned a corner, every time I looked up from whatever I was doing, there he was. Glaring. "Maybe what you saw in your vision was a manifestation of your worry over Cameron."

"Maybe." I hadn't thought of it that way. I was pretty new to the whole stalking thing.

She opened her red locker door then halted again. "Well, let's think about it. You had that vision the same day Cameron started following you."

I nodded, letting my eyes wander back to the picture. Even with my amateur style, the boy appealed to every cell in my body, drawing me in like a magnet.

"And Cameron's been your constant shadow for three days now, right?"

I nodded again, running a fingertip over the corner of his mouth, barely visible.

She shrugged. "Makes sense to me. Your subconscious is reaching out for someone to save you. You obviously have genuine feelings of vulnerability."

"True, but I had the vision before I saw Cameron."

"Oh, well, that does throw a wrench into our parade."

"Still, it's not a bad working hypothesis. You're good at analyzing things."

"That's because I have an anal retentive personality," she said in complete seriousness.

I tried not to laugh at her as I peeked around the wall of bright red lockers to see if stalker boy was nearby.

"And on that note," she said just as I spotted him, "I need to ask you something."

"Shoot."

"Okay, so I was wondering, if Cameron kidnaps you, kills you, then buries your lifeless body in a shallow grave in the desert where your remains lay decomposing for several decades until they're accidentally discovered by some guy on a journey to re-awaken his spirit at the Salinas Pueblo Missions, can I have your iMac?"

I gaped at her. "You've really thought this out."

"I love your iMac."

"I love my iMac too, and you're not getting her."

"But you'll be decomposing," she said, her voice more whiny than usual.

Fighting a bubble of laughter, I shook my head. "I had to save a whole year for iPrecious. She stays with me no matter what state of decomposition I'm in."

"Well, I hate to be the one to tell you this," she said, clearly enjoying the task, "but that's a ridiculous name." She rifled through her books. "I mean, iPrecious? Seriously? You sound like the Apple version of Gollum."

I smiled even though evil butterflies had started dive-bombing the lining of my stomach the moment I spotted Cameron. Being stalked was wreaking havoc on my innards.

"Is he there?" she asked.

"He's there, all right," I said through slightly gritted teeth, my voice tainted with a combination of resignation and fear. Cameron stood leaning against the trophy case, ice blue eyes smoldering as usual. Anger radiated off him, white hot and tangible. Despite his crystalline gaze and shoulder-length blond hair, his features were forever darkened by it.

"Well, crap." Brooke closed her locker door, then nudged up behind me to look over my shoulder. "That boy needs a hobby."

"Stalking is a hobby."

"So is serial killing."

My stomach clenched tightly in reflex. I'd never really thought of Cameron as a serial killer, but I'd never thought of him as a stalker either. "Aren't you supposed to make me feel better? Isn't that what friends are for?"

"Lorelei, friends don't let friends get killed by serial killers." She paused to take inventory of her belongings, cursed under her breath, then marched back to her locker and spun the combination wheel again. "Seriously, what if your grandparents had seen him? I mean, who does that? Who stands outside someone's window all night long in the freezing rain?"

I'd called Brooke late last night and again the minute I woke up this morning. Cameron had been outside my house when I went to bed and was still there when I woke up this morning, even though it'd rained all night. Stalker Boy was nothing if not dedicated.

"I don't get it any more than you do. Cameron Lusk hasn't said two words to me since he stopped Joss Duffy from pasting my eyelids shut in kindergarten."

"Joss Duffy tried to paste your eyelids shut in kindergarten?"

"Only that one time. So why—?"

"With actual paste?"

"Yes."

"Wouldn't it take a really long time to dry?"

I'd lost her. "Brooke," I said, placing a hand on her shoulder to steer her back to me, "please try to focus."

She blinked out of her stupor. "Sorry. That just seems really counterproductive. Superglue, on the other hand—"

"So why," I said, picking up where I'd left off, "after years of living in the same town, going to the same schools, sneaking into the same drive-in theater, has Cameron all of a sudden decided to stalk me?"

"Most likely because he's nutty as a PayDay." She grabbed the notebook she forgot, a matte rust-colored thing that just matched her sweater.

"Least he's committed," I offered.

"Or needs to be. Lorelei, we have to do something. I mean, yeah, today you're alive and abduct-free. Kudos. But who knows what the guy is capable of?"

The situation definitely sucked. Brooke would get no argument from me there. "I thought about putting a contract out on his life."

She closed her locker again and offered a dubious grin. "That's a great idea."

"Yeah, but I don't know where to find that kind of contractor."

Her enthusiasm wilted. "Me neither. But we have to do something. I mean, what if this whole stalking gig evolves into kidnapping? Or worse? Do you even *watch* the news?"

"I know." I turned back to Cameron, the little stalker that could. "I suppose I'll just have to talk to him."

"Well, you can't do it now. The tardy bell's gonna ring any second," she reminded me. "We'd better get to class."

Class was the furthest thing from my mind. I probably should've been grateful that, for the first time in three days, stalker boy was glaring at something other than me, but his glaring had me curious. He looked totally pissed. Okay, he always looked totally pissed, but it was the *way* he was staring, like a

raging fury lay just behind those icy blues. Even at his most intimidating, he'd never stared at me that way, thank the heavens.
So what had him so riled?

I craned my neck and peered across the hall. Most of the kids
were already in class.

"You go on ahead," I said. "I'll be there in a jiff."

"You're gonna be late."

"I'll be right there," I promised, looking back at her. But her
mouth slid into a doubtful smirk. I raised my hands in surrender. "Two minutes, tops. I swear."

"Fine, but don't say I didn't warn you." She gave a sassy toss
of her hair as she headed to class. "And don't even think I'm going to cover for you."

I couldn't help but smile as I turned back to figure out what
Cameron was spending so much energy frowning at.

Then I saw him, a boy, leaning against the wall opposite Cameron. The two were staring each other down, gazes locked like
predatory wolves on the verge of battle. The boy was tall—as tall
as Cameron—strong and solid and . . . breathtaking.

Suddenly the boy's piercing glare darted toward me. I was
still hiding behind the lockers, but in that instant before I could
duck back, his angry eyes fixed on mine.

I had never seen eyes so dark, nor a face so perfect. As I pressed
my back into the red metal lockers, I slammed my lids shut. A
mental image of his flawless face materialized in my mind.

Was he angry with me? Had I done something to offend
him? Or was he just annoyed with stalker boy? Something we
had in common. Of course, I *had been* staring. Maybe he didn't
like being stared at.

"The bell rang, people." Principal Davis stepped out of the
front office in his usual brown suit and browner tie that matched
his brown hair and browner mustache to a tee. He was tall and
broad and built more like a professional football player than like a

high school principal. But I could see where the bulk would come in handy. Several of our students were built like professional football players as well. I risked another peek as he spurred students to class with a practiced snarl. "Let's get to class. Move it."

Then he turned to assess the stare-down taking place in his well-disciplined halls. He studied tall, dark, and beautiful for a moment, then let his gaze slide to Cameron.

"Lusk," he said with more force, "get to class. Now."

Cameron hesitated, blinked, then tore his attention away from the boy to acknowledge Mr. Davis. He lowered his blond head, forcing a smile of mock submission before leaving. Cameron was an odd addition to our little community. He was our resident loner by all rights and counts, but he never lacked for female attention. If anything, he got too much, and it seemed to annoy him most of the time. I watched him leave, wondering if he would actually go back to class.

"Where did you get that?"

The boy turned to the principal. "Sir?"

"Your tattoo. Where did you get it?"

"Tattoo? I don't have one." He brought his arm around as Mr. Davis stepped closer.

What some kids could do with a white T-shirt and blue jeans bordered on sinful. He'd rolled up the sleeves, just enough to show off the fluid curves of his biceps. They flexed slightly as he held out his arm. The principal's brows slid together, his expression baffled.

He glanced back up. "I could have sworn—"

"I want one," the boy said with a shrug, "but my mom says I have to wait." His voice was deep and smooth. It slid over me like warm water and caused a sharp tug in my belly.

"You're new," the principal said after sizing him up for a long moment.

"Yes, sir."

"And your name is?"

The boy paused, hesitated. His dark gaze slipped back to me. I didn't jump back this time, because it quickly glided past me to land on something farther away.

"Jared," he said, returning his attention to the principal.

Jared. I liked it. Though Supernova would've been more to the point.

"Jared?" the principal asked, pressing for a last name.

With an almost imperceptible sweep of his lashes, Jared scanned past me again. "Kovach, sir. Jared Kovach."

The principal wavered. He glanced in my direction but seemed unconcerned with the fact that I still hadn't gone to class. Odd. Mr. Davis lived for herding stragglers to their respective cells.

"Well, Mr. Kovach, I'm Principal Davis." He offered his hand. Jared hesitated, then took it in a firm grip. Even though Mr. Davis was tall, Jared seemed to tower over him. The principal had to tilt his head back to look at him. "Have you filled out a registration packet?"

"Yes, sir. Would you like it now?"

"Please."

A backpack slid off Jared's right shoulder. I couldn't remember seeing a backpack before that moment. Apparently I'd been blinded by muscles and exquisitely fitted jeans. After Jared produced the packet, Mr. Davis took out a few pages and thumbed through them.

"My parents couldn't be here today. I hope that's okay."

"Shouldn't be a problem. Los Angeles, huh?"

Los Angeles. Cool.

"Yes, sir."

"Well, I hope small-town life won't disappoint you."

"I like small towns."

There is a God.

"Good," the principal said. "Let's just hope small towns like you."

Jared wrinkled his forehead, his head tilting slightly. "Let's hope," he agreed.

"See that door over there?" Mr. Davis pointed past me to the counselor's door across the hall.

Jared nodded.

"Why don't you take these papers to Mrs. Geary. She'll help you with your class schedule while we get your information entered into the system."

"Thank you," Jared said, accepting the packet of papers then slinging the backpack onto his shoulder.

When he started toward Mrs. Geary's office, I thought my knees would give beneath me. Every move he made was powerful, full of strength and dangerous grace.

Mr. Davis called to him. "You wouldn't have any relatives around these parts, would you?"

He stopped and turned back. "No, sir."

With an unconvinced nod, Mr. Davis dismissed him again.

And Jared started toward the counselor's office again. Toward me again.

In an act of desperation, I jumped back and tried my darnedest to become a corner. But as he walked past, he slowed his stride and sent a whisper of a glance over his shoulder. Then he smiled. The slimmest smile lifted the corners of his full mouth. Did he see me? I was certain the corner thing would work beautifully.

Without hesitation he stepped inside the counselor's office and I eased out of my disguise. That's when I noticed the poster beside Mrs. Geary's door.

A photograph of Jaredan Scott, a Riley High football player, hovered underneath a snarling wolverine. His name stood out in red and black 3-D font as most valuable player. The parts I found most interesting were the letters *J-A-R-E-D*. And the fact that Jaredan Scott had been sponsored by Kovach Plumbing and Supplies, as stated at the bottom of the poster.

Jared Kovach. Now what were the odds of that? Two more questions sprang to mind immediately. First, why would he lie about his name? And second, how could he have read the fine print of that poster from so far away?

I scanned the distance back to see if Mr. Davis was still standing watch. Instead, I found Cameron Lusk. He hadn't gone to class. I could see him through the plate-glass windows that lined the front of Riley High. He stood leaning against the building, looking directly at me, a strange expression I couldn't decipher shadowing his face.

I offered my own glare, completely perplexed. The guy had never shown the slightest bit of interest in me. Then, out of nowhere, I couldn't turn around without finding him waiting for me, watching, like he was mentally calculating how long it would take to strangle the life out of my body. A cold chill shimmied down my spine with the thought.

And worse, I didn't know what to do about it. I didn't want to alarm my grandparents. They had enough to worry about. The anniversary of my parents' disappearance always put them in a strange state, as it did me. I didn't want to call the police. Naturally, they would have to tell my grandparents. And I was nowhere near moronic enough to pretend I could take him. Boys, no matter how lanky, were generally strong.

"I'm stronger."

I jumped at the sound of a male voice behind me and whirled around to slam face-first into a brick wall. My notebook flew out of my arms, launching a ticker tape parade of science notes into the air. They floated down to land in whispery chaos on the ground.

For a second I just stood there in shock until humiliation

took hold and surged through me with a fiery vengeance. I could feel my cheeks heating as I looked up. And up. Into the eyes of the offending wall.

I stilled.

It was the new guy. And his eyes were amazing. Dark, steady, penetrating.

Penetrating?

"Are you okay?" he asked.

Where'd *penetrating* come from? I felt my cheeks grow even hotter. "Of course," I said, glancing down to hide my face and my bruised pride. I tucked a curl behind an ear and bent to gather my notes.

Supernova knelt to help me.

"You don't need to do that," I said, even more embarrassed as he scooped up my messy notes before I could get to them. Honestly, why couldn't I at least try to write neatly?

"I don't mind," he said, lifting the drawing I'd done that morning.

I snatched it out of his hand before he could get a good look.

He glanced at me but not in surprise at what I'd done. More like curiosity. His dark gaze was startlingly intense. The contrast of molasses-colored eyes and hair made his flawless skin appear almost translucent. The effect was haunting.

I forced my thoughts back to the present. "I'm Lorelei," I managed at last.

He hesitated as he had with Mr. Davis. After a quick glance over his shoulder, he stood and offered his hand. "I'm Jared."

I almost looked at the poster again. Instead, I shut my eyes as a slow dawning crept over me. I recognized his face. I'd drawn it that very morning. I'd been dwelling on it for three days. It was him. The boy. Only the puzzle was complete, and what a puzzle it was.

After an eternity, I realized how rude I was being and rushed to place my hand into his for a boost. The contact electrified me. One minute I was kneeling on the floor; the next I was standing in front of him, as if we had slipped forward in time.

When I felt my feet on solid ground again, I smiled and pulled my hand back. "Thank you."

He watched me a long moment, his brows furrowing in thought; then he blinked as if coming to his senses and handed over a stack of notes. "You should be more careful."

His deep voice, velvety and rich like hot chocolate, tugged at my insides, warmed them. It took a great deal of concentration to focus on anything but the visceral reaction every inch of my body was having as a result of his nearness. Finally, after a couple of false starts, I said, "My grandmother tells me the same thing."

A half smile that didn't quite reach his eyes lifted one corner of his incredible mouth. I couldn't seem to look away. His lashes lowered to fan across his cheeks as if overcome by a sudden jolt of shyness. They were long and thick, just like in my vision, and made his eyes sparkle. I felt that sharp tug at my insides again as I recognized every curve of his face, every contour. My vision had actually manifested right before my very eyes.

I fought to stay focused. "So, you're new?" I asked, pretending I hadn't just heard his entire conversation with Mr. Davis.

"Yes." His gaze meandered back up. It paused a moment on my mouth, just long enough to make my heart miss a beat, before boring into mine again.

"Well, then, welcome to Riley High," I said a tad breathlessly.

He continued to study me and I was beginning to wonder if I had something on my face. Why would anyone that gorgeous spend so much time looking at me? My thoughts jumped back to the vision, replayed it in my mind. The boy. The monster. The sword. And the blood pooling in the valleys of his muscles, dripping down his arm. My attention drifted to his chest, wondering if he took off his shirt right then and there, would he have three slashes across his torso?

With an airy sigh, I came to my senses. Of course not. What I saw wasn't real. Could never be real.

"Oh, my," I heard from down the hall. "Did you fall again, Lor?"

Heels echoed off the walls as the creature whose name shall not be spoken aloud decided to goad me. Again. I glanced around the corner to see Tabitha Sind heading our way with her long, perfect legs, perfect blond hair, and a perfect face to back up her 'tude. I only had Brooklyn and Glitch to back up mine, but that was okay. I really didn't have much of an attitude anyway. Except for when my grandmother said, "Don't give me that attitude." Then I guess I had one. But since nobody could make me feel more ill equipped to be human than Tabi, I decided to access my usual coping mechanism and avoid her at all costs.

"I better get to class," I said, backing away from the most beautiful thing I'd ever laid eyes upon, but Tabitha rounded the corner before I could make my escape. In a heartbeat I was face-to-face with my archenemy, and I had to wonder if it was just me or if her head really was too big for her body.

"Have you considered physical therapy?" she asked, her voice syrupy sweet. "She does that a lot, you kno—"

Tabitha stopped berating me midstream as her vulturous eyes locked on to Jared, and I couldn't help the fierce reaction that bucked inside me. I ground my teeth, biting back the jealousy that leapt onto my nerve endings. I could just chalk this up to one more encounter that would add to the debilitating ulcers I'd someday have as a result of Tabitha's existence.

"H-hi," she said, holding out her hand to Jared. "You must be new here."

"Yes." His hand practically swallowed hers, but just as quickly he tried to pull it back. Apparently, prying his hand out of Tabitha's grip was easier said than done. When he pulled, she stepped. Way closer than was acceptable in a public school setting. PDA anyone?

"I'm Tabitha," she said, making the short statement sound more like an invitation than an introduction. Then she offered him her nuclear smile—the one that melted boys' hearts and had every girl at Riley High wishing she could afford cosmetic dentistry—and I groaned inwardly. There'd be no getting him back now. I may as well cut my losses and make a hasty exit while I still had enough self-esteem to walk upright. Crawling was so demoralizing.

I'd stepped around Tabitha and started down the hall when I heard, "Can I walk you to class?"

I looked back and Jared was looking at me. Not at Tabitha and her big fat head, but at me and my tiny pixie head with squiggly hair. He'd managed to free his hand and was leaning around her, eyeing me with the slightest tilt of his mouth.

"Me?"

"Her?" Tabitha seemed just as surprised as I. She cleared her throat when his brows shot up. "I have to get to the office anyway. I'll see you around, then?"

"Sure," he said, stepping around her. Unfortunately, my class was only three doors down. I thought about pretending it was farther to get more alone time with Jared, but the teacher in whatever classroom I chose at random would only look at me funny when I walked in.

Jared followed beside me, taking one step to my two, the act emphasizing the length of his legs. One arm hung at his side while the other kept hold of the strap of his backpack, and I couldn't imagine why I would notice that, other than the fact that to notice anything higher would have me looking up at an awkward angle. And I so very much remembered the power in those arms. The strength in those hands. And the blood dripping off them.

I shook the memory from my mind. It wasn't real. I had to remember that.

"This is me," I said, stopping beside my first hour.

He read the sign on the door. "Science."

"Yep, science. Where I'm being forced to memorize completely useless particles of information that will never actually apply to any real-life situation I might encounter."

A lopsided grin spread across his face at last. "Sounds like fun," he said, and for a moment I forgot how to breathe.

"Oh, yeah," I managed. "Molecular structure, does a body good."

He rewarded me with the most charming smile I'd ever seen. Dimples. He actually had dimples.

"Well, thanks for helping me with my notes."

"Anytime, Lorelei McAlister." He offered a genteel dip of his head.

I stepped to the door and inched it open. "I guess I'll see ya round," I whispered.

"I'm counting on it," he whispered back, his voice echoing softly in the hall.

I almost tripped.

The moment I sat down in Science, I took out a sheet of paper and scribbled a note to Brooke, who sat behind me. I could hardly wait to tell her about Jared. About how the guy from my vision had just started high school here. I had to word my masterpiece using science jargon, in case our teacher caught on. I passed back the note and had a reply about five minutes later.

What about its molecular structure?

I almost snorted out loud. Brooklyn *would* ask about Jared's body. I folded the note in half and replied on the back.

Structure is solid. Molecular height unbroken. Clearly over six elements involved. Massive covalent bonding. High melting point . . . supernova.

I refolded the note, which basically stated Jared was built like Adonis, well over six feet tall, and could melt a girl with a mere glance. Course, the word *supernova* said it all. A supernova, in Lorelei and Brooke lingo, was a guy so gorgeous, so sumptuous, he defied the delicate laws of nature, created an imbalance in the universe, existed as an explosive force that could shatter the very foundations of our world.

I'd never christened a boy I just met with such a high ranking, but Jared clearly met all the criteria, and then some.

I slipped the note back to Brooklyn and continued working on the papers I'd dropped in the hall. The plan was to put them back in order, but when I thumbed through them, I found that they were already in order. Not one stray page in the bunch. How could that be? My papers had been hit by a hurricane. A hurricane named Jared Kovach.

Within seconds, I felt Brooklyn's note brush across my arm. I reached back and suppressed another chuckle. She'd written the reply across the front in bright red marker.

Holy Häagen-Dazs, Batman!

"I'm glad to see you've taken such an interest in global science."

I jumped at the sound of my Science teacher's voice, then raised my best innocent, doe-eyed expression toward her. It didn't work. Ms. Mullins took the note from me just as the bell rang.

"So, how is your grandmother?"

"My grandmother?"

"Yes," Brooklyn said from behind me. "I told her why you were late. Your grandmother wasn't feeling well."

She did cover for me. "Right, sorry, I was on the phone. But she's much better now."

Students filed out of the classroom while Ms. Mullins examined my coded masterpiece. To the untrained eye, there was nothing on that note but science jargon. And an expletive about ice cream.

I stood with confidence. Absolute faith. Heck, my best friend was by my side. What more could I ask for?

"Well, I better go."

Brooklyn—my very best friend since the third grade, my most trusted companion and confidante—turned tail and ran out of the lab like a chicken with her head cut off. Only in a much straighter line.

I stared after her, aghast. I tended to do that when abandoned by the only person on earth I'd ever tell my deepest and darkest secret to. If I had a deep, dark secret, that is.

Ms. Mullins refolded the note and handed it back. "First of all," she said with a patient smile, "covalent bonding has a low melting point, not a high one. That would be ionic bonding. Second, we covered our review of physical science two weeks ago, though I am glad to see the enthusiasm linger. And third, I have to agree with your assessment, Ms. McAlister. Supernova, indeed."

If I hadn't clamped my mouth shut, my jaw would have dislodged and fallen to the floor. I tried to think of something to say, but the thought of Ms. Mullins ogling Jared was more than a little disturbing. She was elderly. Probably, like, forty or something.

"What?" Ms. Mullins protested. "I'm not dead yet."

I felt my mouth stretch across my face. I loved Ms. Mullins. The mischievous sparkle in her eyes added a dash of delight to the day, like colored sprinkles on a cupcake.

"Sorry about the note," I said, actually remorseful.

She smiled. "I know what today is, Lorelei."

My eyes fluttered in surprise. How could she know?

She placed a sympathetic hand on my shoulder. "If you need anything, please don't hesitate to ask."

Her empathy sent an invisible force pressing into my chest as sadness flooded my lungs. I stood cemented to the spot for a solid minute before I managed a soft, "Thank you."

Then her smile turned a little wicked. "And if I ever catch you writing notes in my class again . . ."

"You won't. Never, I promise." I recovered and tucked the evidence into my back pocket.

She laughed and pointed toward the door.

With a grateful sigh, I gathered my books and headed that way. "See you tomorrow," I said.

"If you're lucky," she shot back.

When I walked out of the classroom, Brooklyn was waiting for me in the hall.

"What happened to you?" I asked accusingly.

"Oh please," she said with a dramatic roll of her eyes, "Ms. Mullins loves you."

"True."

"Besides, I'm much more interested in supernova." That got my attention. She leaned in to me and lowered her voice to a seductive purr. "So he's hot."

"Can you say blazing inferno?"

"Oh, man, I can't wait to see this guy. Sucks it'll have to wait. We're going to be tardy to second hour. If we play our cards right, we might get lunch detention today. I know, I'm aiming high, but—"

I'd stopped dead in my tracks.

Brooklyn looked back at me, bewildered. "I meant we should step it up, not come to a full stop, Ensign McAlister."

Several things had been bothering me about that morning. The poster. The fact that I caught Principal Davis eyeing that very thing when I asked to be excused to the bathroom during first hour. What I could have sworn Jared said to me before I turned around. Didn't he say he was stronger? And finally, how I seemed to have floated up from the ground when Jared took my hand. Course, that last one could be chalked up to hormones.

But . . . "McAlister. My name is Lorelei McAlister."

Brooklyn pursed her lips. "Lorelei, I've known your name since I kicked your butt in the third grade."

"Right." I flashed her an astonished look. "Only you didn't kick my butt, and he's never met me. He called me Lorelei McAlister. He said, 'Anytime, Lorelei McAlister.'"

"But you told him your name."

"I told him my first name, not my last. How did he know my last name?"

Brooklyn grinned and pointed to the back of my notebook. When I turned it over, LORELEI MCALISTER—written in huge black and red letters—jumped out at me.

"Are you okay?" she asked.

"Yeah." I shook my head as if trying to clear cobwebs. "This day has just been, I don't know, weird. Like the world tilted just enough to make me lose my balance."

"You need a caffeinated beverage."

I smiled. "Caffeine would be good."

"Caffeine is always good."

"You're so logical," I said as we headed to second hour.

"Thank you. I was going for logical. It seemed like the logical thing to do."

"Though we really should get straight whose butt got kicked that day and whose butt did the touchdown victory dance."

"Your butt can do the touchdown victory dance?" she asked.

"It could the day it kicked yours."

"Can it do the alphabet?"

I nodded with a giggle, then sucked in a soft breath as my

hand brushed against someone and received a spike of energy in return. I looked back, but there were too many kids in the crowded hall to pinpoint the source. An instant later, a vision flashed in my head. It was short, just the smallest image of a scene, but in it someone was standing watching a girl in a ragged apricot shirt and bloodied khaki capris kneel on the side of a road. She was heaving into the dirt, the contents of her stomach pouring onto the ground in one of the most disturbing visions I'd ever had.

As we entered the classroom for second hour, I glanced down at my apricot shirt and khaki capris. A sickly dread came over me as I realized I was the girl heaving into the dirt. I checked my forehead for a temperature. I didn't feel sick. And why would I be on the side of some random road? Thank goodness my visions were more entertaining than predictive. Still, I totally should have worn my blue shirt.

TALL, DARK, AND FLAMMABLE

"Did you see the new guy?" Glitch slid beside Brooklyn and me at our usual lunch table.

"See him?" I asked. "I almost killed him." I reached over and stole a fry off his tray.

"Bummer."

Glitch had to be the geekiest cool kid I knew. He was smart, funny, and short, and everyone at school liked him. It was weird. And he was filling out, becoming *manlier*. He'd grown three inches over the summer. What the heck was that about?

Even Brooke was developing normally. While she stood on

the cusp of womanhood with guns blazing and heart pounding, I seemed to be stuck in the land of bubble gum and lollipops. I still had to pray every night for the girl-part fairy to get off her butt and do her job. I just wasn't *blossoming* like the others. And to top it all off, I had infuriatingly curly hair that resembled rusted metal, gray colorless eyes, and translucent skin the sickly tone of baking flour. Other than the fact that my chin was too small, my eyes were too big, and my mouth was too wide for my face, I didn't have a lot going for me. Unless looking like an elf suddenly took the fashion industry by storm.

But Brooklyn Michelle Prather was gorgeous. An exotic blend of ethnicity gave Brooke an air of dark mystique. She had almond-shaped brown eyes, long black hair, and a delicate feminine build. I had a build too, just not a particularly feminine one.

"Have you heard anything I've said?"

I shifted back to the present and squinted at Brooklyn's cinnamon eyes as they questioned me. I said, "Sorry, I was calculating how much this whole pasty-white-girl thing sucks."

"Uh-oh." She turned to Glitch. "She's on her pasty-white-girl kick. She needs chocolate." She peeked at the ever-popular snack counter. "Cover me."

Glitch watched the crowded lunch hall with narrowed eyes, searching for possible enemies. "Okay, but hurry before she starts mentioning the girl-part fairy."

I chuckled and stayed Brooke with a hand on her arm. "I'm fine."

With a doubtful expression, Glitch reached over and pulled my lower lid down to study my eye. That'd help.

"Yeah, all right. She looks okay." He shrugged and added, "Least her eyeball does."

I stole another fry and leveled a baleful look at him. "No one asked for your opinion, *Casey*."

Brooklyn snorted. "I love it when you call him Casey." She reached over and stole a piece of chicken off my salad. Eating at our table was kind of a communal effort.

"I don't," Glitch said with a pout. "How am I supposed to embrace my Native American ancestry with a name like Casey?"

"Well, maybe your Native American ancestry will benefit from a little Irish temperament thrown into the mix," she said. "You guys are so calm."

His eyes widened in horror. "Are you psychotic?"

"You mean today or just in general?"

He glanced around to make sure no one overheard her. "You can't say crap like that. Do you want to get me killed?"

"You should totally talk with an Irish brogue," she continued, unconcerned.

"That's a great idea." I nudged him and wriggled my brows. "Brogues are sexy."

He shuddered in disgust. "I'm going to be tomahawked before the day is over."

"So, did you get a chance to have that little talk?" Brooke asked me, able to switch subjects in a single bound. In all honesty, I hadn't seen Cameron since he stood glowering at me through the plate-glass windows.

"What little talk?" Glitch asked, his voice muffled from a mouthful of hamburger.

"No, he hasn't been in class all day."

"Who hasn't been in class?"

"I just don't know about that boy." Brooklyn shook her head and added a few *tsks* to emphasize her disappointment.

"What boy?" Glitch took a noisy gulp of soda, then glared at us, annoyed that he'd been left out of the loop.

As I thought about the inevitable confrontation with Stalker Boy, a sickly kind of dread consumed me. What did one say to a stalker? *Um, pardon me, Mr. Stalker, but could you, like, not?*

Frustrated, I let a sigh slide through my lips. "Why does *he* have to be stalking me?" I half questioned, half whined. "Why couldn't it be someone like Jaredan Scott or Joss Duffy?" *Or Jared*, I thought, but dared not say aloud. I could totally deal with Jared Kovach stalking me.

Glitch's eyes hooded. "Didn't Joss Duffy try to paste your eyelids shut in kindergarten?"

"Stalking is stalking," Brooklyn said after licking salt off her fingertips. "Doesn't matter who it is, it's creepy. And wrong."

She had a point.

"Okay," Glitch said, holding up a finger to get our attention, "I'm going to take a shot in the dark and ask, is someone, perhaps, stalking you?"

"Glitch," I said, finally glancing his way. "There are some things you just don't need to know until we're in trouble and we need your boy abilities."

That struck a chord. An evil grin spread across his face. "Speaking of my boy abilities," he said under his breath, "they're available to either of you twenty-four slash seven, for a small processing fee."

"Noted," Brooklyn said. "Next time I need a jar opened . . ."

He raised his hands and mimicked choking her.

I couldn't help but snicker as my two best friends went at it. I also couldn't help my gaze from roaming the area for the thousandth time, looking for Riley High's newest arrival, wondering where he might be. It hadn't escaped my attention that Tabitha Sind was absent as well. If he was with her, who could blame him? Tabitha was gorgeous, even with her bobble head. It was hard to compete with near physical perfection. Now, if Jared was more interested in IQs, I might have a chance.

"That's an interesting look for them." Brooklyn gestured with a nod toward the door as the Southern twins, Ashlee and Sydnee, walked in. They looked utterly exhausted, their clothes disheveled and their hair barely combed. Until about a month ago, the Southern twins rarely looked like anything less than cover models, but lately, they looked more like homeless teens. Since their father was the richest man in town and they rarely wore anything but designer shoes, I doubted they'd gone belly up. Their shoe collection alone could buy me a new wardrobe. Or a car. Or a house on the Riviera.

"What's up with those two anyway?" Glitch asked.

"I don't know," I said, "but something's not right."

"Hell-o." Brooklyn waved a hand in front of our faces. "Their mother practically abandoned them, running off with that investment broker like she did. And I heard the divorce was heartbreaking. She didn't even ask for custody of the girls."

"That had to be painful, I know, but that was months ago, Brooke. This is different. They're different. Desperate." I tapped my fingers on the table in thought as Brooke took another bite of my salad. "I'm telling you, something is very wrong."

"That's too bad. I'd be more concerned if I weren't so busy breathing." When I cast her a look of amazement, she continued, "Those two are evil, Lor. Did I ever tell you about the time they tripped me in the sack race?"

Only 729 times. While my archenemy was Tabitha Sind, Brooke had always felt a tad resentful toward Ash and Syd. Things had never been the same since they took the sack race trophy at the fall festival. True, it happened in the third grade, but things like that were hard to get over. Apparently.

"Well, here," Glitch said, interrupting our conversation to hand me a small box.

"What's this?" Glitch wasn't exactly the gift-giving type. I had to force him to buy Brooklyn a birthday present every year, and I was pretty secure in the knowledge that she had to do the same thing for me on mine.

He shrugged. "Just something to maybe help you feel better."

Feel better about what? I opened the lid to find a shimmering gold pendant on a delicate chain. It was a sculpture of a mother and a father with a child in their arms. After a soft gasp, I lifted it out of the box and turned it over. It read FOREVER.

I sat stunned for a solid minute, astonishment sucking the air from my lungs, before looking back up at him.

"It's nothing really," he said, playing it off as only a guy could. "You know, for your parents and all."

After swallowing back the lump that suddenly formed in my throat, I said, "Glitch, I don't know what to say."

"Neither do I," Brooklyn said, baffled. "Way to score brownie points, G." She raised her hand for a high five, but he hit her with an annoyed glower instead.

Lifting her brows in pure attitude, she took the necklace from me and fastened it around my neck as I held up my hair.

I turned toward them when she'd finished. "What do you think?"

Brooklyn nodded. "You did good, Glitch."

He shrugged again and stuffed the last of his burger into his mouth. Boys were so funny.

Letting the cool metal slide between my fingers, I was just about to thank him when a thick hush blanketed the cafeteria. I looked up just in time to see Jared walk in. My stomach clenched at the sight of him.

"Holy Häagen-Dazs," Brooklyn said, repeating her earlier sentiment. Every head swiveled toward the new guy as he strolled to the counter serving pizza. Brooklyn sighed. "He wears jeans so well."

I nodded, mesmerized.

"And his muscles gather in all the right places."

"Please," Glitch said with a snort, "my muscles gather just as well as his." We both gave him a quick, dumbfounded look, and he hugged himself self-consciously. "Stop."

Slowly the dull roar of conversation gained volume again. Everyone around us seemed to be talking about Jared. Except for the Goths. They were still staring. Then again, so was I.

"You know, when you told me he was good-looking," Brooklyn said without taking her eyes off Jared, "I had no idea you meant *godlike* good-looking."

I simply nodded again and continued my vigil. Jared's white T-shirt hung past the slim waistband of his jeans, gathering at his hips. His biceps rose and stretched the material at the sleeves, and his forearms corded with taut muscles as he stepped into the line for pizza. Then I locked on to the dark hair that curled over his ears, the touch of shadow along his jawline.

The server said something, and he looked to the side, appearing bashful. My heart stopped in response.

"Heaven help us," Brooklyn said.

He clearly affected Brooke the same way he did me.

"Uh, Lor . . . ," she said, elbowing me again.

I was right there with her. Jared had turned with his tray and was staring straight at me as though wondering if he should join us or not.

After a moment—and a light head rush—I resupplied my red blood cells with oxygen and waved him to our table rather enthusiastically. If the bashful smile he flashed me was any indication, he didn't seem to mind.

"Oh, my god," Brooklyn said. She swung a surprised look at me. "Just what did you two talk about this morning?"

I beamed, not daring to breathe, as he walked toward us. "Oh, you know, the usual. School. The weather. How many children we want."

I expected Brooklyn to at least giggle, but apparently her current state of shock had immobilized her vocal cords. What I hadn't expected, however, was the faint laughter from Jared. He lowered his eyes like before, as though embarrassed by what someone had said. As if embarrassed by what I'd said. No way could he have heard me. Not from that far away.

"Jared," I said when he got close, "sit with us."

But before he could respond, Cameron cut him off. He stepped right between us, his tall frame blocking my view of Jared. I had to scoot to the side to see past him.

"Cameron, what are you doing?" I asked, stunned by his behavior.

But Jared didn't seem the least bit surprised. He eyed Cameron for a moment, seeming more curious than alarmed, then turned to put his tray on our table.

Cameron saved him the trouble. He knocked the tray out of Jared's hand with a sweep of his arm. It flew several feet before crashing onto the floor. The loud clatter brought all conversation to a standstill as part of the tray's contents landed on a table of freshmen. Three of them jumped up and swiped at their clothing until they too saw what was happening. They stilled and looked on in fascination.

I glanced back at Jared, but he only sighed, as though Cameron's outburst was more of a nuisance than an outright attack.

My feelings were a bit stronger. "Cameron, are you nuts?" I yelled as I bolted out of my seat.

Glitch grabbed my arm and pulled me back down.

The entire room had fallen into an eerie silence for the second time that day.

Cameron wore a menacing grimace as he leaned into Jared. "That whole walking-and-carrying-a-tray-at-the-same-time thing must really have you baffled."

Jared smiled. He smiled . . . and stepped even closer. "I was walking before you were even a speck on the horizon."

Cameron's mouth tightened. "Just making sure I had the right guy."

"And do you?" Jared asked with raised brows.

"Oh, yeah."

Jared closed the distance between them. Every person in the room stopped breathing. Anticipation glistened in their eyes as they waited to see what would happen next.

"You know," Jared said in a husky whisper I could barely hear, "your heart's beating a little fast." His smile disappeared. "I can take care of that for you."

As though steeling himself for some mortal blow, every muscle in Cameron's body tensed. He clenched his fists and tightened his jaw. "Do whatever you want to me," he said under his breath, "just stay away from Lorelei."

Lorelei? Me? I snapped to attention. Did he just say stay away from me?

"I think you're the one who needs to stay away from her. Stalking, Mr. Lusk, is not a pretty habit."

Wait. How did Jared know that? How did he know Cameron had been following me? And how did I suddenly become the topic of conversation?

"You can't have her," Cameron said.

"Really."

"I swear to God," Cameron continued, his blue eyes watering with emotion, "you'll die screaming if you try."

Jared's features darkened. His lids narrowed and he lowered his head to watch Cameron from underneath his lashes, like a cougar preparing to attack. "Let's take care of that heart thing, shall we?" He raised a hand toward Cameron's chest.

"What's going on here?"

At the booming sound of Principal Davis's voice, Jared straightened and dropped his arm. Anger lined the principal's stern face as he charged forward.

Cameron eased back too, though just barely. His chest rose

and fell as adrenaline rushed through his body. Then the side of his mouth crept up, suggesting a smile. "Don't worry, Reaper, we'll continue this later."

"You just stay alive that long."

"Wouldn't dream otherwise."

"Lusk, is there a problem?" Mr. Davis asked as he crossed over to them.

Both young men ignored him for what seemed like an eternity before they finally looked away from each other. I'd never felt such palpable tension in my life.

"Mr. Kovach," Principal Davis said through his teeth, unused to being ignored, "I would hate to see your first day here at Riley High turn out unfavorably."

Jared released a slow breath then looked at him at last. "So would I, Mr. Davis."

"I suggest you get something else to eat. And you," he said, jabbing a finger toward Cameron, "come with me."

Cameron chuckled then leaned toward Jared again. "You can't do it here anyway, Reaper. Too many witnesses. I know the rules."

"Lusk," Davis warned.

Cameron turned to follow him out the door. As he stepped past, his stare locked with Jared's again. Their shoulders brushed and each gave a light shove, reiterating the fact that their confrontation was far from over.

After Principal Davis escorted Cameron out of the building, the room erupted in dozens of conversations. They echoed against the walls, but through it all, no one could take their eyes off Jared. They watched, waiting for his reaction. Just as I did.

With a frustrated sigh, Jared scrubbed his face with his fingers, then raked them through his hair, his muscles still contracted, ready for a fight.

"Jared," I said. He turned and looked at me, his dark eyes

pinning me to the spot, his gaze so intense, I forgot what I was going to say. After a moment, I improvised. "Jared, I—"

"It won't hurt, Lorelei," he said, interrupting me. Confusing me. "I'll make sure of it."

"What won't hurt?"

When I tried to rise again, he stepped back, his expression suddenly guarded. Glitch's death grip held, so I didn't get far before being pulled back to my seat.

"What are you talking about?" I asked.

He didn't answer. He just stared, observing me so fiercely, I struggled to breathe under the weight of it. Then, without another word, he backed away, turned, and strode out a side door.

"Okay," Brooklyn said, "that was weird."

I sat stunned for a long time before Glitch's grip on my arm registered. "Ouch, Glitch," I said, slapping at his hand.

"Oh, sorry." He let go but took hold of me again as I stood and started after Jared.

I turned on him with a glare. "Glitch, I need to talk to him."

"I doubt he's in the mood for small talk."

"Let go."

"Just give him time, Lor. Call it a guy thing."

I stood there scowling at him a solid minute before giving in. With a jerk of my arm, I freed myself and sat back down. The fact that he was probably right didn't make it any easier to swallow. "Who does Cameron Lusk think he is?" I asked, incredulous and more than a little baffled. "Why would he do that?"

Glitch drew in a deep breath and held it before offering his version of an explanation. "You have to consider the source," he said, grabbing the ketchup bottle. "Lusk is different."

"That's for sure," Brooklyn said.

I watched as Glitch busied himself with a sudden urge to

smother his fries in ketchup and realized he was holding some-thing back. I felt a disturbance, like an undercurrent just below his too-calm exterior. "What do you mean?"

"He's just different," he said, shrugging one shoulder. "You know. Not quite like the other kids on the playground."

Brooklyn knitted her brows. "You're going to have to give us more than that, Glitch. We've already seen the fruit. We need the juice."

He paused his assault and looked up, his mouth a thin line. "I don't know," he said, trying to dismiss our inquiry. "He probably has anger issues. Not unlike the average juvenile delinquent, if you ask me."

Brooklyn sat back in her chair and crossed her arms. "That's the best juice you got?"

"It's pretty much the only juice I got. On Lusk anyway."

"Oh, no, you don't." She wagged an index finger at him. "Didn't something happen between you two once?"

Glitch stilled.

She was right. The spring break of our second-grade year, he'd gone on a camping trip in the mountains with his Boy Scout troop. Something happened on that trip. Something bad. And I'd known that Cameron was involved, but no one would ever tell me more, including Glitch.

Brooklyn hadn't moved to Riley's Switch yet and didn't know him then. But he changed, withdrew. He stopped com-ing to school and almost had to repeat the second grade, but his parents got him through summer school despite his total shut-down.

I remembered it so vividly because he'd stopped talking to me. We used to play at the park a lot or he would come hang with me at my grandparents' store. When he stopped talking to me, I was too hurt and too lame to realize he'd obviously expe-rienced something very traumatic. My grandparents had to point it out. They convinced me to just be his friend, explained that he would come back to me when he was ready.

When third grade started, he slowly became himself again. He started joking and horsing around. And when Brooklyn moved to Riley's Switch and joined our group, he seemed to bounce back like nothing had ever happened. Still, I couldn't help but wonder if it was all just a cover. The light in his eyes had never shone quite so bright as before that spring break.

Could this have something to do with what happened to him? Now that I thought about it, he and Cameron had been friends in the second grade. But not afterwards. They hadn't spoken two words in eight years.

I studied him as he studied his fries. In the softest voice I've ever heard him use, he said simply, "He's strong."

"Strong?" I asked, almost as softly. I scooted closer. "Strong like how?"

Tension creased his face. "Just strong."

Brooklyn seemed to sense his distress as well. She moved closer too. "You know you can tell us anything, right?"

I'd told her the story. She knew that Glitch had gone away one person and come back an entirely different animal. We were only seven, but in those few weeks, he seemed to grow older, become hardened, almost jaded. And lost. It took a long time for him to find his way back, and as badly as I didn't want him to regress, at the same time, I wanted to know more. Cameron's name seemed to be cropping up a lot in the last few days, and I wanted to know why.

Glitch rubbed his mouth. He did that when he didn't want to admit something. After a long moment of contemplation, he said, "He's not just strong, he's, like, really strong."

"You totally need a thesaurus," Brooklyn said, giving up on the empathetic approach.

He sighed. "I don't know how else to put it."

"Exactly why you need a thesaurus."

"Do you mean in an unnatural way?" I asked, a little more understanding. After all, I'd been there. I'd seen what he went through, what that camping trip had done to him. And I'd wondered a thousand times what happened. I'd even touched him. Nonchalantly, so he wouldn't know, but I'd touched his hand to try to get a vision. Unfortunately, my visions seemed to pick for themselves where and when to show up.

His cheeks reddened. "It's going to sound stupid."

That piqued my interest even more. "You know that's not true."

"Yeah, it is, because when I say strong, I don't mean a normal strong. I mean strong in a supernatural way." When Brooklyn's lips pursed, he tightened his jaw. "Told you it would sound stupid."

"No, it doesn't," she said. "I'm just not sure what you mean."

Since Brooke didn't shut him down or make fun of him, he seemed to grow more confident. "Think about it," he said, straightening in his chair. "Have you ever noticed how he never gets into fights? How nobody ever messes with him? How when he walks through the halls, it's like Moses parting the Red Sea?"

We both half nodded and half shrugged. Clearly Brooke had never really noticed either—Cameron was such an outcast and rarely garnered any attention—but we were both eager to hear more.

"There's a reason," he said, "no one will fight him. No one would dare. Even Isaac Johnson, the biggest defensive lineman Riley High has to offer, steers clear of Cameron Lusk."

"Ha," Brooklyn said, pointing at him. "You almost had me. Isaac Johnson doesn't steer clear of anyone."

"And Cameron Lusk isn't just anyone," he whispered loudly. He glanced around the room, making sure no one was listening before he continued. "That's what I'm trying to say. You don't know what he's capable of."

"Okay," I said, seeing my chance to find out what happened that year and going for it, "so what is he capable of?" I held my breath, hoping beyond hope he'd open up.

But instead of opening up, he withdrew once again, as he had so many times before. "I don't know. Just stuff."

"Fine," Brooklyn said, her tone questioning, "let's suspend disbelief for just a moment and say you're right. He's unnaturally strong. First, how do you know all this? And second, why haven't we heard of this great and unusual strength before?"

"I don't know," Glitch repeated defensively. "Maybe it's a guy thing."

"Another one?"

"We don't go around talking about how strong other guys are, you know?"

"But if he's that strong," I said, pushing just a little, "surely we would have heard something."

"We just don't talk about it, okay? We just don't."

I suddenly realized he hadn't been avoiding the topic of Cameron's strength, but downright hiding it. I leaned in and looked into his hazel green eyes. "What happened, Glitch?"

His shoulders lifted as he took in a deep breath, and I thought he might give in. He gazed at me without blinking, like a memory had taken hold. Then he glanced down at his massive pile of ketchup.

"Never mind," he said, shaking his head as if annoyed with himself. "I shouldn't have said anything."

I put my hand on his, partly to be supportive and partly hoping for a vision. "Glitch—"

"We need to warn Jared," Brooklyn said.

I gasped. I hadn't even considered what all this would mean to Jared. "You're right. We have to find him."

"I don't know, Lor," Glitch said, taking hold of my hand before I could get out of my seat. "Your Jared seems perfectly capable of handling himself. But you still haven't answered me: Is Cameron Lusk stalking you?"

"No, it's nothing." I fished a fry from the carnage and ate it while trying to ignore the doubt on his face.

"I think the more pressing question," Brooklyn said, concern lining her eyes, "is what the bloody heck was Jared talking about? What won't hurt?"

My gut tightened at the mention of Jared's statement, knotting painfully. Both of them looked at me as if I'd know the reason for such a bizarre promise. Well, I didn't. But I did know it was bothering me a lot more than it was bothering them.

WAKING UP DEAD

For the first time in three days, Cameron Lusk seemed nowhere to be found. I walked out of the Java Loft and glanced around warily, expecting to find my stalker skulking in the shadows.

"Want me to walk you home?"

I turned as Glitch poked his head out of the coffee shop, whipped almond toffee cappuccino with nonfat milk in hand.

He raised his brows in question. "My pie'll be out soon. What's your hurry?"

With a smile, I said, "No, you and Brooke enjoy. And don't fight! I have some research to do." We hadn't seen either Jared or

Cameron since lunch, and Glitch's confession about Cameron had me super curious.

His gaze traveled across the street to the town square. "What are they doing?"

A camera crew had set up shop in front of the old Traveler's Inn, a historic and—according to town gossip—haunted hotel. It was the biggest tourist attraction Riley's Switch had to offer, *big* being a relative term.

"I think it's the Tourist Channel," I said, shielding my eyes from the sun. "They're doing a special on haunted hotels in America, and ours made the top ten."

"Cool . . . and yet, creepy."

"This coming from a guy afraid of turtles."

Taking offense, Glitch straightened and pointed a finger at me in warning. "Turtles are not the innocent, harmless creatures everyone thinks they are. Mark my words. They're secretly planning to take over the world. And then where will we be?"

I couldn't help but giggle at the seriousness of his admonishment before shrugging my shoulders.

"Taken over! That's where." He glanced at his table. "Oh, my pie's ready. Sure you don't want some?"

"Positive."

"Okeydokey, then. We'll be over later."

Just like every year, I was apparently still under a suicide watch and would be for the next week. I had to admit, with those two around, I didn't have time to get too terribly depressed about my parents. Still, the minute they left my company, the sadness leached back inside me, as if it had been waiting all along, lurking in the shadows until it got the chance to slither inside. My dependence on their presence was getting ridiculous. It was high time I grew up and learned to cope with my parents' disappearance on my own.

With a wave to shoo him inside, I turned and headed toward the library, determined to overcome the blahs all by my little lonesome. The public library stood in the middle of the town square in what was once the courthouse. Though I often went there to read and relax and just catch my breath, I usually ended up chatting with the director of the library, and my grandmother's best friend, Betty Jo, instead. But what better place to do research? Librarians had an uncanny knack for amassing not only the talk around town, but the talk's history to boot.

As I approached one of the three stoplights Riley's Switch had to offer, an overenthusiastic skateboarder decided to stop right behind me. He failed. He tumbled off his skateboard and crashed into me, knocking me off the curb.

After almost twisting an ankle, I turned and stared him down, impatiently waiting for an apology. He was young and Asian with a slight build, which was probably a good thing. I could have been crushed.

"Sorry," he said as his friends snickered behind his back, joking and shoving one another.

"No problem." I stepped up and turned back to the light. Freshmen.

An October chill had settled in the air, making me wish for a jacket. My thin apricot shirt did nothing to block the crisp wind, and my capris left my ankles exposed and goose bumpy. I totally should have listened to my grandmother this morning. She always seemed to know what I should and should not wear in an eerie, sixth-sense kind of way.

As I waited for the light to change, the skateboarder, who'd been practicing tricks on a park bench, lunged into me again. I couldn't believe it. I turned and narrowed my eyes on him, forcing him to mumble another insincere apology between laughs. This was getting ridiculous. Still, as a sophomore, I needed to exude a certain level of maturity. Maybe it would rub off, though not likely.

When I turned back to the light, I heard his friends teasing him, and a pang of empathy stabbed me. I shouldn't have given him such a cold glare. He was just being a boy.

Probably more to save face than to retaliate against any actual offense, he pushed one of his annoying comrades. The friend pushed back, hard, ramming him into me for the third time.

But this time the force was too great to keep my balance. I stumbled into the street, dropping my backpack and skidding across the graveled road on my palms and knees. Before I could even conjure an emotional reaction, I heard my name behind me, like a whisper on the wind.

I struggled to my feet and turned to see Jared, tall and solid, on the curb where I had just been standing. My breath caught at the sight of him. The breeze tousled his dark hair. His full mouth curved into the suggestion of a smile, just enough for a dimple to appear at its corner. He stepped off the curb and walked to me, an animalistic grace controlling his every move.

Looking down into my eyes, he asked, "Do you trust me?"

I smiled warily. "Shouldn't I?"

"Close your eyes," he commanded gently.

I wanted to ask why, but found it impossible to question him. Unable to disobey, I let my eyelids close and lifted my face toward the sun. Its warmth soothed me, but Jared's presence comforted me as well, lulled me into a state of abandon.

"It won't hurt, Lorelei. I'll make sure of it."

I frowned in question. "What won't hurt?"

Before he could answer, I felt the impact.

Something very large and very heavy slammed into my body. It ripped me from gravity's selfish hold, and I flew through the air an unfathomable distance. My body quaked violently when it landed, broke as it slid into a lamppost.

I waited a short time before asking, "Can I open my eyes now?"

I heard Jared kneel beside me. "Yes."

I peeked and then laughed at the glittering, magical air around me. "This is strange."

He smiled at me again, a smile that seemed to know everything unknowable. "Yes, it is." He placed a careful hand on my chest. "Close your eyes again."

"Uh-uh. Not this time."

"Please."

I tried to shake my head, but my neck seemed to be broken. Curiosity drew my brows together. "Am I dying?"

"Yes," he said, regret softening his voice.

"How odd. I didn't think it would feel like this. And it's the anniversary of my parents' disappearance."

"I know." He seemed sad and I wondered why.

As I watched, he lowered his head and squeezed his eyes shut in concentration. Then, after a brief hesitation, he removed his hand from my chest and shook it. He sighed in frustration and watched me a long moment before looking up toward the heavens.

"I'm sorry," he said, speaking as though sure someone was listening. He glanced back at me. "I'm sorry, Lorelei." He placed his hand on my chest again. "Please, forgive me."

I wanted to say I would forgive him anything. I could feel power emanating from him. I could feel the conflict warring inside him, ripping at his resolve. But before I could respond, he closed his eyes again. And in an instant, life began to flow back into me in great, pulsing waves. I gulped huge rations of air as the stifling weakness I felt evaporated. Strength flooded every atom in my body.

I rested a hand on his, and he opened his eyes again. They were ablaze, bright, like fire at midnight. It startled me at first. As he looked on, an electric current passed between us. It rushed over my skin, causing my insides to tingle in almost painful delight. Slowly the fire in his eyes faded to smoldering embers before the deep darkness emerged again.

"Is she gonna be okay?"

The skaters had gathered around, all color drained from their faces.

Jared winked at me before turning to them. He placed a finger over his mouth. "Shhhh," he whispered.

Their eyes opened and shut as though trying to clear their heads. They stood up straight, then went back to jumping anything unfortunate enough to be in their paths, laughing and shouldering one another as they rolled down the street. The fact that I lay on the pavement after being hit by a truck seemed to have been forgotten.

I beamed at him. "How did you do that?"

A dimple appeared at the side of his mouth. "Magic."

His eyes sparkled like the air around us, and I had to force myself to focus.

A male voice intruded into my thoughts. "I know a little magic myself."

I looked up and gasped. Cameron was standing on my other side, aiming a rifle point-blank at Jared's chest.

Jared raised his hands instantly as if to block the gunfire. "Be still," he said in a harsh whisper. And the air thickened, the world slowed to a surreal halt, a frozen labyrinth of objects and people—either out of place or out of time, I couldn't decide.

Despite this, Cameron discharged the rifle. Bullet after bullet collided with Jared's chest.

I jumped wide-eyed with every shot fired, feeling as though each deafening sound struck me physically. But no bullets hit me. They hit Jared, each round punching through his body.

The shock of witnessing such violence immobilized me. But only for a minute. Instinct took hold. Without thought, I tried to get to my feet, to block the lead from entering Jared's body. Before I could lift myself off the ground, however, Jared placed his knee on my chest and held me down.

"What are you doing?" I screamed, clawing at his leg, trying to squirm out from under him, to no avail. I turned my head from Jared to Cameron. "Stop!" I tried to be heard above the roar of the gun. "Cameron, please stop!"

When the rifle was spent, an eerie silence echoed off the buildings around us. The acrid smell of gunpowder stung my nostrils and left a smoky trail in the air.

Cameron grinned at Jared. "Be still?" he asked with a chuckle. "That's the best you got?" He pulled back the bolt and began reloading the rifle. "News flash, Reaper, that crap doesn't work on me."

Jared stood and I took the opportunity to scramble out of the way. Then I realized he'd just done the impossible: He stood.

"I wouldn't say that's the *best* I've got," he said with a shrug, "but it impresses the girls."

"Yeah, so do bottle rockets."

"There's no blood." I stared up at Jared in disbelief, unable to blink, to comprehend what had just happened. "There's no blood. He just shot you."

I studied the frozen world around us: A mother peered into a store window as her daughter giggled and licked a dripping ice-cream cone, a sizable dollop inches from the ground. A skateboarder hung suspended in the air, his skateboard clinging to his feet as he jumped a park bench. His friends cheered, their laughter captured in time like a movie on pause. The camera crew across the street was staring as if in shock at a delivery truck as it passed through the intersection.

Still lying on the ground, I looked back at Jared, at the holes the bullets had torn into his chest. Yet he was standing, breathing. None of it made any sense.

Especially the smile on his face.

He eyed Cameron from underneath his lashes, flashed him a menacing grin. Then he changed, almost glowed, became so transparent, the bullets fell through him to land on the ground in a succession of light taps.

"That wasn't very nice," he said, becoming solid again. His white T-shirt still bore the holes of its recent abuse, each blackened by the blast of gunpowder. But not even a blush of red stained it.

Cameron sighed as he dropped another shell into the chamber. "I know," he said in almost bored contemplation. "My manners suck. I like to chalk it up to a dissatisfying childhood."

"I'd chalk it up to that narcissistic personality disorder laced with a smidgen of schizophrenia. Your mother would be proud."

Cameron's head snapped up in disbelief. Anger watered his blue eyes and hardened his strong features as he chambered a shell and again pointed the gun at Jared.

I leapt to my feet. "No, Cameron!"

Without unlocking his gaze, he shoved me roughly back to the earth, too intent on baiting Jared to bother with someone so apparently inconsequential.

"You'll tell Mom hi for me, won't you?" Cameron asked as he eased the trigger back. He received only a click for his effort.

"Magic," Jared said with a wink.

Undeterred, Cameron took the rifle in both hands and swung. But Jared caught it millimeters from his face and slammed it back into Cameron's jaw. He stumbled back, tested his jaw, then charged.

The fight that ensued seemed more mystical than real, as though two gods had chosen Earth as their battlefield. Each possessed strength beyond explanation.

I sat horrified. I winced with every throw, tensed with every collision of fist and body. While the earth stood still, a heated battle raged on the quiet streets of Riley's Switch. And with every swing, my breath caught, certain it would cause the death of one of them.

But the battle raged on. A fine sheen of sweat covered Cameron's determined face. Smeared blood trickled from his mouth and temple. He fought as if possessed, as if killing Jared were his one and only goal in life and he was more than willing to die in the process of achieving it.

While Jared seemed physically impenetrable, emotionally he was not so tempered. I felt a war within him. I felt it as easily as I could feel heat carried on a wind. Anger and indignation warred with something higher, something more noble, perhaps empathy or compassion.

The skirmish tumbled across the street, where mother and daughter stood frozen. The only sounds I could hear in the stillness were the raspy breaths of the gladiators and the harsh blows of combat. Even the scents of autumn had ceased to exist in the thick air.

Cameron lifted Jared and threw him onto the windshield of a silver Buick. The car dipped then bounced up and froze, distorted in time as though someone had taken a picture when least expected. The windshield splintered into a thousand shards of sparkling glass, yet held in place, creating a glittering mosaic.

Still on the car, Jared kicked when Cameron charged forward, sending him backwards through the store window, the same window mother and daughter stood peering into. He missed the women by inches.

Again, the glass cracked as if aging before my eyes, fissures webbing throughout the pane. A small crunching sound could be heard; jagged edges surrounded the hole his body created, and yet time held it in place.

Jared slid off the car and eyed the opening Cameron's figure had carved into the window, waiting for his adversary to reappear.

I held my breath, hoping Cameron had been knocked unconscious so the fight would end.

Please, please let it end.

As I watched the window expectantly, I heard a groan from Jared. I looked over at him. He suddenly seemed dizzy. Squeezing his eyes shut, he clutched his stomach and fell to his knees. My heart jumped in alarm. He struggled unsuccessfully to stand, as I ran to him.

I fell to my hands and knees beside him. "Jared, are you okay?" I asked worriedly.

Of course he wasn't okay. He'd just been thrown into a windshield. Yet he didn't have a scratch on him. Cameron bled. A lot. Jared obviously did not. Though his skin remained flawless, his face contorted in agony. He grimaced and doubled over again.

I placed a hand on his shoulder. "Please, Jared. Please let it stop. This is insane."

But he seemed lost, confused. "What's happening to me?"

Just then Cameron kicked through the splintered glass, carrying a ragged piece of wreckage he had pulled from inside the store. He stood over us, bloodied, panting hard with each breath.

I looked up at him. "Cameron, stop."

"Get out of the way, Lorelei," he said, a hard warning in his tone.

"He's hurt."

"Yeah, but it's still breathing." He took the makeshift weapon in both hands like a baseball bat.

"What's happening to me?" Jared put a palm to his head and gritted his teeth. He held his stomach and doubled over for a third time, as if seized by a wave of excruciating pain. "What's happening?"

"What's happening?" Cameron asked with a bright smile. "You're getting your ass kicked, that's what's happening. Now, get out of the way, Lorelei."

"What are you doing to me?" Jared asked, his voice a caustic whisper.

"I just told you, tough guy. I'm kicking your ass. You have a super short attention span." He leveled a warning glare on me. "I won't say it again."

I realized I was crying. Tears blurred the determined face and ice blue eyes staring down at me.

"Put that down, Cameron," I said between pathetic sobs. "I mean it."

Frowning in frustration, Cameron grabbed my arm and jerked me back. I fought his hold with every ounce of energy I had, but he was simply too strong. I felt like a gnat fighting a diesel truck. He tossed me aside as easily as tossing paper into a breeze.

Before I could get my footing, Cameron took the board into both hands and swung. It struck Jared on the side of his head, knocking him onto his hands for balance. Jared looked toward the heavens, as if questioning God Himself, then collapsed onto the sidewalk.

When Cameron brought the board to the ready again, I ran at him. I charged with all my might and rammed a shoulder into his side. It surprised him and was enough to knock him off balance. He stumbled just as the world restarted. And it restarted with a vengeance. The force of time bouncing back knocked the breath out of me.

I gasped for air and glanced around. The skateboarder landed perfectly as his friends applauded his feat. The storefront window shifted with the power surge, showering small shards of glass around mother and daughter. They screamed and jumped back. The everyday noises of town replaced the thick void of silence: cars whirring, birds chirping, people talking—the sounds one becomes immune to until they are no longer there. The Buick's car alarm began blaring too as it bounced back into position.

Behind me, a delivery truck screeched to a halt in the middle of the intersection, its tires smoking in protest. The driver jumped out and ran over to where I was lying before. He scanned the area, confused.

"Wow, what happened to you, dude?"

One of the skaters spotted Cameron. He glanced at Jared, then back again. "Hey, man," he said, showing his palms, "we don't want any trouble."

Without another word, the skaters took off while the mother grabbed her daughter and backed away, her eyes wide and wary. I could hardly blame them. Cameron, spattered with blood and debris, held a board as though methodically planning the deaths of anyone within reach.

I started toward Jared, but Cameron grabbed me again.

"Get to my truck," he ordered, then shoved me in the direction of his pickup parked down the street.

As I stumbled for the kazillionth time that day, fury took hold. A searing heat laced up my spine. My cheeks grew hot with anger. I straightened to my full height—which, admittedly, wasn't much—and strode back to Cameron, purpose apparent in my every move. I had been shoved once too often that day. Enough was enough.

Though he was much too tall to stand eye-to-eye with, my pissed-off attitude seemed enough to get his attention. I stood in front of him, feet apart, fists on hips, and glared as ferociously as I could.

He pointed a finger at me in warning. "Lorelei—"

"If I get hit," I said, interrupting whatever dire threat he had in mind, "shoved," I continued, stepping closer for effect, "or run over one more time today, I swear by all that is holy, I will make it my personal goal in life to have the person responsible sent to prison on charges of kiddie porn."

Cameron stared at me, annoyance working his jaw. "Please, go to my truck," he said at last. "It's . . . not safe."

"You're not safe." Though I rolled onto my tiptoes, I still missed eye-level contact by over a foot. "And I'm not leaving him."

"I have no intention of leaving it. Please, just get to my truck."

A small crowd had gathered and people were beginning to ask questions, but none dared go near Cameron. I could hardly blame them.

"Fine," I said through my tightened jaw. I leaned in and poked his chest with an index finger. "But don't shove me again."

He dropped his make-shift weapon and surrendered with palms up. "You had me at kiddie porn."

Satisfied, I scooped up my backpack and waited for Cameron. He took hold of Jared's ankles and dragged him through the glass on the sidewalk and across the graveled street toward his truck. Their progress made a disturbing crunching sound.

I followed beside them, wanting to help Jared but unsure of what to do. For the first time, blood covered one side of his face, the side Cameron had hit with the store wreckage.

He was bleeding. Why now?

Cameron continued to drag him over the rough, graveled pavement until we arrived at his aging pickup. Rust and splotches of peeling tan and cream-colored paint held it together. A lopsided camper shell sat perched over the bed. The vehicle as a whole looked like it had recently survived a nuclear explosion.

Cameron dropped Jared's ankles to open the tailgate and camper lid. Inside, crumpled blankets and pillows covered the bed floor. Dirty clothes formed a pile in one corner along with a few empty water bottles, soda cans, and a box of crackers. I glanced at Cameron, wondered how many times he had slept in his pickup. And why.

As he bent to grab Jared, I tossed my backpack in the bed and crawled inside. Cameron straightened.

"Get out of the bed. You can't stay back here with it."

"We have to get him to a hospital." Despite my best efforts, desperation tinged my voice. "And stop calling him an it. He's a person, Cameron."

I thought he was going to laugh at me. Then he heard the sirens.

"It's no more a person than your backpack is. And I was thinking more along the lines of the morgue." He lifted Jared with little effort and shoved him beside me in the truck.

"That's not funny."

"It wasn't meant to be. Now, get out." When I refused, he reached in, grabbed my wrist, and pulled me roughly until I stumbled onto the pavement. "Get in the front seat," he ordered.

My anger ignited again. As he turned to close the tailgate, I swung a fist and hit him on the arm. Though it hardly fazed him, he did gift me with a quick glance.

"I told you not to shove me again."

"I didn't shove you," he said, reaching for the lid of the camper shell. "I dragged you."

The lid's hinge stuck on one side. When he reached to release it, I scrambled over the tailgate and back into the bed.

"Damn it, Lorelei." He glared at me, but I scooted to the farthest corner from him. If he wanted me, he was going to have to work for it.

"What are you going to do with him?" I asked.

He eyed me for a long time before finally answering. "Whatever it takes."

Just then Jared moaned. Cameron stilled, watched him as though he were a cobra about to strike. He held out a hand without taking his wary gaze off Jared.

"Take my hand."

"No," I said defiantly. "What are you going to do?"

The sirens were getting closer.

"Lorelei, you don't know what it is, what it's capable of."

"What are you going to do?"

He closed his eyes in frustration and sucked in a lungful of air. Without looking at me, he asked one more time.

"Lorelei, please."

"No." My voice was soft, more unsure than I'd wanted. But I refused to move. "I wasn't kidding when I said I wouldn't leave him."

Without warning, Cameron slammed his fist into the tailgate. The pickup lunged forward as the tailgate crunched inward, yielding to his strength, reminding me of his potential.

He reached up and slammed the camper lid shut with the same angry force. I was surprised the glass didn't shatter.

I heard him retrieve the rifle from across the street before climbing into the driver's seat. He started the pickup then backed onto a side street to avoid the approaching police cars. With tires squealing, he turned and headed toward the highway.

PARADOX

Jared lay unconscious on his back, his face turned toward me, his thick lashes forming half circles across his cheeks. He swayed with the motion of the truck, like a child sleeping, oblivious of the world around him. His breathing, deep and steady, helped me relax, even if just barely. Blood streaked over his jaw and mouth. I took a dirty T-shirt from the corner to wipe it off, but only managed to smear it. He looked darker. His skin wasn't as light as it had been, like something had changed.

He was a paradox, I thought, a self-contradiction. He looked so young, so new to the world, but when he touched me, he seemed centuries old. I saw knowledge in his eyes of things no one could know. And my vision. Had it been real? Had that really happened? Maybe he was from another dimension, another time.

The glass between the camper and cab slid open. I looked up. Cameron was trying to keep an eye on the road and me at the same time.

"Climb up here," he said.

Eyeing the minuscule opening, I gave him my best look of incredulity.

"If it wakes up," he continued, "we'll both be in a world of trouble."

"I can't fit through there."

"Give me a break. You weigh, like, two pounds."

I rolled onto my knees and glanced through the window at the road. We were headed down into Abo Canyon. "We have to get him to a hospital," I said, panic threading through my words. "Where are we going?"

"Lorelei, please. If you'll just get up here, I'll explain what I can."

"No. Where are we going first?"

"I don't know yet," he said with an irritated sigh. His hands, stained with the dark reds of human blood, tightened on the wheel.

"Cameron, just turn around. He could die."

He frowned into the rearview mirror at me. "It'll take a lot more than that to kill it." He looked back at the road, his brows kneading in thought. "I may have to use a chain saw."

I sucked in a sharp breath. "That wasn't funny."

"Good thing I wasn't kidding, then." He checked his sideview mirror. "Damn it."

"What?" I looked out the back glass as an eighteen-wheeler bore down on us, so close that all I could see was its chrome grille. The steep grade of the canyon made it difficult for trucks to maneuver through its twists and turns.

"Nothing like a rectal exam by an eighteen-wheeler."

"Cameron, turn around," I said, searching the area for a place to pull over. There just wasn't one, and wouldn't be for a few miles.

"Look, as soon as we get out of the canyon, I'll explain, okay? I have to get you to a safe place."

"Me?" I asked, stunned. "Why me? What's this all about?"

I glanced over my shoulder. The eighteen-wheeler was struggling with its speed, but it did manage to back off a few feet.

"Would you just quit arguing and get up here?"

I looked down at Jared. Blood had pooled on the blanket beneath his chin. "He's bleeding really bad."

"Yeah, that was kind of the idea when I hit him with that board."

Exasperated, I leaned in through the window to look at him point-blank. He concentrated on the road, but slanted his eyes toward me as I came into his peripheral vision.

He was an absolute mess. His blond hair hung in clumps caked with blood. Scratches and cuts and some rather impressive bruises covered his swollen face. His mouth bled from a deep gash in the corner, as did his right eye.

I had to reason with him. I needed answers, and Jared needed a hospital. "Cameron," I said, my voice pleading, "why is this happening? Why are you and Jared so strong? Why are you trying to kill each other? And what does any of this have to do with me?"

He squeezed the steering wheel as though uncomfortable with my proximity. After wiping his face across a shoulder, he turned away to look down the side of the mountain. We were coming off the grade. The ground leveled and the truck backed off even more.

As I waited for a response, some kind of explanation, I heard

Jared moan again. Before I could ease back into the bed, Cameron reached over with lightning-quick speed and grabbed my arm.

"Gotcha," he said as he tried to drag me into the cab.

But Jared had grabbed me also. He had hold of my leg and clearly had no intention of letting go. As they played tug-of-war with my body, the thin metal strip along the ledge of the sliding glass window cut into my ribs. A searing pain slashed through me.

I screamed and used my free hand to try to push myself up off the ledge. "Cameron, let go!"

He hesitated, worked his jaw, then finally let go and scanned the area for a place to pull over. In the meantime, Jared jerked me through the small portal. I landed on top of him and gasped as he clutched a fistful of hair at the back of my head. He wrapped a steel-like arm around my waist to lock me to him then eyed me with something disturbingly similar to hatred.

"What did you do to me?" His voice was harsh, raspy. He looked scared, like a little boy lost and alone—and pissed as Hell because of it.

His arm was like a metal vise, making it almost impossible to breathe. I pushed against him, gasped for air. But the more I struggled, the tighter the vise's crushing hold became.

I cried out in pain for a second time. Lack of oxygen sent the world spinning around me.

I heard Cameron call to me. "Lorelei, hold on!"

Jared wound his fist deeper into my hair and pulled me closer. "What did you do to me?"

"I . . . I don't understand," I managed between gasps.

In a smooth unhampered move, he rolled on top of me, pinning me down with the weight of his solid body. He held me there for a long time.

Though no fires burned in his eyes as before, there was enough heat from his piercing gaze to sear me to the spot. He jerked my head back and wrapped his long fingers around my throat, slitting his eyes as if daring me to defy him again.

"I could break your neck," he said in a husky whisper as he moved so close, I thought his lips would touch mine, "before you even felt the twitch of my hands." His breath, sweet and warm against my mouth, felt so at odds with the cold, cruel sincerity of his words. "I could boil the blood in your veins and fuse your bones together." His eyes were knives, stabbing me with hot anger. "And I could make sure you lived long enough to feel every surge of pain, every nuance of agony."

Fear engulfed me as it never had before. After what I'd seen today, I didn't doubt a single word he was saying. "I'm sure that you could," I said with a nervous swallow, then added, "Please don't."

He was shaking violently, or perhaps it was me. I wondered if he had stopped time again, because everything seemed to stand still as he stared down at me, a contemptuous rage glittering in his eyes.

"What did you do to me?" he asked again.

I raised a hand—praying he wouldn't take it as a threat and carry out the aforementioned atrocities—and placed it on the side of his face.

He tried to back away, but I held my ground, kept my palm on his warm face.

"Jared," I said, my voice quivering uncontrollably, "I would never hurt you." He peered curiously at a tear as it pushed past my lashes. "I couldn't hurt you even if I wanted to."

He watched me warily as though struggling with some inner demon before saying, "You're the only one who can."

A sound above caught our attention. Cameron was trying to aim his rifle and drive at the same time. Jared grabbed the barrel just as the gun went off, startling me to the core. It blew a jagged hole in the top of the camper.

In one fluid movement, he jerked the gun from Cameron's hand, chambered a round as he rose to his knees, and pointed it at Cameron's head.

"No!" I scrambled up and lunged at him, trying to push the rifle aside. I shouldered myself between him and the pickup—between him and Cameron. Clutching at Jared's T-shirt, I coaxed his sight down to mine. "No more." I spoke softly but firmly. "This has to stop." I turned to Cameron. "Both of you. This has to stop."

Cameron grinned. He had no intention whatsoever of listening to me. "Not in this lifetime, love."

He reached below the seat and took out a nasty-looking pistol, the kind that held six fat rounds.

The instant the gun went off, I found myself on the bed of the pickup, facedown. Jared was over me, but only for a split second. Before Cameron could get off another shot, he kicked down the tailgate and slid out the back of the pickup.

After a brutal fall to the pavement and a few rolls, he sprang up to land solidly on his feet. My breath caught as the eighteen-wheeler behind us tried to brake, sliding and skidding in helplessness. My hands flew to my mouth, sure Jared would be crushed.

He stood eyeing me, unconcerned. Just as the truck bore down upon him, he sidestepped calmly out of its way.

The relief that flooded my senses sent an unwelcome darkness washing over me. I shook my head to keep it at bay, forced myself not to pass out.

When Cameron screeched to a halt on a narrow pull-off, I flew forward and hit the cab. Pain exploded in my head. For the second time I almost lost consciousness, but I fought it with every ounce of determination I had.

I glanced back at Jared. He hadn't moved. He was still standing there, eyeing me, his powerful stance testifying to his strength, to the might he held in his grasp.

Cameron jumped out of the cab and retrieved the rifle from the bed. He turned and pointed it.

Jared stood his ground.

But again I lunged and knocked Cameron off balance. The shot fired harmlessly into the air.

Jared bared his teeth.

As Cameron chambered another round, Jared turned and sprinted toward the caves in the red canyon wall, disappearing behind a hill.

With a curse, Cameron threw the rifle onto the ground. "Why did you do that?" he yelled, engulfed by anger and frustration. "Don't you see what you've done?"

I shook my head in disgust. "You're crazy. You're both crazy."

He stepped toward me and I tensed. He must have seen me flinch, because he stopped himself. Tension dug furrows into his forehead as he glared at me. "Better crazy than dead," he said at last. He turned and latched the abused tailgate. "Get in the cabin."

"I'm not going anywhere with you. You're absolutely nuts. Here you've been stalking me for days, and now—"

"Him!" he said harshly. "It! I've been stalking that thing for the last three days."

His confession stunned me. I stared at him with mouth agape. Why would he have been stalking Jared?

Growing impatient, Cameron tried to take hold of me again, to drag me back into his pickup. I fought him with a wicked kick to his shin.

Success at last. Finally something got his attention. He let go with a string of curses any rapper would be proud of and fell back against the tailgate, rubbing his shin vigorously. After a moment, he slid to the bumper and cast a malevolent look at me, breathing hard, his patience clearly dissipating.

"Whose blood do you think you're covered in?" he asked, raw emotion ragging his voice.

I glanced down at myself for the first time and gasped. He was right. I was practically drenched in blood. My apricot shirt had become dark crimson. My capris had huge ugly spots and hung in ragged tatters over my knees. I swiped at the blood, tried to get it off as a latent state of shock consumed me.

"That thing's?" he continued. "Mine? It's yours, Lorelei." He leaned forward. "You don't know what it is, why it was sent here."

"Sent here?" I asked as I peeled my shirt away from my skin. Nothing. Not a single scratch, and yet at some point I'd been drenched in blood.

"For you. It was sent here for you," he said with fury.

"Of course," I said as realization dawned. How else could I have survived without a scratch? "To save me."

Cameron scoffed aloud and shoved away from the truck. "Man, I wish I lived in your world." He picked up the rifle and threw it in the bed. "I'll tell you what, shortstop, when you're ready to return to Earth, you let me know. Until then, get your ass in the cab. I'm not leaving you out here."

"He saved my life, Cameron."

In an instant he turned on me, whirled around and stabbed me with a glare that made the blue in his eyes ignite with anger. "It doesn't do that!" he yelled, waving a hand toward the spot where Jared had been standing. "It doesn't save lives, Lorelei. That's not what it does."

"Then what?" I asked, growing more irritated by the second. "What are you talking about?"

"That's it." He raised his face toward the heavens as though asking God for patience. After sucking in a deep breath, he acknowledged me again. "I'm not doing this here. We have to go. Now, you will either get into this truck voluntarily, or you will get in by force. I'm up for either. But let me assure you, one way or another, you will get into this truck."

He was serious. Arguing with him had come to an end. With a sigh of resignation, I lifted my chin and strolled to the passenger's side, pretending it had been my idea all along. I needed to sit down anyway, before I collapsed.

Cameron climbed in and slammed his door shut to emphasize his sour mood. The sound sent a shock wave jolting through me. It sounded like the rifle as it fired into Jared's chest. I flinched and molded myself into the corner like the Cowardly Lion.

When Cameron started the truck, a wave of nausea washed over me. Everything that had happened that day hit me in one massive assault. From waking to find Cameron crouched by the tree outside my window—still there from the night before—to crashing into Jared in the hall; from being shoved into the street by skateboarders to being given a second chance at life by an angel; from witnessing the most savage acts of violence I had ever imagined possible to enduring the raw hatred and anger in Jared's eyes; from all of that to this. To not knowing why any of it was happening, to not knowing who Jared was, or how he did what he did.

"Wait," I said in a whisper as I felt my stomach lurch. "Wait, pull over."

"No way."

"No, I'm going to be sick. Pull over."

When I covered my mouth with both hands, Cameron reluctantly pulled over. Bile burned the back of my throat before I could open the door. Stumbling out of the pickup, I heaved onto the side of the road. I threw up the cappuccino I'd had at the coffee shop and a few other contents I dared not identify.

Cameron came around to stand beside me and tried to sympathize, but I held up a hand. "Don't," I said as I started to cry. "Just don't."

For reasons unknown even to myself, a sadness welled up

inside me. I couldn't hold it back. Tears glided past my lashes and trailed down my blistered cheeks. I fell raggedly to my knees and cried on the side of the road like a two-year-old.

I shook with trauma, with shock, with fear and doubt. And I longed for my parents, mourned their deaths. There were so many questions left unanswered. In the years since their disappearance, I hadn't forgotten what it felt like to be in their arms. It was like being embraced by love, enveloped by warmth and safety. I wanted them back so much, now more than ever.

I could feel Cameron at my side, but he didn't try to touch me again. Instead, he handed me an oily rag, probably one he used to work on his engine. But it was better than nothing. I wiped my face and mouth and after several embarrassing moments, I pulled cool air into my lungs and forced myself to calm.

A thought had emerged. A thought that, however disturbing, would explain a lot.

I looked up at Cameron, swallowed back the lump in my throat, and asked with more curiosity than fear, "Am I dead?"

He crouched beside me with a grim smile and, in the most understanding voice, said, "Not even close."

THE GIRL IN THE MIRROR

As Cameron cut through the dirt parking lot of Wild 'n Wonderful, my grandparents' health food store, I hunkered down in the passenger's seat.

"It's your grandmother," he said, letting me know who was in front running the store. It should have been me. I was scheduled to work at four. Guilt washed over me, adding to the turmoil churning in my already upset stomach.

"Was Grandpa with her?"

"I didn't see him."

"Darn. He may be in the house." My mind raced as Cameron pulled around to the back of the store where I'd lived since I was six. The store had an attached apartment. After my parents' disappearance, I moved in with my grandparents. I'd practically lived there anyway. My mom ran the store most of the time while I was being spoiled rotten by Grandma and Grandpa. Mom always said it should have been criminal to be so pampered. My chest cinched tightly with the memory. Shaking it off, I turned back to Cameron. "I'll just have to chance it. He could be at the church." Grandpa was the pastor of the Sanctuary, the only non-denominational church Riley's Switch had to offer, and it kept him pretty busy. "I need to get upstairs and change my clothes before they see me."

After he stopped and killed the engine, I crawled up into the seat and glanced around for Grandpa.

"Are you gonna be okay?" Cameron asked.

I looked at him, surprised. "Oh, sure," I said lightly. "Who doesn't enjoy a good violent brawl while drenched in the warmth of her own blood?"

He bowed his head in what appeared to be genuine regret. "I'm sorry about everything, Lorelei. I wish none of this had happened to you."

I didn't know what to say. It wasn't his fault. At least, I didn't think it was his fault.

He reached through the sliding glass window and grabbed my backpack for me.

"Thanks. What are you going to do now?" I asked, changing the subject.

He shrugged. "Take a shower."

"Me too," I said, crinkling my nose at my appearance. "And brush my teeth." Even though I had a million questions, the two of us were making a shaky truce. It was enough for now. "You're not going to do anything stupid, are you?" I asked.

"I'm pretty much the poster boy for stupidity, in case you haven't noticed."

"I haven't."

My statement caught him off guard. I could see it in his expression. That and appreciation.

I pursed my lips at him. "You know what this is called, don't you?"

His expression turned wary. "No, what?"

"It's called the Stockholm syndrome. You know, where the captive identifies with the captor?"

He shifted uncomfortably and glanced out his window. "I'm not your captor, Lorelei."

"Then what are you?" I knew he wouldn't give me a straight answer, but I had to try.

He continued to stare out his window. "I'm the same guy you've known since kindergarten."

"Dude, you may be many things, but one thing you are not is the same guy I've known since kindergarten."

He lowered his head. "I know. I just wish I were."

I needed to lighten the situation again. I liked it better light. And I needed a shower. Bad.

"Well," I said as I opened the door, "at least you don't have vomit aftertaste in your mouth."

He chuckled. "And at least I'm not covered in blood."

I gaped back at him. "Have you even looked at your face?"

He frowned and glanced in the mirror.

I couldn't help but laugh as I jumped out of the pickup and ran into the apartment.

Grandpa must have been out running errands or at the church. I sighed in relief, quietly so Grandma wouldn't hear me. With that miraculous stroke of luck, I managed to make it to my room unnoticed.

After sliding past the full-length mirror by my bed, I paused and stepped back for a better look. The shock that jolted through me caused a sharp intake of breath. Dried blood caked my hair and stained my skin and clothes. The back of my shirt hung in tattered strips, probably shredded when I landed on the street and slid into that lamppost. I lifted one ragged strip. The skin underneath remained unmarred.

And it hadn't hurt.

Jared had promised it wouldn't hurt, and it hadn't.

With a start that caused a wave of nausea to wash over me again, I realized I had been hit by a truck. A huge green delivery truck. I didn't actually remember being hit by a huge green delivery truck, but the knowledge was there nonetheless. I had been hit, no doubt about it. One minute I was at the light, the next I was lying under a lamppost a block away. An entire block away.

The realization set my world spinning again. Drained both physically and mentally, I suddenly felt exhausted to the point of delirium. The world darkened as it had when the eighteen-wheeler missed hitting Jared by a heartbeat. Only this time I couldn't stop it. The bones in my legs dissolved, and the floor tilted beneath my feet, rising to meet me as I lost all track of consciousness.

In what seemed like moments later, I found myself struggling to wake up, fighting my way out of the dark. My senses reemerged—thick and fuzzy around the edges—and I tried to open my eyes.

My lids, however, were not cooperating. Clearly they'd learned nothing from all those years in the Girl Scouts. I sucked air into my lungs and tried again, harder this time. Conjuring every ounce of strength I had, I managed to pry open one eye but only for a split second before it slammed shut again.

The room had darkened. In that instant, I did get a glimpse

of my surroundings, and the room had definitely darkened. I must have been out longer than I thought.

"She's waking up."

Brooklyn?

"We need to call an ambulance."

Glitch? No, Glitch, don't call an ambulance.

"I don't think any of this blood is hers. I can't find a scratch on her."

"But her ribs are really bruised. They could be broken."

"Lor, honey?" Brooklyn smoothed a warm damp cloth along my brow. It felt wonderful. "Can you hear me?"

I tried to speak, but words just wouldn't budge. A dry, scratchy sound erupted from my throat instead.

"Oh, my god," Glitch said, "they've turned her into a frog!"

Despite my predicament, I laughed. Leave it to Glitch to lighten even the darkest situation. I finally managed to pry open my eye again.

"A one-eyed frog! What kind of monsters—"

"Glitch!" Brooklyn said impatiently.

"All right," he acquiesced.

But it was too late. I was giggling. I saw a flash of pearly whites on Brooklyn's face as she propped me up with a pillow. I was on my bed with no memory of how I got there.

"I know, I know," she said. "What would we do without him?"

Glitch brought me some water. "Seriously, what's up with your eyes?"

I tried to shrug, but my limbs felt weighted, like someone had filled them with lead when I wasn't looking.

"Okay, never mind. We have about seven thousand questions. You up for it?"

I grinned behind the glass and finally pried the other eye open. "What time is it?"

"A little after nine," Brooklyn said.

With that, I bolted upright. "Nine? Nine o'clock? Nine o'clock at night?"

"Oh yeah, she's just fine."

"Glitch, believe it or not, your comments are rarely helpful." Brooklyn tried to ease me back down onto the pillows. "Yes, nine o'clock at night. We got here about six and found you sprawled all over the floor. Lor, what happened?"

"Oh my gosh, did my grandparents see me?"

"No, you begged us. Don't you remember?"

"I begged you? When was this?"

"When we got here. You begged us not to tell your grand-parents. You said you were fine, that Jared had saved you and not to call an ambulance. We helped you to your bed, then you passed out again." Brooklyn tucked the blanket around me. "It's a good thing your grandma can't get up and down those stairs very easily. She didn't even know you had come in."

"And you've been here this whole time?"

"Yeah," Glitch said from behind Brooklyn, "and so has the sheriff."

Once again, I bolted upright. "The sheriff? Here?"

"He's come by a couple of times," Brooklyn said, biting her lower lip. "But we told your grandparents you weren't feeling well. He's supposed to come back at . . . well, now. And your grand-mother's making you chicken soup. We didn't tell her you've been unconscious for the last three hours."

"Why?"

"Because you begged us not to," Glitch said as though I were simple. "Are you paying attention at all?"

"No, I mean the sheriff. What does he want?"

"I don't know," Brooklyn said, concern lining her eyes, "but he's been looking for you since this afternoon. Since right after that earthquake."

I choked on a half-swallowed gulp of water and coughed a good minute before I could speak again. "An earthquake?" I asked between gasps for air. "They're calling what happened on the streets of Riley's Switch this afternoon an earthquake?"

"I knew it wasn't an earthquake!" Glitch raised his arms triumphantly and did a victory stroll around my room. It was a short stroll. My room was tiny. "It was a tornado." He turned back to me in question. "Am I right?"

"In a way," I said, squirming to find a less lopsided position. "Only there were two tornadoes. One named Jared and one named Cameron."

That snapped them both to attention. Brooklyn gazed at me wide-eyed, a mixture of worry and curiosity in her expression.

"Okay, I'll tell you everything," I said, "but you have to keep an open mind. That means you too, Glitch."

He scoffed as though offended. "When has my mind ever been anything but open? And don't even bring up that whole turtles-are-innocent-and-kind thing. That doesn't count."

"All right," I said. "Do you remember this morning . . ."

And so began the tale of my most improbable, most impossible Tuesday. I told them everything I remembered in great detail, finding no need to elaborate. The story itself pushed the limits of human comprehension.

When I finished, both Brooklyn and Glitch sat staring at me. For a long time. A really long time. They were either absorbing the information I'd just imparted or sleeping with their eyes open. I wasn't sure which.

With tears sparkling beneath her lashes, Brooklyn spoke at last. "You mean, that truck really did hit you?"

"You heard about that?" I asked, my voice squeaking.

"Yes. Well, no. Kind of. One of those cameramen from the Tourist Channel burst into the café while we were sitting there. He said he could have sworn a truck hit a young girl with long auburn hair. He said you were gone, but he literally went around to all the customers and asked them if they'd seen anything. He said the town looked like an earthquake had hit it."

"I don't understand, Lor." Glitch sounded hurt. The look on his face proved it. "How could this happen? Any of it? You could have died." He stood and looked out the window. "You could have died."

My heart swelled. My two best friends in the world had sat with me for three hours. Their concern warmed me. Their very presence made me feel new again. Well, maybe not new. Maybe more like a really good-quality secondhand. But still.

"I *was* dying," I admitted.

"Don't say that," Brooklyn said, visibly shaken by my story.

"No, I was. Jared brought me back. I felt a life force surge through my body. I felt it."

"What did it feel like?" Brooklyn asked.

"I don't know exactly. Warm. Strong." After a moment, I confessed with a whisper, "It felt like him, pushing inside me, healing." I shook out the memory of his majestic touch with a forlorn sigh. "All I know is I was leaving and he brought me back."

"Then why did Cameron try to kill him?" Glitch was angry now, and I had to keep him calm. The last thing I needed was another angry male to contend with. Even a short one.

"That's exactly what I intend to find out."

"Well, I don't think you're the only one."

I glanced back at Brooklyn in question. "What do you mean?"

She looked at Glitch, then back at me. "After the cops came roaring through town this afternoon, we went back to the café. We kept trying to call you to make sure you were okay."

"Oh, right, sorry. I turned my phone off. I was going to the library." I fished it out of my pocket and turned it on. The screen was broken. Darned big green delivery truck. My grandmother was going to kill me.

"Well, that reporter was there, the one from the Tourist Channel doing the story on the hotel who kept asking everyone if they'd seen anything. He was sitting at the booth behind us, talking on the phone for-like-ever while we were trying to track you down. He kept going on and on about how this was it, about how he had found what they'd been looking for, and how he had it all on tape."

I inhaled sharply. "He got it on tape?"

"Not everything," Glitch said. "I think he was talking to some big-time producer. He said the tape screwed up right when the truck was about to . . . about to run you down." His voice faltered, proving the subject upset him. For some bizarre reason, I felt guilty.

"Yeah," Brooklyn said. "He was so excited, he was shaking, but I could tell the tape thing pissed him off. He argued with one of his technicians, told her to fix it or find another job. He had such an attitude."

"He did," Glitch agreed. "And he was saying that after the truck screeched to a halt, he saw this one kid, a blond, drag this other kid through the glass that just happened to shatter for no reason, then through the gravel on the street like he weighed nothing, while this girl, *the* girl, who should be dead, is following alongside them arguing with the blond guy and fussing over the dark-haired one, and that they were all covered in blood and—"

"In other words," Brooklyn said, interrupting, "someone else knows and is more than interested in what happened today. He said he would get the evidence, that he just needed more time."

"He seemed very determined, Lor," Glitch warned.

I nodded. Whoever he was, he definitely wanted the story. This was getting worse by the minute. "What did he mean, he found what they'd been looking for?"

"I have no idea," Brooke said. "He was like a dog with a bone."

"Darn. I'll just have to figure out this whole thing before Mr. Butthead Reporter does. But this time, I need some help." Both Brooklyn and Glitch perked up at that thought. "I don't suppose either of you would be up for an investigation of sorts?"

"Investigation?" Brooklyn asked, her eyes brightening. "I was born for it."

"And I was born for fame and fortune, but that's beside the point. I'm in."

I smiled and felt for the necklace Glitch gave me in memory of my parents. It wasn't around my neck. "My necklace is gone," I said, glancing around in alarm.

Brooke and Glitch scanned the room as well before Glitch said, "You know, you were hit by a truck. There's no telling where it is now."

My shoulders deflated in disappointment. "I really liked it, Glitch."

"I can get you another one," he said with a shrug. "My dad made it for you."

I pulled in a soft gasp. "Your dad made it?" Now I really felt guilty.

"Yeah, but now he has the mold. It won't take him any time to make another."

But I wanted that one. The first one. The one made just for me and my parents. I tried to brush my hair back with my fingers, but they got tangled in the blood-caked mess on my head. Gross. "Okeydokey, it's definitely shower time."

HYBRID

"In a million years I never thought I would say this, but . . . are you sure we should be skipping?"

Brooklyn and I both turned to Glitch, our faces a snapshot of surprise. We were in his sad excuse for a Subaru, heading to the spot where Jared had disappeared. I didn't know where else to start, so retracing my steps seemed the most logical thing to do.

"Glitch," I said after the shock of his statement ebbed, "have you gone mad? You skip for any reason under the sun."

Brooklyn laughed in remembrance. "I especially liked the one where the nightmare about the giant turtles made him too tired to concentrate on his schoolwork, and he felt he would be a distraction to the rest of the class, so in the interest of everyone's educational experience, he should be allowed to go home."

I snickered. "That was a good one."

"Yeah," Glitch said, "but the sheriff wasn't looking for me on turtle-nightmare day."

"And he's not looking for you today either. He's looking for me," I said. I had managed to wiggle out of my talk with the sheriff once again the evening before, complaining to my grandmother that my stomach was upset. Unfortunately, I hadn't been lying. Though her chicken soup did help. It always helped.

"And when he finds you in my car . . ."

Brooklyn snorted. "Looks like macho boy's cool just melted like a Slush Puppie in August."

Glitch rolled his eyes as he drove his ancient Subaru through the canyon. "Don't try to pull your peer-pressure Jedi mind tricks on me. Are you sure it was this far?"

"Yes. It's just up here," I said, pointing ahead redundantly.

"How are your ribs?" Brooklyn asked.

I tested them with my fingertips. "Better, I think. Just a little sore." I touched a tender spot and winced. "Or a lot sore."

"They're really bruised. I still think you should have them checked out by a doctor, or at least the school nurse," Glitch said.

"How can I have them checked by the nurse without my grandparents finding out? She'd call them. She would have to."

Brooklyn shrugged. "You know, Lor, they're a lot stronger than you think."

"I know they are, but they can't find out. Ever. My parents disappeared off the face of the earth. Just vanished. How do you think they would feel if they knew I almost did the same? In a roundabout way."

"I know. I'm just saying—"

"Here! Right here!" I pointed with more enthusiasm than I'd intended. "See the skid marks?"

Glitch pulled to the side of the road and turned toward us. "Okay. What now?"

The hill that Jared had disappeared behind was only about a quarter mile back. I opened my door, grabbed my water, and said, "Now, we search."

Four hours later, I sat in the Java Loft with two slightly annoyed friends eyeing me.

We'd skipped school for nothing. After looking all day, we didn't find even a trace of Jared. My feet hurt. I'd almost sprained my ankle seventeen thousand times trying to traverse the uneven ground of the canyon. And worry gnawed at me, twisting my insides into knots. Where could he have gone? He was hurt and alone and probably cold and hungry.

And why on planet Earth did the white news van for the Tourist Channel keep circling the block?

"Have you given any thought to their strength?" Glitch asked, jarring me out of my musings. "Because I have. I'm thinking maybe this Jared's an alien. The Roswell crash site is just around the corner. Or maybe he's a supernatural entity. You know, like a demon or something."

"A supernatural background would definitely fit with the vision I had, no matter how crazy it sounds, but what about Cameron?" I asked. "I mean, Cameron Lusk? Come on. We've known him since kindergarten." I nursed a mocha cappuccino, my imagination running amok.

"This bites," Brooklyn said. "Cameron's hot."

Glitch and I glanced up in surprise, though Glitch did seem a little more annoyed than surprised.

"He is," she said defensively. "He was hot when I moved here in the third grade, and he's still hot now."

"Well, I can't argue that," I said with a shrug. While he definitely had the tortured, brooding teen down pat, there was a reason girls fawned over him. Sadly, they usually ended up disappointed. He took the loner bit to a whole new level. "He's just so antisocial."

"Man, but that smile of his." Brooklyn seemed to slip into a dream, her stare looking but not seeing.

"His smile?" Glitch asked, irritated. "Cameron Lusk hasn't smiled in years."

"I wonder what his home life is like," Brooklyn said, ignoring him. "It can't be good. I mean, look at the way he dresses."

Normally, the look of utter disbelief plastered on Glitch's face would've lifted my spirits. But his expression held something more, something desperate. Something close to agony lined his eyes. He relaxed his facial muscles almost immediately, wiping away any evidence that Brooke's impression of Cameron had hurt him. "Isn't this the same guy who tried to murder another human being yesterday?"

Brooklyn snapped out of it and cast him an angry look. "You just said Jared is probably an alien. There are no laws against killing aliens." She tilted her head in thought. "Least none that I know of."

"Great," he said, his jaw flexing. "That just makes everything peachy."

I understood Glitch's point, but this was not the time for personal biases. Whatever happened between him and Cameron during that camping trip, if anything, it couldn't hinder us now. But I found it impossible to tell if Glitch's gut reaction to Brooke's sentiments had anything to do with that or if he'd been hurt for different reasons.

Either way, I couldn't worry about it now. I needed Glitch on the bandwagon 100 percent. I wanted more than anything to find Jared. Needed to find him.

"Look," I said with determination, "Cameron said he was following Jared, not me. I don't know how and I don't know why, but I do know he is our best bet in finding him. I say we look for Cameron and hopefully find Jared along the way."

Glitch shook his head. "I don't want you anywhere near Cameron Lusk."

"Well, I think it sounds like a plan," Brooklyn said. "Got any idea where to start?"

"Absolutely not," he said, bitterness creeping into his voice. "We are not going in search of a certified psychopath who takes better care of his guns than he does his truck."

I leveled a hard stare on him, my face tightened, my expression unyielding.

Moments later, he caved. "Fine." He tossed a napkin onto the table. "But I can't miss football practice."

"You're the manager. You can't miss one practice?" I asked.

"Do you even know Coach Chavez? You two'll just have to lie low until practice is over. Then we can *all* go in search of the mighty Cameron together."

"We're big girls, Glitch," I said, more than a little perturbed.

He choked on his cappuccino, coughed for like twenty minutes, then turned back to us. "Big?" he asked. "You're barely five feet tall."

"I meant age-wise."

"You're five-zero."

"Glitch."

"Five-nada."

"You're missing the point."

"Five-nil, zip, zilch . . . aught."

I sighed long and loud, letting my aggravation ooze into the atmosphere. "What time is practice over?"

———

"This is so cool," Brooklyn said as we eased up a path cleared of brush to Cameron's front door. "We're like the Three Musketeers, searching for truth and justice and the American way."

Glitch snorted. "More like the Three Blind Mice, stumbling around trying to find a hunk of cheese in the dark. This is crazy. Cameron's a tad psychotic, in case you haven't noticed. And besides, the Three Musketeers were French. They would not have been searching for the American way."

Even though Glitch knew where Cameron lived, it took us a while to find the small mobile home tucked into a forest grove on the valley floor. Its olive green exterior, camouflaged against the backdrop of evergreens, sat perched on cracked tires, deflated for years by the looks of them. Junk metal formed an intricate pile of rusting artifacts at one end of the house, glistening in the setting sun.

"I guess this answers my question about his home life," Brooklyn said, her nose scrunching in distaste.

"Maybe." But it didn't really look like the stereotypical poverty-stricken household to me. Except for the junk metal, the yard was pristine, well kept. There was no trash, no overgrown brush, no empty beer cans or broken lawn chairs in the front yard as I would have expected. True, Cameron dressed like he lived in a perpetual state of poverty, but I felt his wardrobe was more a choice than a product of his upbringing. He liked grunge.

I raised my hand and knocked on the vinyl-covered door.

When it didn't open immediately, Glitch asked, "Can we leave now?"

He really didn't want to be there. Just as I was about to answer, a stocky dark-haired man opened the door. He wore a dirty gray T-shirt and held an unopened bottle of beer in one hand. He eyed us suspiciously at first, then allowed a small upturn of his lips to soften his mouth.

If this guy was Cameron's father, he looked absolutely nothing like his son. Where Cameron was ridiculously tall, blond-haired, and blue-eyed, this guy was average height with black hair and brown eyes. His skin had dried to the consistency of leather—clearly having worked in the New Mexico sun all his life—and his thick arms and neck were nothing like Cameron's lanky frame.

"Um, Mr. Lusk?" I asked in a whispery, uncertain voice.

"That would be me," he said easily. "But I don't have any cash if you're looking to sell something. Don't keep much around the house."

"Oh, no," Brooklyn said from behind me. "We were just wondering if Cameron was home."

"Really?" he asked, surprised. "You came to see the kid?" He looked directly at me then, calm, knowing. "I didn't figure he'd have let you out of his sight for anything."

I stilled in bewilderment. "You know about that?" I asked. "About how he's been following me?"

"Why don't you kids come in." His smile was gentle and re-assuring, not unlike a serial killer's, from what I'd read. "Can I get you something to drink?" he asked as we stepped across the threshold.

The interior was actually very nice. Light beiges, ashen wood accents. It was all very warm and inviting. And a soft fire crackled in a wood-burning stove on the far wall.

"I'll take a beer," Glitch said, his tone completely serious.

The man laughed. "And I'll take a one to five in the state pen. I don't think so. There's soda in the fridge. Help yourself."

As Glitch shuffled to the kitchen, I checked out Cameron's house in fascination.

"I know," the man said with a smile. "You expected olive green carpet and gold filigree wallpaper. I get that a lot."

Despite all efforts to the contrary, I felt myself blush. Clearly my surprise could've been taken as an insult.

"Please, sit down," he said.

Glitch had grabbed an orange soda, our absolute favorite, for us to share, then sat beside Brooklyn on a small sofa. I sank down into a comfortably overstuffed chair, the kind you could sleep in for days.

"Sorry about my attire," he said. "I was working on the house. Didn't know I would have such auspicious guests."

We should have called first. I knew it. Grandma said it was rude to just show up on someone's doorstep uninvited, but I didn't want to give Cameron a heads-up, so we went with a surprise attack. Not that it had done any good.

"You were working on this house?" Brooklyn asked.

"Oh, no." He grinned as if the thought amused him. "I was working on Cameron's house. We've been building a house for him since he was about, oh, eleven I guess. Good thing we started early, eh?" he added with a wink.

The man's behavior floored me. Based on Cameron's personality, which was mostly angry with a side of angry, I'd expected an ogre. Possibly an abuser. Instead I found a charming, sincere, hardworking gentleman.

I cleared my throat. "So, can I ask what you meant?"

"I figured you might." He put his unopened beer on a side table, apparently unwilling to drink in front of us. "He's been on this mission for several days now. He does that from time to time. Told me he was watching you."

"Yes," I said, "he was. But do you know why?"

"Kind of. But I don't see the things he sees. And I'm all the happier for it."

The things he sees? My chest tightened with hope. Finally, I might get some answers.

"I don't have any answers, though, if that's why you've come."

Just as quickly, my hopes plummeted.

He seemed to pick up on my distress. Leaning forward, he looked at me like he understood how I felt. "I'm sorry I don't know more," he said quietly. "I'd help you if I could. Heck, I'd help the kid if I could. He doesn't let me in much. Never has."

"Why?" Brooklyn asked as though desperate for answers herself. "Why is he so . . . well, he's just so—"

"Bullheaded?" he asked.

"Yes!"

He shook his head, unfazed by Brooklyn's zeal. "Been like that since his mom passed away. Stubborn as the day is long."

"I'm so sorry," I said, regret softening my voice, "about your wife."

"And I'm sorry about your mom and dad," he said. "I knew them both."

I gasped softly in surprise. "You knew my parents?"

"Sure did. I used to work at the railroad with your dad. Hard man to please, that one. But fair. Your mom kept his britches pulled up tight. She was a firecracker." He beamed at me. "Just like you, from what I hear."

I couldn't help the proud smile that spread across my face. Or the lump that suddenly formed in my throat. I swallowed hard. "I only remember them a little."

"Naturally. You were a young one when all that happened."

"How old was Cameron when your wife passed away?"

A sadness clouded his eyes, and I regretted the question the instant I asked it, wished I could take it back. But he didn't seem to notice.

"He was two, almost three. He saw it even then. Saw it come for her, take her."

I froze and something squeezed tight around my chest. "What did he see?" I asked, my voice barely audible.

He looked up. "Are you sure you don't know?"

Glitch passed me the soda, then sat back and crossed his arms over his chest as though refusing to listen. I took a quick swig, the acidic fizz of orange soda making my eyes water. After a moment—and a light cough—I answered, "Mr. Lusk, I don't know anything right now, other than the fact that I don't know anything."

An understanding smile spread across his face. "Please, call me David. And that would put us in the same boat. I only know bits and pieces, the parts the kid yells out in his sleep. I learned a long time ago not to ask questions."

"He yells in his sleep?" Brooklyn asked, her face a picture of concern, and I suddenly realized how much she cared for him. I couldn't believe I didn't pick up on it before. I couldn't believe she didn't tell me. And I couldn't believe the tension that had Glitch grinding his teeth together. Was he jealous of Cameron or just worried about Brooke? We'd been friends for so long, it had never occurred to me that he could have genuine feelings for her.

"Sometimes," Mr. Lusk said, "yes, he does."

Brooklyn sank back against the cushions.

"Mr. Lusk," I said, then corrected when he gave me a teasing glare, "I'm sorry, David, whatever you know, I promise it's more than we know. Anything you can tell us would help. I'm just trying to understand what's happening," I added when I could see he was going to protest.

He leaned back in his chair with a sigh, his dark skin a shadow against the light fabric. After a long moment, he finally said, "He calls it the reaper."

Brooklyn perked up, but Glitch seemed a thousand miles away. I handed her back the soda then braced my elbows on my knees as Mr. Lusk spoke.

"Says it's enshrouded in darkness," he continued, staring into the fire in thought, "and that it comes to take people before their time. For some reason he can see it, could always see it, among other things. His mother said he had a special gift. She believed him even when he was two, when we were at a restaurant in Albuquerque and he told her there was a dead woman sitting in the booth next to us."

My breath caught with the image, but I forced myself not to react, not to show Mr. Lusk how much the mere thought of that statement disturbed me. "You didn't believe him?" I asked softly, changing the subject, so to speak.

"Not at the time." He seemed to regret that. "But his mother knew. She tried to tell me. It was all just so hard to swallow."

"He's really strong," Glitch said, his expression venomous. "Is that part of his gift?"

If Mr. Lusk picked up on Glitch's disrespect, he didn't show it. "I suppose." He lifted his shoulders in a half shrug. "Don't really know for sure. Kid's darned near indestructible. Always has been. His mom told him it was our little secret. She thought if people found out, they would begin to ask questions, maybe even take him away from us."

"Do you have any idea where he might be right now?" Brooklyn asked.

He shook his head. "Not even a smidgen of one."

"What about you?" Glitch raised his brows at me, as though everything was normal, as though he hadn't seethed all the way home after visiting Cameron's dad the night before.

I dropped my books on my desk, deciding to drop the line of questioning I'd planned as well. We had enough going on without adding fuel to Glitch's fire. Even though our lives were in utter turmoil, school started at eight in the A.M., sharp as a thumb tack, unwilling to cease its relentless weekday schedule despite our extenuating circumstances.

To top it off, I'd had one of my recurring dreams, the disturbing one where I swallowed something dark and it ripped me in two, trying to escape. I woke up panting and sweating as I always did when I had that dream. Then I tossed and turned the rest of the night, wondering where Jared was, if he was okay.

So, with only three hours' sleep under my belt, I turned to him in frustration. "Not only am I sleep-deprived and cranky, I've also been grounded for life."

"Me too," Brooklyn said as she walked into first hour. "My mom was totally pissed. She acted like I committed armed robbery or something."

"How do you do it?" I asked Glitch, a master at ditching and other nonproductive ventures. "How do you skip school and get away with it?"

With the spotlight on him, Glitch brightened. He took a moment to slick back his hair and polish his nails on his Riley High jacket, then leaned in as if to impart some ancient guarded secret. "Skill, ladies," he said under his breath. "Pure, unmitigated skill."

Brooklyn squinted at him. "You were so busted, weren't you?"

"Yep," he confessed. "Grounded for two days past forever."

I whistled, impressed. "That's longer than life."

"Bummer, huh?" he said. "I gotta get to class. See you at lunch."

After he left, I asked Brooklyn, "Think we'll get detention?"

An older feminine voice behind me answered. "I wouldn't make any immediate plans."

I turned to Ms. Mullins, my science teacher, as she handed me an official-looking slip of paper. I opened it with dread. "The principal wants to see me?"

"It would seem so," she said, peering at me from over her glasses. "Hurry down there."

"Man," I whined as I left the room, "my grandma is going to kill me."

So this was the hot seat.

I eyed the stuffed bear perched atop Principal Davis's computer as I sat waiting in his office. Appropriate. Everyone called him the Bear, a fact that did nothing to ease my discomfort. My nerves were becoming more frazzled the longer I sat there, staring at that bear, questioning my inane decision to take the previous day off to investigate Houdini. Jared had disappeared. Vanished. And Cameron seemed to have joined him.

I rolled my eyes in annoyance for the fiftieth time at having to be in the principal's office. As if last night wasn't bad enough.

Apparently, the school's automated system called the house when I missed class without an excuse. By the time I got home, which was past my curfew, my grandparents already knew I'd skipped and I was promptly and thoroughly grounded for the rest of my natural-born life.

But Grandpa had faith in me. He couldn't believe his pixie stick would skip for no reason. Surely I had a good explanation.

Unfortunately, I couldn't come up with one on such short notice. I hadn't expected them to find out so soon, and I couldn't tell them the truth. They would have called their psychologist friend from Los Lunas in a heartbeat. So I lied. I told them I skipped because I forgot to study for a test.

"Okay," Grandpa said, turning against me in a disappointing instant, "ground her for life. But for heaven's sake, Vera, don't take the girl's phone. I don't think she'd live through it."

I laughed at the thought. Grandpa, all bark and no bite. But I had to watch out for Grandma. That woman could put the shrew in shrewd when she wanted to. Thank goodness she didn't want to very often.

My phone vibrated in my pocket. I took it out and flipped it open, then squinted as I tried to decipher the text from Brooklyn through my broken screen.

"Sup? R u toast?"

I smiled and texted her back. "Bear not in cave yet. Pray 4 me. Pray hard."

As I closed my phone and stuffed it back into my pocket, I scanned Principal Davis's office. Even though it never met the standards of the school's administrative assistant—she fussed about it constantly—it had always been fairly organized. But not today. Books, newspaper clippings, and scraps of paper with scribbled notes engulfed his desk in a huge, mountainesque formation.

I realized the books were old Riley High yearbooks. A couple were open and written in with thick black marker. With curiosity piqued, I eased up to get a look at what the stalwart principal had been up to. Just as I scanned to a face in a crowd he'd circled and starred, the book slammed shut in my face.

I leapt back in surprise.

"Find anything interesting?" Mr. Davis asked.

With a hand on my chest, I said nonchalantly, "Not really. Are those old yearbooks?"

He took a moment to get situated in his chair before answering. Principal Davis was a tall man, dark and broad. He could charm a snake one minute and send the toughest football player at Riley High home in tears the next. But I'd always liked him. I hoped this meeting wouldn't change that.

"Yes, Ms. McAlister, they're old yearbooks. I didn't mean to startle you. I just have a couple of questions, then you can go."

I sat in amazement. "You mean, I'm not in trouble?"

"Should you be?" He set a piercing gaze on me, one I knew would come in handy if a Riley High student was ever suspected of international espionage.

"Oh, no," I said with a light giggle, trying my best to sound utterly innocent of any wrongdoing. Like, say, skipping. He must not know yet. "I was just kidding."

He eyed me momentarily before asking, "What do you know about that new kid, Jared Kovach?"

No way. Why on earth was he asking me about Jared? "Oh, Jared? Well, not much, I'm afraid. I just met him a couple of days ago."

"I see. I saw you talking to him. It seemed like you two were friends."

"Well, we are. I mean—"

"Do you know his parents?"

"Not personally. Is he in some kind of trouble?"

His gaze slid surreptitiously to the yearbook he'd slammed shut before returning to me. "He hasn't attended a single class since the day he arrived. I just thought maybe you knew something about his situation."

"His situation?"

"I can't get hold of his parents. The number he gave has been disconnected."

"Oh, right." I was trying desperately to stay one step ahead of him, but it was hard to outrun a bear, especially on uneven ground. I considered doing the fetal-position thing and playing like a rock, but he might think that odd. "From what I understand, his parents are having some problems."

"What kind of problems?" he asked, clearly intrigued.

"Mr. Davis, I'm not sure I should be answering for Jared."

"I can assure you, Ms. McAlister, anything you say will be held in the strictest confidence."

"I understand, but I just don't know that much. I mean, all he said was that his parents were having problems and—" I tried to think up an excuse for his absences, any excuse. "—and they were trying to work things out, and he just wanted to be with them. That's probably why he's been absent."

I couldn't tell if Mr. Davis was biting or not. He tapped a pen on his desk and sized me up with a hard stare. Without warning, he shot from his chair and held out a hand. "Thank you for coming in, Ms. McAlister."

I stood and watched his huge hand swallow mine in a firm shake. "No problem." With as much tact as I could muster, I looked down at the yearbook then back.

Got it. 1977.

"You can get a pass back to class from Connie."

"Oh, okay. I'll let you know if I hear anything."

His smile held more suspicion than sincerity. "You do that."

As I left the office, I wondered how I was going to break the news to Glitch and Brooklyn that we would be skipping again today.

ELLIOT

"So this is the library." Glitch turned in a full circle, taking in the Riley's Switch Public Library, recently remodeled and modernized. Softly muted colors added to its quiet ambience. "Nice."

"Yes," Brooklyn said in a teasing tone, "and they have books, too. They're made of paper with words inside and you read them."

He turned to her in disbelief. "Surely you jest."

She snorted and socked him on the arm for good measure. He rubbed his shoulder and smiled to himself, clearly enjoying the attention.

"Is it just me," Brooklyn said, gazing thoughtfully out the glass doors, "or is that reporter guy following us?"

We turned back for a better look. Sure enough, a white van with the Tourist Channel's blue logo sat idling out front.

"I've been seeing that van a lot lately," I said, my suspicions growing.

Before we could discuss that fact further, my grandmother's best friend, Betty Jo, spied us from behind the circulation desk and brightened.

"Okay, guys," I said in a low tone as Betty Jo headed toward us, her large body lumbering across the thick carpet, "remember the plan."

"Got it," Glitch said, lowering his voice to match mine. "Should we synchronize our watches?"

"Hi, Betty Jo." I couldn't help a quick kick to Glitch's ankle. He cursed under his breath as Betty Jo pulled me into a hug.

"How have you been, precious?" Before I could answer, she asked, "Are you out of school?"

"Well, not especially," I hedged, uncomfortable with lying to my grandmother's very best friend, the woman who helped both my grandparents through the roughest time in their lives, my parents' disappearance. "We're doing research for a school project."

"Oh, wonderful. How can I help?" She clasped her hands in a prayer position, ever ready, willing, and able to help on school projects.

"Does the library keep old copies of the Riley High yearbooks?" Please, oh please, oh please, oh—

"Sure does."

Yes!

"We have them all. They're in the special collections area. I'll get the key."

"Thanks so much," I said with an excited smile.

"Not at all, darling." We looked on as Betty Jo circled the desk to retrieve the key.

"I wish I had someone who thought of me as a precious or a darling," Glitch said almost dreamily.

Brooklyn snorted again. "There are just so many things I could say right now."

Glitch's mouth narrowed to a thin line of annoyance as Betty Jo hurried back with the key. "Okay, it's right over here." We followed her to a special room at the back of the library. "I've already signed you in. Let me know if you need any help."

As Betty Jo left the room, I turned and spotted the yearbook. "There it is—" I pointed to the top shelf. "—1977."

"So, what are we looking for?" Glitch reached over Brooklyn, jumping to grasp the book she was struggling to reach. When he landed, he wrapped a hand nonchalantly around her waist as though to make sure she didn't fall.

I'd started noticing all kinds of these little touches, details I always just dismissed as the everyday remnants of close friendship. After all, didn't he do the same to me? But the more I thought about it, the more I realized his attention to me was just that: the everyday remnants of close friendship. His encounters with Brooke were much more deliberate and happened much more often. When on planet Earth did his feelings for her morph into downright infatuation? He'd had a bit of a crush on her since she moved here in the third grade, but it seemed to have evolved. I wondered if Brooke knew.

As soon as he landed, Brooke snatched the yearbook from him and sat at the round table that took up most of the space in the closetlike room. She seemed completely oblivious of Glitch's advance. Probably a good thing at the moment.

With a mental shrug, I dropped my notebook and sat beside her as she thumbed through the pages. "I really don't know for sure. But the way Mr. Davis was guarding it . . . wait." She'd turned the page to find the words IN MEMORY OF ELLIOT BRENT DAVIS headlining a memorial layout for a Riley High student who had passed away. I quickly scanned the collage that had been put together to honor him. Both candid and professional shots bordered the main photograph of Elliot Davis. It was a studio shot of him holding a football, and I realized who Elliot Davis had to be. "This is Mr. Davis's brother."

"Oh, my gosh," Brooke said, leaning in closer, "you're right."

"He looks just like him," Glitch said, hovering over us from behind.

I tapped the page with my fingertips. "And this is the page Mr. Davis was looking at. I remember. He'd circled a face with a—"

"Lorelei," Brooklyn interrupted in a hushed whisper. Her finger slid up to one of the photos bordering the main picture. In it, a crowd of students stood around the flagpole of the old high school. They were laughing, as though in disbelief, and I realized it was a shot of Mr. Davis's brother. In what must have been some kind of a prank, he and some friends had chained themselves to the pole and were holding a sign I couldn't quite make out.

But they were laughing, too. Every student in the photo was laughing, except one. A boy. He was standing closer to the camera yet apart from the rest, his stance guarded, his expression void, and then I saw the unmistakable face of our newest student.

Jared Kovach.

I felt the world tip beneath me, my head spin as I stared unblinking.

"It can't be him," she said.

But there was no mistaking the wide shoulders, the solid build, the dark glint in Jared's eyes.

"It can't be him," she repeated.

He had the same mussed hair, the same T-shirt with the sleeves rolled up, the same arms, long and sculpted like a swimmer's. The only difference I could see in this picture was the tattoo. Two, actually. Wide bands of what looked like a row of ancient symbols encircled each of his biceps.

"It just can't be, right, Lorelei?"

He was just as breathtaking, just as surreal. And somehow, it made perfect sense. I swallowed hard and asked, "What if it *is* him?"

"Lor," Glitch said, shaking his head, "that's impossible."

"Maybe it's his father, or even his grandfather." Brooklyn glanced up. "Lots of kids look like their grandparents."

"Think about it," I said. "Think about all the things he can do." I studied the photo again. The caption below it read, *Taken the day we lost our beloved brother and friend.*

"What if it is him and he was there the day Mr. Davis's brother died." I thought back to what Cameron's father had said. "Cameron calls him the reaper. Maybe he really is."

"Is what?" Brooklyn asked, pulling away from me.

In hesitation, I pursed my lips. Then I said it, what we were all thinking. "What if he really is the grim reaper?"

"Then wouldn't you be dead?" Glitch asked, suddenly angry. He'd set his jaw, and I could tell he'd slipped into a state of denial. Heck, I'd considered moving to that state myself, but the facts were hard to dismiss.

First the vision, then the accident, the fight, the gunshot wounds that didn't faze him, didn't leave a scratch, and the way he'd rolled out of the bed of Cameron's truck and landed solidly on his feet when he escaped. And just the way he walked, the way he moved. So ethereal. So dangerous.

"Nothing about Jared is normal," I said. I looked up at Glitch. "Or Cameron, for that matter. He's different. You said so yourself. Always has been."

Glitch offered me a sardonic smile. "Okay, so if Kovach is the freaking grim reaper, then what the heck is Cameron?"

I certainly didn't have the answer to that. "I just think we should at least consider this a possibility."

"Yeah, a crazy one." He raked his fingers through his spiked hair.

"You weren't there, Glitch. You didn't see what I saw. What kind of entity can stop time?"

Glitch's face softened. "Lor, you said it yourself. You had been hit by a truck."

"And I don't have a single bruise to prove it." Despite my best efforts, I was getting frustrated.

"Have you looked at your ribs?"

"Do you honestly believe a delivery truck would only bruise my ribs? I told you how that happened. I was being torn through a tiny sliding glass window." After a moment, a shocking real-ization burrowed into my thick head. I eyed him, dismayed. "You don't believe me."

Guilt lined his face as he tried to convince me otherwise. "I didn't say that."

"You didn't have to." I stood and strode out the door with the yearbook, searching my pockets for change for the copier. As Glitch approached, I turned to him.

"Of course I believe you," he said softly. "It's just—"

"Don't worry about it." Though the revelation hurt, I could hardly blame him. It *was* an incredible story. Seriously. Stopping time? Jared shot at point-blank range without a single bullet wound to show for it, then rolling from a truck going sixty only to land on his feet and sprint up a mountain? Yeah, incredible.

"It's not that I don't believe you," Glitch said, regret lacing his voice. "Please, don't be mad at me."

His sincerity squeezed around my heart. So did his lost-puppy expression. He was such a cheater.

"And besides," Brooklyn said as she walked up, "when you're mad at him, he totally ignores my insults. Those insults serve a social function. They reinforce the hierarchy of our little threesome here." She opened her hands, indicating our merry band of misfits.

"I'm not mad in the least," I said, offering Glitch a half smile. "But when I prove I'm right?"

He grinned. "Then I'll be your love slave forever."

Brooklyn chortled, "You're grounded forever. And a couple of days beyond that. How can you be anybody's love slave?"

"And just think," I added as I turned to make a copy of the memorial page, "when your parents find out you skipped again today, they're going to be even more upset. You may have to do yard work. Or worse," I said with a soft gasp, "the dishes."

"That's not funny." Glitch's grin evaporated. "If you're gonna crack jokes, they should really be funny."

"I thought it was funny," Brooklyn said with a shrug.

"You think the *Teletubbies* are funny," he said.

I raised my brows. "He is right, you know. For once."

"I know," she said, her tone flat. "I hate when that happens."

I wrapped a supportive arm around her shoulders. "Cheer up, kid," I said, brushing a fist across her chin in jest. "Even a broken clock is right twice a day. It was bound to happen eventually."

"Of course," she said, brightening. "I feel so much better."

"Here." Glitch grabbed the yearbook, feigning annoyance at the jokes made at his expense. "I have some change."

He didn't fool me. He loved every minute of it.

As he turned to make a copy, Brooklyn asked, "So what's next?"

That was a good question. I could only come up with one answer, the only trail we had to follow. "Don't they keep all the old newspaper articles on eight-track tapes or something? We could try to look up the report on Elliot Davis's death. Find out what happened."

"Good idea. We can see if there was anything suspicious about it. Not that we'd actually know if it were suspicious, but it wouldn't hurt to check."

I nodded my head in agreement, then lowered it, almost afraid to ask my best friend's thoughts on the matter. But I had to know. "So, what about you, Brooke? Do you believe me?"

Brooklyn's face split into a brilliant smile and she leaned into me. "With every bone in my body."

Relief washed over me. I needed Brooke to believe me. It surprised me how much I needed it. "And where do I stand?"

"Stand?" Her huge brown eyes looked at me, confused.

"Yeah, you know, in your social hierarchy."

"Ah," she said, propping an arm on my shoulder, "the way I see it, we're co-presidents, and Glitch there is on the bottom rung of the political ladder. He's pretty much pond scum."

"Perfect," I said as Glitch growled over his shoulder. "Nothing like a society with two heads of state and one poverty-stricken, uneducated, mentally ill constituent to back us."

"Exactly," she said, polishing her nails on her blouse, quite proud of her governing hierarchy.

THREE LAWS AND A SUBARU

It took a while, but we managed to find a newspaper article on an ancient cell of microfiche that described the sudden death of Riley High's star quarterback. He'd apparently died of an aneurysm while sitting in his car after school, waiting for his brother, Alan.

Elliot Davis, the oldest child of James and Anne Davis, died moments after his brother found him. A later article explained that he spoke to his brother right before he died, but that Alan Davis was in shock and couldn't tell his parents what their son had said. How awful his father must have felt. How awful

Principal Davis must have felt as well, his older brother dying in front of him, so suddenly, so tragically.

The mental image of the scene played over and over in my mind as we walked home, wondering how Jared fit into the picture. It made no sense. Elliot Davis died of an aneurysm. What did that have to do with anything?

Brooke and I decided to do a little more investigating by way of my grandparents until Glitch got out of football practice. I couldn't imagine what a team manager did, but the guy rarely missed a practice and never missed a game. His job must have been really important, whatever it entailed.

"Hey, Gram," I said, strolling into the kitchen with Brooke in tow. Grandma was a couple inches taller than either of us, but that wasn't saying much. She was thin with light gray hair and soft baby blues that Grandpa said made all the boys' hearts go pitter-pat. He would wriggle his brows and assure me she'd been the prime catch of the season. It cracked me up.

"Hey, kids. I'm trying a new recipe for the gang."

The gang she referred to was her bingo group. She and Grandpa played bingo at least once a week at the church Grandpa pastored, so that made it almost a religious experience in their eyes.

"It smells wonderful," I said, plopping my books onto the kitchen table. The store and our kitchen were separated by a pocket door, so Grandma could work in the house when we didn't have customers. I often did the same on my shifts, concocting all manner of salsas in the kitchen until the bell rang, announcing a potential sale. My peppered red *chile* was the best.

Brooklyn tiptoed to look into the pot. "You need any taste-testers? We're available all afternoon and have excellent taste buds."

Grandma chuckled and handed us a bowl of chips as she stirred. We dipped freely of the *chile con queso* and sank our teeth into a spicy, crunchy kind of heaven.

"Oh, my gosh," Brooke said, her mouth half full. "This is incredible."

"Mm-hmm," I agreed, going in for another test.

"I made plenty, so I'll leave you a bowl."

"Thanks, Grandma," I said.

"You girls aren't double-dipping, are you?"

I turned as Grandpa walked in through the back.

"Hey, Pastor," Brooke said, wiping at her mouth with the back of her hand.

"Hey, Grandpa."

He placed his cap on its usual hook and walked over for a hug, squeezing both of us at the same time. "Well, now that you two have tested the fare, I guess I can have a go without the threat of imminent death hanging over my head." When Brooklyn looked up at him in surprise, he said, "Oh, yeah, this woman has been trying to kill me for years." He shook an accusing chip at Grandma. "Didn't pix tell you?"

She turned toward me, her brows raised in question.

"He's right," I said between bites. "She tried liquid Drano once, but he could taste it in the food, so she had to get more creative."

"Now, now," Grandma said. "That Drano thing was just a big misunderstanding." She winked at Brooklyn, and we both laughed at my grandparents' teasing. They were so fun.

While Grandpa was a pastor, he made preaching look more like stand-up comedy than a lesson on the teachings of the Bible, so we had a pretty big congregation. He had a thick head of white hair, soft gray eyes, and a wide, solid frame. He wasn't particularly tall either, but at least my grandparents could see over the seats in the movie theater. They were my mom's parents. I'd never met my other set of grandparents. They died before I was born. But I had this set, and I was perfectly happy with them. When they weren't lecturing me.

"Can I ask you guys a question?"

Grandma spared me a quick glance as she poured us our own bowl of *queso.* "Absolutely."

"You know down in the Abo Pass where it turns three times really sharp and then levels off?"

"Right," Grandpa said, wiping his mouth on a napkin. "The turns past the Missions?"

"That's it," Brooke said, heading to the fridge for a soda.

"Sure do. That's pretty far," he said, wondering what we were up to.

"We're not going out there or anything," I assured him. "We were just wondering what's there." I couldn't help but think Jared might have found some kind of shelter nearby, if there was any to be had, maybe in someone's barn or shed.

He rubbed his chin in thought, but Grandma beat him to the punch line. "The old Davis mansion is out there," she said. "And the Aragon homestead."

Brooklyn's head popped up from behind the fridge door. "The Davis mansion? I'd forgotten about that."

So had I. And it was in the same area Jared had last been seen.

"Far as I know, nobody's lived there for years," Grandpa said. "Probably nothing but ruins now."

"Do you know how to get out there?" I asked as nonchalantly as possible.

"There's a turnoff right past that last curve. Have to be careful, though. Foreigners are always taking that curve too fast." Grandpa called anyone not from New Mexico foreigners. He cracked me up. New Mexicans took those curves just as fast as anyone else, but hard as we tried, we never convinced Grandpa of that. "What's all this about?" he asked, munching on another cheese-covered chip.

"Oh, it's for our science fair project," I said before biting the bullet and trying my hand at a big black lie instead of the little white ones I was so fond of. "Speaking of which, I know we're grounded and all, but we were wondering if we could go back to school and help Ms. Mullins set up for the science fair this afternoon."

"My mom said it's okay with her if it's okay with you," Brooklyn added. Man we were getting good with the lying.

"Science fair, huh?" Grandma said as she hurried to clean the kitchen before they set out for a wild night of legalized gambling. Bingo players were hilarious. "I guess if it's for science. Just be home before dark."

Grandpa winked at me behind her back and whispered, "She's so easy."

I had to agree. My grandmother would let me rob a bank if it was in the name of science.

"I've always wanted a peek inside this house." Brooklyn bounced in the front seat of Glitch's car, giddy with excitement.

Glitch looked at me in the rearview mirror as we wove through the menagerie of ponderosa pine and alligator juniper. "So, no one has lived there since the Davises?"

"According to my grandma. After Elliot Davis died, his parents closed up their business, boarded up their house, threw the kids in the car, and moved to South Texas. They didn't sell it or anything. I think Mr. Davis was a freshman at the time."

"I wonder if they still own it," Brooklyn said.

"I wish we knew," I agreed before explaining more of what we'd learned to Glitch. "Elliot Davis was younger than my grandma, but she remembers him, remembers what happened. She said the Davises were devastated. It broke her heart."

As much as we'd found out about the Davises and the incident, we still had nothing to tie Jared to Elliot Davis's death. We'd asked my grandparents what they remembered. I thought they might know something, might have heard something that wasn't in the papers. I was surprised at how much she remembered, but just as the paper reported, it was a medical condition. Nothing suspicious.

"If they do own it, why wouldn't Mr. Davis have moved into it when he came back?" Glitch asked. "It just seems odd."

Mr. Davis had moved back to take the principal job when it opened up a few years ago. Apparently, the whole town was surprised when he moved back.

"Grandpa said it's in shambles now and would cost more to repair than it would to just tear it down and start over."

Brooklyn turned and peered around the passenger's seat at me. "And why do we think the boys might be here?"

I shrugged. "Just a hunch. It's a straight shot from where Jared jumped out of Cameron's truck to here. And it's abandoned. What better place to take refuge?"

"That's true, I guess. If I were seeking refuge, I'd want to hole up in a cool old mansion."

"Can you believe this?" I asked, my mind wandering back to Jared, to everything we'd learned so far. "The first guy I've ever really liked, and he could be some supernatural bringer of death. I should just give up."

"Give up on boys?" Brooklyn said. "That'll be the day."

"I should. I should just quit while I'm ahead."

"Lor," she said, crinkling her nose with skepticism, "you have to actually be ahead to quit while you're ahead. Besides, they're boys. They're big and clumsy. They're in a constant state of flux that makes them almost interesting. Why quit now?"

"Because she's tired of unrealized expectations and fruitless endeavors?" Glitch said, wriggling his brows.

I pretended to be appalled. "What are you talking about? My endeavors are totally fruity."

Glitch chuckled, and I wondered why he was helping me if he didn't believe a word I'd said. He even left football practice early for me. He had never done that before. I wasn't sure how the team would manage without him. How would they carry on? Of course, with the lot of us being grounded, the only way he could go with us was to pretend he was at football practice and skip out.

His ancient Subaru groaned in protest when we hit a pothole. Poor thing. Its maroon paint had long since faded to a brownish gray, and its rattles and squeaks made it impossible to hear the radio. But it got us where we needed to go.

He looked at me in the rearview mirror again. "Do you really think he'll be here?"

I gave a halfhearted shrug. "I have no idea. I just don't know where else to look."

"I'm game either way," he said in an obvious attempt to reassert his support. I loved him for it.

I was just about to tell them I'd remembered something else from the vision—Jared's name, his real name—but Brooklyn sucked in an awestruck breath.

"Here it is," she said.

Tucking the info away for future reference, I looked up at the huge Spanish ranch house looming before us. The earthy tones of the two stories had faded with time. Thick adobe walls crumbled to expose interior blocks mixed from mud and red native clay. Mammoth wood pillars supported the second-floor balcony from where it was said Mrs. Davis would sit for hours to paint the landscape.

"Wow," Glitch said, agreeing with Brooklyn's awe. "It's beautiful."

"Yeah. Grandma said Mr. Davis's grandfather built it in the forties."

The car crawled to a stop before two twelve-foot wooden doors. We piled out and stepped through the massive portal onto a veranda long overtaken by brush and vines.

"We should have brought another flashlight." Brooklyn staggered to my side and took hold of my arm as I was holding the only flashlight we'd brought. "I can't see a thing."

"No kidding. When the heck did the sun set?" I asked, hitting the light against my palm. It finally came on, shining a bright beam through the darkness. "I don't remember it setting. What time is it?"

A neon green light appeared at my side as Glitch checked his watch. "It's after seven."

"Grandma's gonna kill me." My insides seized with anxiety and a special torturous kind of dread. "I told her I'd be home before dark."

"Well, she can't do any worse than my parents." Brooklyn shivered. "When they find out I skipped again . . ."

Glitch pushed open the front door. "It's not locked. Maybe he really is here."

An excited thrill shot through me like a bolt of lightning. What if Jared was here? What would I do? What would I say to him? Somehow, *Thanks for saving my life; sure hope your near-fatal concussion is better,* seemed a tad trivial.

After a thorough search of the first floor, I stood with Glitch and Brooklyn at the bottom of a wide staircase leading to the second. The house was in a sad state of disrepair, crumbling from time and a serious lack of TLC. Trash and debris cluttered the floor, and tattered curtains hung uselessly over dirty windows. If I hadn't known better, I'd have said it looked haunted.

In a word, it was beautiful.

"Do you think it's safe?" I asked nevertheless, studying the stairs doubtfully.

"They look okay." The uncertainty in Glitch's voice did not inspire confidence. "Stay close to the railing just in case."

We tiptoed up the staircase single-file: Glitch, me, then Brooklyn. An eerie creak echoed against the walls with every step, the boards cracking just enough to push our stomachs into our throats. I didn't even want to think about the hundreds of spiders it would've taken to weave the heavy curtains of webs that hung listlessly overhead. Surely they were out doing important spidery stuff.

Brooklyn had a death grip on my arm. "The two key vocabulary words for this evening are *extreme* and *danger*."

"Sure gets the blood pumping," Glitch said.

After we reached the landing, we began our search again. Carefully, as there was a lot of space between the first and second floors. But five rooms, seven closets, and two bathrooms later, my heart began to sink. I'd been wrong. He wasn't here. I was beginning to wonder if I'd ever see him again.

With a sigh of despair, I opened a door to one of the smaller rooms at the end of a long hall. A dark silhouette sitting on a windowsill turned toward me. I knew immediately it was Jared. The knowledge sent a jolt of delight surging through my body. Finally, I had found him. And he was alive.

"Jared," I said, elated. But when I raised the flashlight to illuminate his face, I thought my knees would give beneath me.

His face was swollen, bloodied, and bruised. He squinted against the harsh light and tried to shield his eyes with an arm. The arm he raised was just as bad. His T-shirt was no longer white. Stained with dirt and blood, it looked like something the cat dragged in after the dog had mangled it to shreds.

"You found him?" Glitch asked as he and Brooklyn stumbled into the room.

Without a word, Jared spit into the darkness at his feet,

folded his arms over his chest, and studied me, his gaze unwavering.

I lowered the flashlight and walked to him. "I was hoping we
would find you here."

Despite his bravado, pain lined his handsome face. His jaw
stiffened with every breath he took. He didn't reply, but he
seemed almost pleased that I'd found him, proud.

Suddenly the room brightened. We turned to see Cameron
light an oil lamp. He sat on an old desk in the corner, rifle in
hand as though guarding a prisoner. He was beat to oblivion as
well, holding his side with his free hand, his fingers covered in
blood.

The realization of what these two buttheads must have been
doing for the past two days sparked a fury inside me. I had
been so worried, sick with it. And these two geniuses spent the
entire time in a pissing contest?

I turned on Cameron. "Have you been fighting for two days?"

He shrugged. "Off and on."

I couldn't believe it. After all the anxiety and guilt. I blinked
back my astonishment and turned to Jared. "May I ask why you
two jerks feel the need to beat each other to death? Or do
you think an explanation is too much?"

"What about it, Kovach?" Cameron said. "Got an explanation?" He chuckled humorlessly, then winced. After a moment
of recovery, he added, "Oh, wait, that's not even your real
name."

"No," I said as I turned back and fixed him with a cold, hard
look, "it's Azrael."

Jared snapped to attention. It was his turn to stare in disbelief.

I tamped down the self-doubt that threatened to swallow me,
suddenly worried about what he might think of my visions. Of
my bizarre gift. Would he be appalled? Wary? "I see things," I

explained hesitantly. "Sometimes when I touch people, I see things. I get visions. And I had one with you. In it, your name was Azrael." When he continued to stare, I added, "I didn't remember it at first. I was so shocked by what I saw, but then it came to me. I was in your head and your name was Azrael."

After a lengthy pause, the initial shock of my statement seemed to ebb. He sized me up for another few seconds, then turned toward the thick darkness outside, something more than physical pain haunting his eyes. He didn't seem appalled, so that was good.

"Please, tell me what's going on," I said, my voice cracking with my plea.

Brooklyn stepped to my side, making me grateful my two best friends were near.

I drew air into my lungs and began again. "I was dying. I felt life leaving me, and you brought me back. You have some kind of power."

I inched closer to him. I could almost feel Cameron tense behind me in one of his ill-conceived attempts at protection. Brooklyn turned toward him, ready to fight with all of her five feet if he tried anything. She could never actually faze him, but that didn't matter. She was there for me, as always. God bless her freaky little soul.

"Am I wrong?" When he looked down, listening but not answering, I continued. "You fight monsters," I said, trying to piece together the events as I spoke, "and save girls hit by trucks. But why? Did you come here just to save me?"

Cameron laughed out loud, the sound harsh and out of place in the quiet room. "I'm pretty sure we already covered this, Lorelei. It doesn't do that." He tilted his head to the side, studying Jared. "Tell her, Reaper. Tell her why you're here."

I wanted to get closer, to reassure him he could tell me anything, but I also remembered how incredibly strong he was. And impossibly fast. I decided to plead from where I stood. "Please, Jared. I just want to know what happened."

He turned back to me at last, a vertical line creasing the skin between his brows. "I wasn't there to save your life, Lorelei." He studied me a moment longer, then said, "I was there to take it."

"Bingo," Cameron said, applauding tauntingly, his satisfaction almost eclipsing the disgust he wore. "Give the man a prize."

"I don't understand." I stepped back in shock. "I was dying. I almost died, and you saved me. I felt it."

Jared wiped the back of his hand across his brow, where a stream of blood dripped onto his lashes. "No," he said after a long pause, "you wouldn't have died for another forty-eight minutes. By then it would have been too late. I was sent to take you sooner."

I stood in a daze. A fog of disbelief immobilized me. He was lying. He had to be. Why would he be sent to kill me? What had I done?

Brooklyn wrapped an arm around my shoulders. "What are you talking about?" she asked Jared. "How can you know that kind of stuff?"

Jared's countenance hardened, cementing me to the spot. He began talking about things that didn't happen, things I didn't want to happen.

"After you were hit, you were medevaced to Albuquerque," he said. "You never made it. You died less than two minutes into the flight." He paused again, gave me a moment to absorb his words before continuing. Then, in the softest voice, he added, "But your grandparents didn't know that."

I gasped aloud and straightened. "My grandparents?"

"They were upset. Driving too fast. There was a sharp curve and they crossed the centerline. They collided head-on with another vehicle."

My hand flew to my mouth. Emotion seized me, squeezed my chest painfully. Tears sprang to my eyes and blurred my vision. Glitch and Brooklyn both grabbed me as I swayed, my knees giving in to the weight of his words. They guided me to a rickety wooden crate.

"Everyone involved died instantly," he continued, forging on. "I was sent to take you before they called the helicopter, before your grandparents started for Albuquerque."

"You're talking in past tense like it already happened," Brooklyn said, clearly upset herself. "It didn't."

He frowned as though surprised by her statement. "Time . . . doesn't work like you think." He stood and started toward us.

In an instant, Cameron was in front of him, pain forgotten, their anger ratcheting, and I was sure the fighting would begin again. Fresh tears pushed past my lashes. I couldn't see them fight again. I couldn't be a witness to such brutality, such gut-wrenching violence.

In the movies it seemed so easy. Nothing was real. Men were expected to fight, and the good guys always won. But in real life the violence was sickening, traumatizing. It made no sense. There was no black-and-white, no good-guy–bad-guy scenario, no solid line of virtue with which to keep score. There were only shades of gray. The pain was real. The blood was real. And I would rather die than see that again. I closed my lids, pushing the tears from my eyes to fall down my cheeks and drip from my chin.

"I'm sorry, Lorelei," Jared continued, watching me. "I didn't mean to hurt you."

Cameron scoffed. "Okay, superhero, you saved her." He leaned forward, his face mere inches from Jared's. "So why don't you just leave?"

With the speed of a cobra, Jared shoved Cameron back, his stance offensive, seeming to beg him to retaliate. "Don't you think

I've tried? Do you think I want to be here? I don't know what happened. I shifted and locked on to this plane, but I have no idea why."

Cameron had caught himself before he fell. He turned, brimming with satisfaction. Jared's push was the invitation he'd been waiting for.

But Glitch stepped in between them, whether on purpose or not, I didn't know. "You mean, you can't leave?" he asked. "Why?"

"I would relish that answer myself." He scowled at Cameron, then eased back onto the windowsill, clutching his ribs in pain. "Something happened after I saved you, Lorelei. Something changed."

"What?" Brooklyn asked, trying to coax more information from him. "What changed?"

"This." He lifted his hands to indicate himself, then winced. "Me. Do you know how many times I've bled on this plane? I don't bleed. I don't bruise." He turned on Cameron. "And I certainly don't get knocked out by a boy with a stick."

Cameron grinned from ear to ear in triumph as Brooklyn asked, "Then why?"

"I don't know," he said, working his jaw as though angry with himself. "I broke the law."

After taking a steadying breath, I stood and asked softly, "What law?"

He stared into the darkness, whispered what must be the laws of his . . . profession—*profession* being the only word I could come up with. "We cannot change history. We cannot change human will. We cannot redeem the sins of the father."

Brooklyn frowned in confusion. "What does that mean?"

"It means I broke the law. I changed history. You were supposed to die. I was just supposed to tweak the timing a little."

Glitch exhaled loudly and asked the obvious. "Okay, besides the fact that all this is freaking me out, I have to ask, doesn't that in itself change history?" He bent his head in thought. "I mean, either way, you would have stopped Lorelei's grandparents from dying, right? That's a change."

"Yes, that's a change. But only humans can change history. I would not have changed history. Amanda Parks would have."

We all looked at him even more bewildered than before.

Again, Glitch asked the obvious question. "Who's Amanda Parks?"

A grin softened Jared's battered face. "A five-year-old from Portales, New Mexico, who prayed that her father—the guy your grandparents would have killed in the accident—would arrive home safely from his business trip." His smile widened as though he was picturing her in his mind. "A child's faith. There is nothing stronger on earth, I promise you." He looked at me, seemed to want me to understand. "Because of her request, I was sent to change the circumstances of her father's death. Thus, by association, those of your grandparents. They were directly involved in Amanda's request. That is how their fates would have been altered. Amanda Parks would have changed history, Lorelei. Not me."

Though I still felt like I was trying to catch a minnow in the water only to have it slip between my fingers each time, a glimmer of understanding did seem to be taking root. There were laws, even for supernatural beings.

"But you did," I said with gentle resolve. "You changed history."

"I did." A sudden sadness came over him. "Lorelei, you don't know what I've done to you. I'm so sorry."

"You've changed history for me."

"No, you're wrong." He bowed his head as though ashamed, then said in a soft, husky voice, "I've changed history for me."

MESSENGER

I could not hide my puzzlement. Jared had changed history, had broken one of his laws, for himself? "You act like you've done something bad."

"You don't understand," he said, the full outline of his mouth thinning in disappointment, "you couldn't possibly. It's wonderful, the place you would have gone. You cannot imagine how wonderful. And I took that away from you. I have risked everything." He peeked at me. "I have risked your very soul."

Though I could hardly agree, I had to ask, "Then why?"

"Because if you had died, I would never have seen you again.

You would have gone to Heaven, a place I have not been for a very long time."

My heart stilled in my chest. I couldn't believe what he'd just said. A supernatural being changed history just to see me. *Me.*

Wait, he'd been to Heaven?

The tense hostility held barely in check by Cameron broke free. He picked up his rifle. "I'd say that's reason enough to send you back."

Prepared for such a reaction, Brooklyn struggled to pull a pistol from her coat pocket. Finally wresting it free, she aimed it at him. "We anticipated something idiotic like this from you."

Cameron turned to her in surprise—a surprise that, unfortunately, didn't last long.

I knew she'd brought the gun. My best friend had guts. No one could argue with that.

She scowled at Cameron. "First you wanted to kill him because he was going to take her. Now you want to kill him because he didn't. Bipolar much?"

When he stepped closer, Glitch and I flanked her on either side, a warning glare in our eyes. Probably looking more comical than intimidating, I curled my hands into fists. On our best day, the three of us together might actually be able to bruise him, but what choice did we have? We had to stop him. Or get horribly maimed trying.

Cameron raised his brows at Glitch. "I'm impressed," he said, taunting him with a smirk, "considering what you know about me."

I knew it. Something did happen between Cameron and Glitch. Neither of them had been the same when they came back from that camping trip our second-grade year. Curiosity burned inside me, but it would have to wait. We had bigger fish to fry, as my grandmother would say.

Glitch lifted a shoulder. "That was a long time ago."

"Yeah, I hear you have problems sleeping at night."

"No more than you."

"And that whole bed-wetting thing? Tragic."

I had no idea Cameron could be so cruel, but Glitch didn't waver. He stood unbending in the face of someone who could cause serious damage on his worst day.

"Look," Glitch said, squaring his shoulders, "are we gonna do this or what? I don't have all night."

I was so proud of him. A little worried, but proud.

Cameron raised his hands in mock surrender. "I certainly wouldn't want to upset the Three Musketeers. Or was it the Three Blind Mice?"

Brooklyn's jaw dropped. "You were there?"

He shrugged, feigning indifference.

"You're a jackass."

Cameron's eyes glittered and he stepped closer to Brooklyn. She raised the gun farther, her hand shaking. But Glitch and I were right by her side, Glitch with his bravado and me with my fists. If she got clobbered, we all got clobbered.

"I've been called worse," he said at last, gifting Brooke with a mixture of interest and empathy.

For the first time, I got a good look at him. He resembled Jared to a tee, scraped up, bruised, swollen. I shook my head. No way would I ever understand boys.

"Okay," Glitch said impatiently, "I get you, Jared. Well, not really, but as much as humanly possible at this point. But I don't get *you*." His resentment toward Cameron was obvious. "Why are you so strong? How can you fight like that? It's not any more human than Jared, or Azrael, or whatever his name is."

Cameron's attention shifted to Glitch but he didn't respond. He retreated to his desk and parked himself upon it, rifle still in hand. And our lungs could work again, for the moment.

Jared finally answered for him. "He is of Jophiel."

"He is of what?" Glitch asked.

"Jophiel, the messenger. Cameron is Nephilim. He is only part human, placed upon the earth to protect the prophet."

"What prophet?" Glitch asked.

But Cameron interrupted him, his anger simmering as though he could scorch Jared from where he stood. "You don't know anything about me."

"On the contrary, when we realized a female descendent of Arabeth was to be born," he continued, ignoring the vehemence in Cameron's voice, "we . . . disregarded the laws of our father. We sent a messenger to the believer Hannah Noel."

Cameron shot to his feet, stabbing Jared with a blistering hatred, and I realized whose name Jared had just spoken. His mother's. Hannah Noel Lusk was Cameron's mother.

"But her time came before she could instruct Cameron of Jophiel in his duties. And his earthly father refused the teachings of the believers."

"How dare you even say her name," Cameron said, livid with rage.

Brooklyn raised the gun again and Cameron shot her a look of utter contempt.

"So, who's the prophet?" Glitch repeated, but I was too busy making connections in my head to worry about that.

I sucked in a soft whisp of air when Jared's meaning hit me. "Messengers? You mean like angels? Are you guys angels?"

Jared's brows drew together. "Cameron of Jophiel is Nephilim. But, yes, I am a messenger. I am Seraphim."

How did I not pick up on that in my vision? An angel? An actual angelic being? Here in Riley's Switch, New Mexico? The realization knocked the breath out of me.

Cameron turned away with an angry smirk, refusing to listen. But I noticed he didn't argue. Did he know what he was? Had he always known?

I had so many questions, I could barely decide on which one to ask first. Turning back to Jared, I decided to ask the one that was causing me the most discomfort at that particular moment. "You said you weren't supposed to be here, that you don't want to be," I began, the statement causing a sharp pang in my chest. "Are you in trouble? Because of me?"

Jared took a moment to consider my question. His jaw tightened in reluctance before he said, "I lied."

"You lied?" I asked, confused. "You didn't break a law?"

The corners of his mouth threatened to turn up. "No, I most definitely broke a law."

I wondered what he must think of me. Of all humans. I suddenly felt minuscule, like my small life in my small town meant absolutely nothing in the grand scheme of things. Which kind of sucked.

"Wait," Brooklyn said, turning to me in bewilderment. "Lorelei's the prophet."

"Finally," Glitch said. "Wait, what?"

She blinked up at Jared. "Am I right? Is she the prophet Cameron was sent to protect?"

His head tilted knowingly. "She is."

"What? No," I said, rejecting the idea outright. "That's . . . that's not possible."

While I stood shaking my head in disbelief, Glitch's jaw dropped to the floor and Brooklyn laughed.

"Yes!" she said with an exuberance I found unsettling. "Oh, my god, that totally rocks!"

I could see her mind working a mile a minute, but she was wrong. They were all wrong.

"Can I just call a time-out?" I asked, shaping my hands into that very signal. "Seriously, it's a nice thought and all, but you guys have the wrong girl." I backed away, my shoes crunching as I stepped over decades of dirt and debris. "I'm not a prophet. I will never be a prophet. I don't even know what a prophet does. I'm sorry, but you've made a terrible mistake."

Jared placed his hands behind his back. "You are the last descendent of the prophet Arabeth. The gift of prophecy is in your blood."

"Lor," Brooklyn said, her excitement a tad annoying, "this is cool. You've always had visions—now we know why."

I balked in frustration. "I have visions of nonsense. They're meaningless."

"But they come true."

"Not always."

"What about when Tabitha backed into Mr. Davis's SUV?"

I closed my eyes. "Brooklyn, do you honestly think the heavens would create a member of the Nephilim to protect a girl whose most realized prophetic vision involved a psychotic cheerleader behind the wheel of a Nissan?"

"Well—"

"He's right," Cameron said, polishing his gun with a ripped edge of his T-shirt. "You're the prophet whether you want to be or not." The bitter sting in his words was impossible to miss. "They make the rules, run us through their mazes, whatever they want whenever they want, and we have no choice." His cool resentment made me shiver. "We're pawns, Lor. Game pieces for them to play with. You may as well get used to it."

"Who are *they*? Who makes the rules?" I asked, panic threatening to overtake me.

With an index finger, he offered one, solitary explanation. I followed his finger up and looked toward the heavens, his meaning so clear, so powerful.

I didn't know what to say. For some reason, coming from Cameron, it sounded more believable, and yet surely God would never have placed such a gift in my bumbling hands. Surely there was someone more qualified. "I just—" I backed to the far wall. "—I just don't feel very prophet-able."

Jared's expression was one of sympathy when he continued. "I should explain. But first, let me ask, have you studied the witch trials in history?"

I tilted my head and nodded, wondering what that had to do with anything.

He backed to the wall opposite me and leaned against it, watching me with a stony curiosity. "Long before the most notorious period of witch hunts, twelve centuries before the year of our lord, during the dawn of the age of iron, there was a woman named Arabeth who lived in a small village in Europe."

Stuffing my hands in my coat pockets, I leaned against the wall and listened. Brooklyn sat on the crate and Glitch stood beside her, suddenly very interested in what Jared had to say.

"She had visions like you, a gift that risked her life, but her parents protected her, kept her visions a secret. She grew up, married, and had children of her own. Then one day, she had a vision she could not deny. The water from the main well in the village had been tainted, and she knew if people drank it, an illness of epidemic proportions would spread throughout the countryside. She ran to the well and tried to warn the villagers. But no one listened, naturally."

I didn't like where Jared's story was going. Of all the history I had to learn in school, women and men being executed for witchcraft was among the hardest for me to wrap my head around. I recoiled every time I thought about the injustice, the stark brutality one human could visit upon another in the name of religion.

"When people began dying, their families panicked and blamed Arabeth. Even her own husband accused her of being unclean. And in the maelstrom of fear and superstition, she was dragged from her home and executed on the streets of her village. They claimed she cast spells and raised the dead, a misconception of the disease."

I sank inside myself and shook my head, reluctant to hear any more.

"By that time, Arabeth's husband knew that his three daughters also had the gift. He took them to Arabeth's parents, threw them into the couple's yard, and made his in-laws a promise: If they were still there at dawn, he would kill them all.

"Left with little choice, they took their granddaughters and fled into the night. Your ancestor, Lorelei McAlister, was the first woman in human history ever to be burned as a witch."

I siphoned a sip of cool air, my heart aching for Arabeth. For her parents and daughters.

"What happened to the girls?" Brooklyn asked.

"The couple was elderly and they knew they couldn't care for them much longer, so they gathered every cent they could and sent the daughters of Arabeth to three separate corners of the world. The eldest daughter was adopted by a wealthy couple and later had a daughter of her own. Her lineage continued for six centuries and ended with the last prophet in her line. Though her gift went unrecognized, her talent did not. She was the celebrated poet Sappho."

"Sappho." Brooklyn looked back at me in awe. Sappho was a Greek poet, her work greatly admired and sought after. And she was one of Brooke's heroes.

"The youngest daughter," Jared continued, "was taken in by poor farmers, but she grew up happy and healthy. Her lineage continued much longer and ended with the anointed one, the woman you know as saint Joan of Arc."

This time, even Glitch and Cameron turned to look at me, the shock on their faces apparent.

Brooklyn turned back to him, her eyes wide with wonder.

"So, in a roundabout way, Lorelei is related to both Sappho and Joan of Arc?"

Jared studied me as though I were a new life-form before answering, as though trying to judge my reaction to the current events. "She is."

I didn't know what to say. I had never been so humbled in my life. To know that I shared a common ancestor with such heroines, such absolute champions.

"That's . . . amazing," Glitch said. For once, he seemed to struggle with what to say.

I knew how he felt. When I finally found my voice, I asked, "What about the middle daughter? What happened to her?"

Jared's features softened, his eyes glittering in the faint light. He seemed glad for my interest. Even relieved, perhaps. "Her name was Lara Beth," he said, the soft consonants falling easily off his tongue. "She grew up a slave yet was revered and cherished by those around her. When she was sixteen, she had a vision that saved the life of a local landowner's son. Indebted, he freed her and offered her a place in his household. Soon, she and the boy fell in love and were married. They had three sons, one of whom is your ancestor as well. Lara Beth became a respected healer and advocate for the slaves. She also thwarted a civil war, but that's another story," he added.

"Sons?" I asked, enchanted. "Did they have visions too?"

Jared shook his head. "It seems the gift is inherent only in the female descendants. It should be noted, Lorelei, that this lineage is on your father's side, not your mother's."

For some reason, that surprised me. I wasn't sure why.

"You are the first female to be born in the lineage of Lara Beth in over thirty-two centuries. And yet you are just as gifted as both she and her mother were."

I focused on the ground, unable to fully comprehend, or accept, what he was saying. But he was an angel. Maybe he couldn't lie. Even so, I just couldn't manage to swallow everything he suggested. "I just think you have the wrong person," I said, begging him to reconsider. "There has to be another female descendent from another branch of the family tree. You know, like a long-lost cousin or something."

"All other lines have been severed. You are the last, Lorelei. Heaven has been waiting a long time for you. And you've caused quite a stir." He took in a deep breath. "They were expecting you a couple of days ago, in fact. I've probably caused quite a stir myself."

"And now you're stuck because of me. Because you broke a law for me."

He crossed his arms over his chest, his eyes glistening in amusement. "They're pretty touchy about their laws."

"Yeah, but you only have three," Glitch said, deciding to chime in with his usual genius for timing. "How hard can it be?"

Brooklyn backhanded him on the leg, then raised a hand, gesturing for his help to stand. He pulled her up. "So what now?" she asked, dusting off her backside.

The question stunned me. What now, indeed. I couldn't imagine how he must feel. Jared was stuck on earth with no family, no money, and no home. If I were in his shoes, I'd be terrified. But I wasn't a supreme being with the power of the sun in my left pinkie.

Still, the mere thought of him scared and alone broke my heart. I had to help. Surely the four of us—I glanced at Cameron—the three of us could come up with a solution. But first, the boys' tortured-in-prison-camp getups had to go. Time to get them cleaned, clothed, and fed.

"Okay," I said, forcing the whole prophet thing to the back of my mind and authority into my voice, "first we get you two cleaned up. Then we figure out what to do next. We can go to my house."

"You can't just invite it into your home, Lorelei," Cameron said, suddenly back on full alert.

I didn't need his paranoia or his temper just then. "Yes, Cameron, I can."

"Listen to me." He stood and pointed toward Jared. "He's stuck here because he saved your life. What do you think he'll do to get back? Maybe it's as simple as rectifying his mistake."

"Are you saying he would kill me to get back?"

"I could just kill *you* instead." Jared stepped toward Cameron. "Do you think that would get me back?"

Cameron strolled forward until he was inches from him. They stood on the verge of another battle, each more than willing to begin the game again.

In a moment of sheer frustration, I hauled my right foot back and kicked Cameron's shin. As he cursed and limped backwards, I turned to Jared, with his smug expression, and did the same to him.

He grabbed his leg and let loose a string of what was surely curses in another language, his teeth clenched in agony.

"Stop it!" I said, anger and a throbbing toe bringing tears to my eyes. "Both of you, stop it! No more fighting." I looked at Cameron. "You. Did I ask for your protection? Your help? No! And for your information, I don't care if Jared was sent here to cut me to pieces with a rusty machete. He saved my grandparents' lives. Even if I had died, he saved my grandparents' lives."

I fought back the emotion that tried to take hold of me. My grandparents were all I had in the world. And Jared had saved them. The fact that he'd been sent to take me instead of save me didn't matter in the least. Cameron needed to understand that.

"That's all that matters, Cameron," I said. "He could be a se-rial killer from Pluto, I don't care. But what I do care about is this ridiculous death wish you each seem to have. Why do you guys hate each other so much?"

My question seemed to surprise Jared. He stepped back as though coming to his senses. But Cameron shut down. I could see a curtain being drawn around him, and I knew he wouldn't explain. "Fine. Don't answer me. But you will stop fighting, both of you, or neither one of you will be able to walk when I'm done." I headed for the door. "Now, get to the car."

GRILLED CHEESE SANDWICHES

Because I had ordered Glitch to drive Cameron's pickup to my house, I ended up driving the Subaru home. Glitch didn't want to leave us alone with either one of them, but I threatened to grill him about what had happened that spring break in the second grade. He stopped arguing instantly.

Brooklyn sat in the passenger's seat, which put Cameron and Jared in the back. If I'd been smart, I'd have separated them. But I wanted to be able to watch them both at the same time.

Brooklyn turned to me as I adjusted the rearview mirror,

bringing both the boys into focus. "I am so stoked you're a prophet."

"Yeah," I said with a stifled laugh, "I'm getting that."

"So, we're going to call him Jared, right? I mean, changing his name to Azrael might be awkward right now. You said it yourself, Principal Davis suspects something."

"I know. He's stuck with Jared."

"What do you mean Principal Davis suspects something?" Jared asked, straightening. "Suspects what?"

"I had to go to his office," I explained. "He had every year-book from the seventies in there. He found a picture from the day his brother died. You were in it."

"He'd circled your image," Brooklyn said, "like he knows something."

"That could be problematic." He wrinkled his brows in thought. "I don't know why I've locked on to this plane, but while I'm here, I shouldn't disturb the natural order of things any more than I already have."

"You mean to tell me, someone took your picture?" Cameron asked, taken a back.

"Not really his," Brooklyn said. "It was a picture of Elliot Davis, Mr. Davis's brother, taken on the day he died."

"And, what," Cameron asked Jared, "you struck a pose?"

He turned toward the window. "I was waiting."

"I'm kind of surprised your picture can be taken," Brooklyn said, "you know, that you even show up on film."

"When I shift onto this plane, I take a physical form. I'm solid, like you."

Brooklyn snorted. "I don't think you're anything like me."

Cameron scoffed and leaned his head back against the seat. "So you slither onto this plane to rip some poor schmuck right out of his skin, and you get caught on *Candid Camera*. You aren't the brightest reaper in the universe, are you?"

"He's not the grim reaper," I said, suddenly defensive. And very thankful that we'd been wrong. "He's an angel."

"For Pete's sake, Lorelei." Cameron shook his head as though floored at my naïveté. "He's an angel, all right. The freaking angel of de—"

"Perhaps you should stop talking now," Jared said.

"Or what?"

"I'll make you stop."

"If you didn't hit like a girl in a pink party dress, I might be inclined to worry. Wait a minute." He sat up again, his expression amused. "You don't want her to know."

Jared sat up as well. They'd been shoulder to shoulder in the small space as it was, but now they were facing each other, a murderous scowl on Jared's face, an almost comical one on Cameron's.

Though neither actually made a move to initiate another fight, the last thing I needed was a rumble in the Subaru. I turned to them angrily. "Am I going to have to pull over?" I asked, pointing a finger at each of them in turn.

They both frowned and backed down, turning to look out their windows and pout. Satisfied, I refocused on the road. Which was a good thing, since I was driving.

"Can I ask why you came for Mr. Davis's brother?"

I watched in the mirror as Jared thought back. "Elliot Davis knew he was dying. He felt it and he prayed for just a moment more. He had a message for his brother Alan. Because the message was one of absolute unselfishness and he had such faith, I was sent."

"To tweak the timing," Brooke said, amazed.

"Yes. I waited for him to deliver the message, then I took him."

"What was the message?" she asked.

He grinned. "I cannot say."

"Man." She frowned in disappointment, but my thoughts had veered in another direction.

I slowed the car to a stop. Fortunately, the road was deserted. I turned back to him and asked, "Did Mr. Davis see you?"

He blew out a slow sigh then admitted, "Yes, he did. For a split second in time, he saw me materialize and take his brother."

"Nice," Cameron said.

"We'll definitely have to steer clear of the Bear."

By the time we arrived at my house, it was a little past nine. Glitch and Brooklyn had called their parents to see if they could stay at my house to work on our science fair projects. Since they were both grounded, I was floored when they both got permission. Lesson learned. Throw in the word *science,* and we can get away with anything.

We entered through the back door. My grandparents had already locked up the store. Thank heavens for bingo night.

While Glitch made his specialty, grilled cheese sandwiches, Cameron went upstairs to take a shower.

"Would you like some water?" I asked Jared after gathering some toiletries from the store for him. I made a list of everything I took on a pad by the register so it would come out of my paycheck.

He thought a moment. "I'm not sure. Perhaps."

I smiled and handed him a tall glass of water. He already seemed to be looking better. The swelling had gone down, and the bleeding above his eye had stopped. I wondered if the ability to heal quickly was part of his celestial uniqueness. "You're not sure if you're thirsty?"

"Not really." He took a cautious sip, paused a half beat, then gulped it down and asked for more.

Five glasses of water and three sandwiches later, I gaped worriedly at him. "How long has it been since you've eaten?"

"Since forever," he said, unconcerned.

I was stunned by his answer. "Didn't you say that you changed after you brought me back?"

"Yes."

"That was two days ago. You haven't had anything to eat or drink in two days?"

He shrugged. "I didn't realize I was thirsty."

"Jared," I scolded, "that is very dangerous."

His eyes glittered as he studied me, appreciation for my concern apparent.

Overcome by a shy kind of awkwardness, I pulled away from him. Blindingly gorgeous boys weren't interested in me. He would figure that out sooner or later. I took his glass and plate to the sink. "We have a few touristy items for sale in the store. I'll try to find you something to wear as soon as I check on the shower situation."

Humiliated by my own behavior, I left him with Glitch and rushed upstairs to check on Cameron and Brooke. Fatigue had leached into my muscles, and my bruised ribs ached. But the thrill of finding Jared, of having him in my house, kept my adrenaline pumping strong. And he was an angel. A celestial being. Who would've thought?

I walked into my room as a freshly showered Cameron sat shirtless on my bed, suffering through Brooklyn's ministrations. She was applying antibiotic ointment and butterfly stitches to a nasty cut on his back.

"You're a mess," Brooklyn said.

"So they say."

Her mouth thinned as it did when she wanted to say something but didn't quite know how to put it. Gathering her courage, she took a deep swallow of air and asked, "Why do you hate Jared so bad?"

He stilled but didn't answer.

After a moment, she continued. "Is it because he was sent to take Lorelei? Sent to take the person you're here to protect?"

Keeping his eyes averted, he said softly, "He can't be trusted."

"How do you know?"

He looked at her from over his shoulder. "We have a history."

She smoothed a bandage over the cut. "Can you tell me about it?"

"No."

"Figures. Want a sandwich?" she asked, taking care not to touch the wound when she helped him with the T-shirt he'd confiscated from his truck. "Glitch makes awesome grilled cheeses."

"I guess," he said as his head popped through the opening at the neck.

"Fine. I'll go place the order, but don't think for a minute I'm not furious with you."

"Wouldn't dream of it."

I winked at her as she left the room, then folded my arms over my chest. In obvious pain, he struggled to his feet and turned to me.

"She doesn't like me much, does she?"

"Brooklyn? Brooke's pretty direct," I said, trying to come up with the right words to describe my best friend. "If she didn't like you, you'd know it."

He shrugged. "Guess that's something."

"Am I interrupting?"

I turned to see Jared standing in my doorway.

Cameron answered before I had a chance. "Isn't that, like, your job? Interrupting the lives of others? Creating havoc and despair wherever you roam?"

"Cameron," I said in that warning tone my grandparents used every so often.

"I'm going downstairs." He strolled out, giving a light shove as he brushed past Jared.

Jared ignored him, his gaze unwavering as he watched me watch him. Even beaten and bruised he was stunning. A cut on the side of his mouth did nothing to lessen its beauty, its fullness emphasized by the dark shadows of his unshaven jaw. His eyes—sable shimmering pools framed in thick, impossibly long lashes—sparkled even in the dim light of my room. He was the most sensual being I'd ever laid eyes upon. Yet he was like those guys who didn't know how beautiful they were. It made me like him all the more, and I wondered how his mouth would feel pressed against mine.

With a mental shake, I dragged my thoughts out of the gutter and headed for the bathroom. Just because a god stood in my doorway didn't give me permission to objectify him. Really, it was like I hardly knew myself anymore.

"I'll start the shower for you," I said, suddenly self-conscious. "Glitch has guy shampoo and conditioner in here. You probably don't want to use mine, unless you want to smell like a field of lavender or an apricot tree."

I moved the shower curtain aside and turned on the water. After testing the temperature, I turned back. Jared had followed me and now stood in the bathroom doorway. There was something about him and doorways. He filled them up so completely.

His line of sight meandered to my mouth and lingered there a short while before traveling back up. "Your eyes get darker when you're emotional." He took a step toward me. "They're darker now, like smoke from a forest fire drifting toward Heaven."

"Really?" I asked, my lungs burning inside my chest. "I didn't know that."

His expression, curious and intense, sent sharp tingles arcing through my body. My insides went all mushy and my knees weakened. I couldn't believe how wildly beautiful he was, how powerful and seductive.

He stretched out his hand. "I believe this is yours."

I looked down. My necklace sat resting in his palm, the delicate chain laced over his long fingers. With a squeal of delight, I took it from him. "Where did you get this?"

The barest of smiles softened his features. "It was in my hand when I jumped from Cameron's vehicle."

"Oh, my goodness, thank you so much," I said, fastening it around my neck. I couldn't believe he had it.

He lifted the pendant where it rested, the backs of his fingers brushing the base of my throat, his skin warm against mine. If I let myself, I could look at him for all eternity. His strong jaw. His full mouth. His eyes so dark, they were like the ocean at night.

Realizing I had to get a grip, I snapped back to the present. Holy moly, I could barely think when he was around. "Right, um, I got you a few things from the store." I pointed toward the sink. "A toothbrush, toothpaste. You know, the usual." I smiled, pretending his whisper of a smile wasn't causing a slight head rush. "But if you need anything else . . ."

His demeanor changed in a heartbeat. Pain etched his face as he snaked an arm around his stomach. "I feel wrong," he said, grabbing the doorframe of the bathroom for stability.

"Wrong, how?" I asked, concern raising my voice an octave.

"I don't know. Just wrong." His stomach muscles seemed to contract. He clutched at his midsection and fell to his knees.

"Jared!"

Before I could kneel beside him, he lunged toward the toilet. He swallowed several times and I could almost feel the acidic bile as it rose up and burned the back of his throat. It refused to be squelched. Everything he had just eaten wound up in the toilet in a succession of violent purges.

With empathy guiding my every move, I jumped up to wet a washcloth, then knelt down and rested it on his forehead.

Breathing heavily into the toilet, he said, "Wrong like that."

After I flushed the commode, I wiped the cloth over his face, being careful not to reopen any wounds. "You're human now," I said in my best scolding voice. "At least a part of you is. You have to be more careful."

"I have to clean my mouth."

I helped him to his feet. He shook, suddenly weak and pallid. And he was so tall, well over six feet, but I did my best to get him to the sink.

After he brushed his teeth, I filled a cup with water and tried to hand it to him. His doubt kept him from searching for it.

"You're dehydrated," I said as I placed the cup in his hands. "Take small sips."

"I don't feel dehydrated."

"No matter, you are. Two days without H_2O will do that to a person." When he still didn't drink, I pushed the cup up to his mouth. "We don't have a very big water heater, so we run out of the hot stuff pretty fast. You might want to shower quickly."

"Okay."

I turned and pointed out the necessities. "Soap, shampoo, conditioner, a razor if you need one." I had to admit, I liked the shadow along his jaw, but he might not.

"Thank you," he said as he gingerly lifted his shirt over his head.

I turned from him with a gasp. Did six-packs get any sexier? "Um, okay, then. I'll be downstairs."

"Lorelei?"

I stopped but didn't turn around.

After a moment, he said, "Thank you for the toothbrush."

I smiled. "Yeah, well, you saved my life and all. It's the least I could do."

His silent laugh caused a rush of warmth as I closed the door. Then, with thoughts of melted cheese driving me, I hustled downstairs for a sandwich myself. Glitch had a magic touch with grilled cheeses. I could live off them if I had to.

"How is he?" Brooklyn asked.

"I'm not sure." I took an orange soda out of the fridge and jumped onto a stool beside her. "He got sick."

Glitch had the gall to look offended. "You mean he ate three of my sandwiches and then just threw them up?"

"Pretty much."

"Well, that sucks."

"Yeah, for him," I said with a bit of peevishness. "Not you, sandwich boy."

"Hey, you want one of these or not?"

"Of course."

He studied me suspiciously and pointed his spatula. "You're not going to throw it up, are you?"

"Not likely."

"Wait," he said, suddenly smiling, "where'd you find it?"

I reached for my necklace with a smile of my own. "Jared had it. It must have come off when we were in the back of Cameron's pickup."

"Oh, right," Cameron said, "when he was trying to choke the life out of you. That makes perfect sense."

He sat at the breakfast table in the corner, sipping a Dr Pepper.

I chose to ignore his sarcasm. "Have you eaten yet?" I asked him.

"He doesn't get another one," Glitch said, waving his spatula as if it were a magic wand. "Five is the house limit."

I whistled, impressed. "Well, I'm starving. Pass one over, pretty please."

Sinking into a grilled and cheesy heaven, I devoured Glitch's sandwich in less than five minutes along with a few chips and an apple for dessert. Afterwards, I sat chatting with Brooke and sandwich boy, all the while keeping track of how long Jared had been in the shower. And it was an awfully long time, much longer than the hot water would have lasted. I couldn't keep from looking up toward my room every few seconds.

Brooklyn noticed. "Why don't you just go check on him?"

"Okay," I said, needing little encouragement. I jumped from the stool and raced upstairs. The shower was still on, the door still closed.

I knocked lightly. When he didn't answer, I cracked open the door.

"Jared?"

When he still didn't answer, my heart leapt in alarm. What if he got sick again? What if he'd passed out? Or worse. What if he disappeared back to wherever it was he came from?

With worry driving me forward, I rushed into the tiny room and pulled back the curtain. Then I gasped and stood frozen a solid minute. Jared stood under the rushing water, naked. And not just a little. He'd lifted one arm and braced it against the wall to rest his head upon. The other hand had grasped the pipe that led to the showerhead. His eyes were closed as ice-cold water sheeted off his shoulders and down his back.

With effort, I stopped my gaze from going any lower. "Jared?"

His grip tightened around the pipe as he pecked at me, and the emotion that poured off him, that glistened in his eyes, was none other than regret. "I shouldn't be here," he said, and I couldn't help the guilt that washed over me. It was my fault. He wouldn't be here if I could learn to walk and chew gum at the same time. Really? Falling in front of a delivery truck was the best I could do?

I plastered a hand over my eyes and felt blindly for the shower valves, trying desperately to avoid body parts. After turning off the water, I grabbed a towel off the shelf and handed it back without facing him. "Wrap this around your waist."

He took it from me, and I heard the soft sway of material as he worked to fasten it around his nether region. The fresh scent of soap and shampoo filled the room.

"Okay," he said.

I turned back and was struck speechless by the sight of him, devilish and handsome. Dark wet locks hung over his forehead, dripping water down his face and onto his chest. The bands around his biceps almost glistened, they were so inklike, so sharp. The width of his torso tapered to a lean, sculpted stomach. He'd managed to cover the most pertinent part of his maleness, which I was terribly thankful for. I took another towel, beckoned him to bow, then draped it over his head to dry his hair.

"I shouldn't be here," he repeated, his voice thick with sorrow as I massaged wetness from his hair, and a tightness cinched around my chest. He reached back and took hold of the pipe again, making me realize how low the plumbing was in the shower. I'd always thought it the perfect height. "I don't know why I shifted and locked on to this plane." He looked at me from underneath the towel. "I'm risking everything by being here."

I couldn't imagine what he must be going through. Was he afraid? I would have been. Absolutely terrified. Whatever he was feeling, he would not go through it alone.

"We can figure this out, Jared. I promise you."

What did I expect? That he would want to stay here? That he would revel in his circumstances? Rejoice in the fact that fate had discarded him, like a kid abandoned at a truck stop in the middle of the night?

"At least while I was fighting Cameron of Jophiel," he said, his voice rough with emotion, "everything stopped. I could think of nothing beyond survival."

Fear lurched inside me. "Jared, you can't fight anymore." I leaned in to assess his expression under the towel. "Please, promise me."

He looked at me through slitted eyes. "I would never have hurt you, Lorelei," he said, his voice laced with a sadness that almost brought me to tears. "In the back of Cameron's vehicle when I grabbed you, I would never really have done those things."

I forced a smile past my doubt and continued to dry his hair. "I know."

"Do you?" His long lashes were spiked with water. "You were so scared, it hurt." He placed a hand on his chest. "Inside."

His confession surprised me. "Well, you were pretty convincing."

He lowered his head. "I'm so sorry."

"Don't be. You were scared too." I rubbed his head with the towel. His body filled the room, made it seem small in comparison. "Can I ask you something?"

"Of course."

The towel draped over his head gave me courage. I didn't want him to see me when I asked my next question. "If you had wanted to, could you really have boiled the blood in my veins?"

He froze. After a moment, he straightened and looked down at me. "I don't know. I had already shifted onto this plane. I don't know what I can do now, if anything."

I dropped my arms. "But if you hadn't shifted, you could have?"

He didn't want to answer. I could tell by his expression. He worked his jaw before answering. "Yes," he said at last.

I waited before picking up the corners of the towel and dabbing at the bruises on his face. "Your job must be really interesting."

"Interesting," he said with curiousity. His white teeth flashed, the effect nuclear. "That's a good word for it. Any thoughts on what I might wear?"

I was still wandering around ground zero, struggling to come back to the present. I shifted onto my other foot and cleared my throat. "I found some sweats and a T-shirt in the store," I said, pointing over my shoulder. "They have our logo on it, but they should fit."

His eyes slid down to my mouth, where they lingered like a caress. He leaned forward, and my breath caught as his scent stirred my senses to life. Just when his mouth was close enough to brush mine, he reached a long arm over my shoulder and pushed the door closed.

"Oh, right," I said with a nervous giggle. "Guess you'll want some privacy."

He flashed another smile as he stepped from the tub.

With barely enough room to maneuver, I whirled and headed for the door. "I'll get those clothes now." I almost fell out of the room in my attempt to escape. That boy was just way too gorgeous for my sense of balance. My original assessment had pretty much nailed it.

Absolute supernova.

After I grabbed the clothes, I cracked the door and shoved them through the opening. He thanked me with a soft chuckle. Better that than me making a fool of myself, waiting for him to kiss me, for his mouth on mine. Maybe in an alternate reality.

With a groan, I fell forward onto my bed and buried my face in an overstuffed pillow. A strong mixture of excitement and fear rushed along my nerve endings. I took a deep, calming draught of air and turned over to stare at the ceiling, unable to wipe the grin from my face.

"I feel sixteen." Jared stepped out of the bathroom in the red T-shirt and black sweats I'd found for him.

"You look sixteen." A muscular, godlike sixteen, but sixteen nonetheless.

He regarded his clothes with a forlorn expression.

"Here, you're still wet." I stepped forward to pull down the dampened shirt, but lifted it farther instead. His side had a huge red gash in it. I raised the shirt more to inspect it. "This looks really bad."

"Yes. I can't remember if that was the crowbar or baseball bat."

"Oh, goodness," I said, holding up a hand, "you should probably keep stuff like that to yourself."

"Sorry. Cameron is rather creative that way. I've never felt pain on this plane, though I have on others. I forgot how much it hurts."

I searched his dark fringed eyes. Did he mean the plane I saw in my vision? Could that place have been real?

"I'm amazed at how much I need oxygen," he said. Testing his lungs, he took a deep breath, then clutched his ribs in agony.

I grabbed his arm like that would help. "Are you okay?"

"I believe so."

"I think your ribs are cracked." I inspected them gently with my fingertips. He hissed in a sharp breath and winced. "Yep."

"I'm okay. I'll be fine tomorrow."

"You need something on that wound." Lowering his shirt, I straightened. He absolutely towered over me, his dark eyes warm and interested. "How tall are you anyway?"

"By your measurements and in this form, I am six-five."

"Holy moly. That's tall."

He chuckled softly. "How tall are you?" he asked, his deep voice touching every part of me. The shadows that pooled in the contours of his muscles shifted every time he moved. It was mesmerizing.

"You have tattoos," I said, changing the subject.

He nodded and pushed up his sleeves to give me a better look. "I was able to make them disappear before, but now they're just . . . there. I should not let Alan Davis see them."

"Alan Davis? You mean Principal Davis?" I asked, alarmed.

"Yes. You were right. He'd recognized me that morning, remembered me from when he was a boy, when I came to take his brother, Elliot Davis. Like many others, he saw me in the crowd as I waited, took note of my tattoos. He approached me, fascinated, and asked what they meant."

"What did you tell him?"

"The truth, that they are a testament to the power that was bestowed upon me as well as my station, rank, and mission."

"Oh." I looked back in surprise at the bands just visible under the sleeve edges. They were beautiful, fluid. Crisp black curves sprang into sharp points that wrapped around his arms, forming symbol after symbol like a line of ancient text. "And you think Mr. Davis recognized them?"

"He caught a glimpse before I thought to conceal them. If he sought my image in that yearbook, I know he did."

"Well, then, we'll just have to keep them hidden in the future."

I took the ointment Brooklyn had been using and began spreading it onto his side as he held up the shirt. The gash was horrible and grotesquely deep. And his back was covered in scrapes and bruises. I shook my head again in wonder. Boys.

"May I ask you something?"

"I welcome it."

The way he talked sometimes threw me. Well, that and the fact that he welcomed my questions. No one alive welcomed my questions. I could be very obnoxious.

"You said that you've never felt pain on this plane. But you have on others?" I went further with the ointment, quickly covering the worst of the scratches while I had the chance, just to be on the safe side.

"I have."

That realization made me cringe inside. The fact that he ever felt pain for any reason saddened me. "In my vision, you were fighting something. A huge dark monster." I looked up at him to gauge his reaction. "Was that real? Did it really happen?"

He hesitated as though unsure if he should be honest. His mouth thinned and he answered. "It did happen, most likely. I've fought many."

"But you don't have scars on your chest. It had ripped through you like paper."

He placed a hand above his heart in thought. "Ah, yes, what you saw happened. I was charged with bringing down a rebel demon who had escaped from Hell and made it into another dimension, but that was many centuries ago."

Sputtering, I stepped back. "A demon? Like, a real one?"

His head tilted in curiosity. "I believe they are all real."

I sank onto the edge of my bed and stared at the carpet a long time. "That was a demon. Are they all that . . . monstrous?"

The bed dipped as he sat beside me. "I didn't mean to frighten you."

"Wait, why don't you have scars?" I glanced at his chest.

With a glint of understanding, he placed his hand under my chin and lifted my face to his, commanding my full attention. "Despite our appearance," he said, his tone purposeful, "make no mistake, Lorelei McAlister, we are nowhere near human. Our origin and existence differ vastly from your own. We are powerful and dutiful and execute our orders without empathy or the slightest hint of remorse."

His statement sounded more like a warning than a friendly tip. In spite of everything, the warning he was obviously offering for my benefit, my attention wandered. I noticed the fatigue that had fallen over him like a veil, his heavy lids, his body drained of energy.

"Do you want to try another sandwich?" I asked. "Or maybe some soup?"

When he shook his head, I stood and pulled his shirt back down over the cut. I felt so guilty. What he did for me had obviously cost him a great deal. And there I sat, offering a supreme being a grilled cheese sandwich. A stab of regret shot through my heart. He was there because of me. And he clearly didn't want to be.

"I'm so sorry, Jared. You've lost everything because of me."

He grabbed my hands as they fitted his shirt around him. "Is that what you think?" he asked, his tone full of surprise. "Do you think I don't want to be here because I've lost something?"

The warmth of his hands seeped into my skin. "Of course. You're stuck here because of me. You've lost everything."

"Lorelei, I am stuck here because of me. Because I changed history, remember? Locking on to this plane is the least of my worries." He squeezed, then let go.

"I don't understand. You said you didn't know why it happened."

"And I don't. But that doesn't mean I don't want to be here because of it."

I wound a loose string on my shirt around my fingers. "Then why don't you want to be here?"

He took hold of the string and pulled me closer. "My presence, my reasons and intent, they all risk your soul, Lorelei, your salvation."

"In what way?"

"A seraphim, even an archangel, cannot be with a human. It is forbidden." He stood also and looked down at me. "I don't want to be here, because my presence risks everything I care for. And yet, the thought of being anywhere else in the universe floods me with unbearable pain."

While he said many things, I heard only one. "So, you do want to be here?"

I held my breath as he thought about his answer.

"More than anything," he said. Then his brows inched together. "I have never been tempted. Since the earth was being formed beneath my feet, I have never longed to taste the nectar of humans, the forbidden fruit of seraphim. And then I saw you. My mouth waters every time you are near." He squared his shoulders and confessed, "I can only hope that when you know all there is to know, you can forgive me my trespasses."

I stood utterly mesmerized, lost in his words. How was this even possible, that I was the forbidden fruit of a god? Holy freaking cow. With a mental shake, I tamped down the elation shooting through me and focused on the brunt of the situation. Feeling somewhat like an impetuous child, I asked, "But what about Jophiel? The archangel who visited Cameron's mom? Wasn't that forbidden?"

"His sacrifice was in the service of humankind. My desires are a bit more . . . self-serving," he said with a wry gleam. "So, no, Lorelei, I should not be here. In a thousand different ways, I shouldn't be here."

"Well, that makes two of us, remember?" I said, my brain straining for a solution, some loophole we could jump through. "I'm supposed to be dead. So either join the club or start one of your own." I grabbed the ointment and put the lid back on before looking up at him again.

After a moment, he said, "Did you know your mouth tilts sideways when you're being sarcastic?"

"Oh, yeah, you're trashed." I pulled him around the bed and eased him onto it. He needed to rest. "You can have my bed. I'll sleep with Brooke."

"No." Without another word, he carefully lowered himself onto the floor beside the bed, halting when a jolt of pain shot through him.

"Jared, you can't sleep on the floor," I said, appalled. "You need to rest, not toss and turn all night."

With an evil grin, he reached up and stole one of two pillows off the bed. "I'll be fine." He crossed his arms behind his head and lay back. I chuckled and dragged my comforter off, tossing it over him. "Thank you," he said, his voice soft as though he were almost asleep already.

I watched as his eyes drifted shut, his presence powerful even at rest.

"And if Cameron of Jophiel takes a baseball bat to me in my sleep, I'll snap his neck."

Sobering instantly, I crawled onto the bed, shoes and all. "I'll pass along the warning," I said, surrendering to weariness.

"I should not be here, Lorelei McAlister," he said, his speech slurring with fatigue, "and yet, I have never felt so at peace."

My eyes flew open and I looked over the side of the bed. "You're at peace?" I asked, but he was asleep before I finished the question.

I rested my head so I could examine him, shivering as every nerve ending I possessed tingled. I liked the feel of him close by, the rhythmic sound of his breathing, the clean smell of his breath and hair. But the niggling in the back of my mind grew stronger the more I looked at him. He was utterly magnificent. A higher being. A supreme entity. What would he want with a pixie stick like me? He could have anyone in the universe, literally, and he was stuck on Earth. I squeezed my eyes shut, blocking out reality. Despite the fact that having a real relationship with Jared was supposedly forbidden, and I certainly didn't want to get him into any more trouble than he was already in, I prayed he would still be there in the morning.

VISIONS OF SUGARPLUMS

"Can't you sleep?"

I raised my head and tried to open my lead-filled lids. I was sleeping just fine, thank you very much.

"I can sleep," Brooklyn said. "I just prefer listening to music."

"Really?"

Ah, Cameron. They must have come in after I passed out. I pried my lids open the best I could and looked at them through my mussed hair. Cameron was sitting on the window seat, back straight, alert as always. Did that guy ever rest?

"I have bad dreams," Brooklyn said, "when it's too quiet." She was on her own twin bed that was tucked into the corner by the window seat. Grandma and Grandpa had bought it for her, since she practically lived with us anyway. "Can't you sleep?"

"Not with him here." He indicated Jared with a nod of his head.

I couldn't help but peek over the side of my bed to study the boy sleeping so soundly beside me. He looked almost totally healed already. He had light bruises and scratches where deep cuts and swollen golf balls had been before. I glanced back at Cameron. The same. Healing quickly was definitely part of who they were. It would have taken a normal person days, even weeks to reach that point.

Trying not to be noticed, I raised up and peeked over at Glitch. He was on the floor in a sleeping bag. Pretty much every available inch of floor space had been confiscated.

"Have you slept at all lately?" Brooklyn asked. She had on her favorite pajamas, the ones with tiny turtles all over them, the ones that *disturbed* Glitch.

"Do you care?" Cameron volleyed.

She sighed and hugged a pillow to her. "Cameron, I know what you were doing, why you were following Lorelei. You saw him, didn't you? You knew what he was."

He rested back against the window and looked out of it. "I only felt it at first. Then, about a week ago, I saw it following her."

"You saw Jared? He's been here for a week?"

"No. At first, there was simply a fine dark mist. It was so unlike Lorelei, I knew something else was there."

"What do you mean, so unlike her?"

He rubbed the back of his fingers on the cold glass. "Lorelei's aura is bright, like fire. I've never seen anything like it."

"You can see her aura?" Brooklyn asked, propping her elbows on the pillow.

"I can see everyone's auras, ever since I was a kid."

"Wow." She pondered on that briefly before asking, "So, when you first saw them, when you were a kid, did you know what they were?"

"Not even," he said, shaking his head. "I used to ask my dad why people didn't glow in their pictures like they did in real life. That's when it hit me. Not everyone could see them. My dad made me promise not to tell anyone."

"That's pretty amazing." Pausing thoughtfully, she asked, "So, what color is mine?"

"Oh, no," he said, turning to her with a wary expression. "Trust me. You do not want to go there."

She gasped. "Is it bad?"

"Awful."

Clasping her hands at her chest, she said bravely, "Go ahead. Tell me. I can take it."

I knew from the tilt of his lips, he would give her a bogus answer. He leaned toward her and whispered. "It's purple with pink polka dots."

She threw her pillow at him. "It is not."

He caught it easily. "How do you know?"

"Just tell me, butthead."

He laughed and tossed her pillow back. "What are you gonna do for me?"

"What am I gonna do for you?" she asked, sitting up. "What do you mean, what am I gonna do for you? I can't do anything for you. You're, like, all strong and crap."

With a grin more evil than before, he regarded her a long moment. She braced herself for whatever he might say. "You could tell me your deepest, darkest secret."

She rolled her eyes in disappointment. "I don't have any deep, dark secrets. Least not any that compare with the likes of yours."

"Your aura speaks otherwise," he said. Clearly, he knew something she didn't.

"Yeah, whatever. So, do auras change color?"

"All the time. When someone gets mad or depressed. Pretty much any strong emotion will change a person's aura temporarily. You wouldn't believe how badly a laughing person can be seething underneath. It's . . . intimidating."

"I never thought anything could intimidate you."

He looked at her in surprise. "I've been intimidated by you since the third grade."

Brooklyn stilled, completely taken off guard. "Me? Get outta here."

"No, really. Your aura was so different from any I'd seen before. I didn't know what to think of you."

"Wow." She wiggled her shoulders. "I'm intimidating. That's kind of liberating in a bizarre, dominatrix kind of way. So are you gonna tell me the color or what?"

"I don't know if I should. I could use it as leverage someday."

"Fine," she said, feigning disinterest. I could tell she was dying to know—especially since it was so intimidating and all—but she decided to drop it for now. "I order you to get some sleep, then."

"Another order?" He raised his brows, amused. "You gonna pull that water pistol on me again?"

With a soft gasp, she asked, "You knew that was a water pistol?" After he shot her a *duh*-like smirk, she said, "I can't believe you knew it was a water pistol."

"Oh yeah," he said sarcastically, "the differences between a water pistol and a Glock are really subtle."

"Okay, then why did you back down?"

He lowered his head and asked quietly, "Didn't you want me to?"

Judging by the look on her face, the question stunned her. I know it stunned the heck out of me. She didn't seem to know how to answer.

After a moment, her expression changed. "Tell you what," she said, jumping down, "I'll take the window seat, and you take the bed. I'm shorter."

Ouch. That was a big sacrifice for Brooke. She loved that bed. But I totally agreed. Cameron needed to get some Z's. He was grouchy enough without sleep deprivation adding to his moodiness.

He shook his head. "I can't go to sleep."

She walked to him and grabbed his shirt. "Come on, Rocky."

He let her pull him over to the bed. With a reluctant sigh, he lay down. She tossed a blanket over him and giggled at his feet dangling over the edge. Twin beds and super-tall guys did not go well together at all.

"But I'm not sleepy," he argued.

"I know, I know." She took a blanket from a shelf and lay down on the window seat.

Personally, I gave him fifteen minutes tops, but his breaths were deep and rhythmic before Brooke even settled in.

She lifted her head and looked past Jared's sleeping form at me. "Not sleepy, my left butt cheek," she said.

I laughed.

"It's her."

Oh, no. Not again.

"The prophet," came another hushed whisper. "I told you we would see her."

For the love of carrot sticks, let me sleep.

The voice, a child's, whispered again. "She looks like fire."

I squinted into the darkness, confused by the soft voices, before looking over at Jared. He was awake, sitting against the wall beside me, one leg bent with an arm resting on his knee. What a heavenly vision.

"Do you feel them?" he asked in a hushed tone.

I glanced around. "What?"

"They're coming."

"Who?" I tried to sit up straight, but a sharp pain shot through me, causing my teeth to slam together in agony. My ribs hurt worse today than they had yesterday.

"They're excited to see you."

"Who's excited?" I asked again.

He said nary a word, smiled and, without releasing my gaze, gestured to a point behind me.

I glanced back and started in alarm. A child was sitting on the wall just past my head, as though on a levitating bench. He giggled, turned to his friend beside him, and whispered into her ear. She looked at me and giggled too. They covered their mouths with tiny hands as their laughter sparkled and danced around us, illuminating the room, casting shadows on the walls.

Then the boy glanced at Jared and sobered instantly, tucking his chin and averting his eyes.

"Shhhh," someone said in a faint whisper, and I looked toward Glitch's sleeping form. A child stood beside him. He pointed up. "She's coming."

I scanned the room and counted a dozen children sitting here and there, all dressed in white linen like little angels-in-training. I half expected to see tiny wings and tarnished halos. A few were looking at me in absolute curiosity, but most were gawking at Jared, and I couldn't help but see fear in their eyes, uncertainty. They watched him warily, huddled close to one another. Then I realized Cameron was awake. He looked on, his eyes wide, uncertain.

"Do it," one of them said, egging his friend on. "Get closer." The other one shook his head, so the boy said, "Fine. I'll do it."

He took a wary step toward Jared, then another, but the minute Jared focused on him, the boy scrambled back to the corner with his friend.

"You didn't even get close."

"I got closer than you," he said defensively.

Jared shot me a conspiratorial look and winked. "I have a way with children."

I was about to ask him what was going on, when a bright glow infused the room with a light so brilliant, it woke Brooklyn and Glitch too. They opened their eyes just in time to see a beautiful elderly woman materialize. Her skin was dark, her eyes golden, warm and magnificent. Her robe, thick like liquid pearl, flowed past her feet.

The children looked on adoringly, as if they couldn't get their fill of her, as though each secretly hoped she would cast her attention their way.

She smiled at Jared. When she spoke, her voice was smooth, unhurried. "Azrael, the noble son, created from the resplendence of light and the void of darkness—"

Jared dipped his head in acknowledgment.

"—you have not been abandoned." Her smile was like life itself: pure and bright, nurturing and intoxicating. The children echoed her words as she spoke, like whispers in an empty cavern. All except one. I'd noticed a boy, smaller than the rest, who'd tucked himself behind my dresser. He emerged from his haven to slowly creep toward the woman, all the while keeping an eye on Jared as though afraid he would jump up and bite him.

"You have more power, more freedom than any of your brethren," she continued, a loving shimmer sparkling in her eyes, "and you used it to save her."

Me? I jumped to attention.

"But I did so for selfish reasons," Jared said.

"You are of light and darkness. Only you can decide where your true intentions lie."

"Why am I here?" he asked, suddenly angry.

"Why should I answer what you already know?"

"I'm . . . not human." He shook his head in frustration. "I can't be here."

"And yet you are."

"Is He angry?" he asked, regret thickening his voice.

Her expression changed to one of sympathy. "With you? You know He isn't."

"Then—"

"He is pleased, Azrael."

Her words seemed to jar him. He sat up straighter, tightened his jaw in thought, his eyes wide, uncertain.

"Sometimes," she said, seeming to sense his confusion, "we must swim against the current to find our true purpose. You have proved yourself beyond anything we could have hoped for. Because you have a singular power, one that transcends any of your brethren's, you alone are best suited to carry out this mission. You know what is to come, and now you are charged with its success."

His head whipped up in disbelief. "There's no way to succeed, no way to win. It is written." He shot to his feet, his fists clenched. "You have sent me to fail."

She stepped forward, her movements like a soft breeze, as the little boy peeked around her skirts to view Jared. With her nearness, Jared sank onto one knee in reverence. "It was also written that the last prophet of Arabeth would be crushed and would drown in her own blood."

Jared glanced at me when I made a sound of alarm.

She turned toward me for only an instant, then placed her fingers under his chin and lifted his face to hers. "Perhaps it is time to rewrite what is to be."

Jared sat back on his heel and frowned, as though trying to make sense of it all.

"You said it yourself: Only humans can change history."

He focused on her again, a dawning creeping into his eyes before the little boy caught his attention.

Peeking from behind her skirts, the boy smiled at him and held out his hand. Jared's head tilted in curiosity; then he held out his own hand, palm up.

"Silas, no," the other children warned, but the boy slid his shaking hand forward. "Silas," they repeated, but when the boy's fingers brushed against Jared's, they all inhaled in disbelief. He had done what they'd been afraid to do. All eyes turned toward the boy in awe, and I realized that these spirits, these supernatural beings, were terrified of Jared.

"But we have sent you help," the woman said as she surveyed the room, taking in each of our awed faces one by one. Then she turned to Cameron. "Cameron of Jophiel, you have been charged with a great responsibility. It is why you were chosen, why you were created. Do you accept?"

"Yes," he said without hesitation, completely mesmerized by her, as though he knew exactly what that responsibility might be.

With a mischievous glint in her eyes, she looked from me to Brooklyn then to Glitch and crossed her arms in thought.

"Uh-oh," one of the children said. "Someone's in trouble."

"And you three." She frowned with feigned severity. "I have waited a long time to meet you. I am honored to be in your presence."

She was honored? I sat there, staring in awe at the most magnificent being I had ever seen—so bright, I could hardly look at her; so loving, I thought my heart would burst—and *she* was honored?

She leaned toward me. "You, the last prophet of Arabeth, are of fire, an element that can also bring light or darkness, that can do good or cause harm, that can tip the scales or bring balance. Combined with the powers of Azrael, the possibilities are limitless. You may even, given the right circumstances, save the world. You must decide now. Do you accept?"

"Yes." I answered even faster than Cameron had.

"Lorelei."

"Yes. Yes, I do."

"Lorelei."

I bunched my face up, confused again.

"For heaven's sake, young lady." Grandma's voice broke into my dream. "It's time to get up. You're going to be late for school."

I awoke with a start and took in my surroundings. Everyone else was just waking as well. I looked at Jared. He flashed a sleepy, boyishly gorgeous smile at me and I almost seized with the jolt of pleasure that shot through me.

"My heavens. You kids must have been working for hours." Grandma stood in a flannel button-down and loose slacks, otherwise known as her cleaning duds, her soft blue eyes concerned as she surveyed the room. Glitch was on the floor, Brooklyn on the window seat, and Cameron in Brooklyn's bed. Rumpled clothes and bed-heads gave us each that much-sought-after, all-night-kegger look. And as amazingly healed as both Jared and Cameron were, their appearance still had a certain bar-brawl quality to it.

Grandma took it all in, pausing a long, long moment on Jared, then looked back at me. "I'll make some breakfast while you kids get ready for school."

"Oh, no, Grandma, you don't need to do that," I said, trying to sit up without cringing outwardly. Freaking ribs.

"Lorelei Elizabeth McAlister," she scolded, "you never let me make you breakfast. It'll just take me a minute."

I acquiesced. "Thank you, Grandma."

"I get the first shower!"

Before I could argue, Glitch jumped toward the bathroom.

He glanced back, eyeing Cameron, his expression hard, before he locked the door.

"So much for hot water," Brooklyn said, oblivious.

The morning progressed in a rather tense, tight kind of awkwardness. My grandparents hovered over us throughout breakfast, asking a million questions about the most bizarre things, which was very unlike them. And I didn't miss the odd looks cast in Jared's direction, or the quick glances they cast toward each other. I couldn't blame them. He *had* been sleeping on my floor. Thankfully, the T-shirt he wore had sleeves just long enough to cover the tattoos around his biceps. It was one thing to have a boy in my room. It was another to have a tattooed boy in my room.

The five of us drove to school in utter silence. Glitch reluctantly drove Cameron's truck again so I could keep an eye on the middleweight contenders in the backseat. But they didn't say two words to each other. It seemed no one knew quite what to say.

Even though Jared and Cameron were both sore, they weren't in nearly as much pain as they should've been. Their scrapes and bruises were nothing but light marks on their perfect faces now. I wanted to comment on it, but everyone was so quiet, I couldn't bring myself to speak.

I also wanted to ask about the dream. It felt so real, so warm and intoxicating. But, again, the silence was like a rock wall, cold and impenetrable.

As we pulled into the parking lot, I noticed a crowd gathered in front of the gym. Then I saw a guy with a microphone and another with a camera.

"That's him!" Brooklyn screamed, proving the wall wasn't that impenetrable. "That's the reporter!"

"What reporter?" Jared asked.

"Well, crap," I said, and made an illegal U-turn.

"Where are you going?" Cameron asked.

I decided to answer Cameron's question first. It was easier. "I'm going to the faculty parking lot."

"Students can't park in the faculty lot. Quite the little felon these days, aren't we?" he said.

I chose to ignore him. "And as for that reporter," I said, responding to Jared's question, "he apparently saw me get hit by that delivery truck and then saw Hercules over there drag your unconscious body to his pickup." I narrowed my eyes on Cameron before refocusing on the road. "Let's just say he's very curious. He's been following us around."

"And he has a tape," Brooklyn said.

"A tape?" Jared asked, suddenly alarmed. "What's on it?"

Brooklyn turned to him. "We don't know. But we do know there's just enough on it to make him dangerous."

Even though I parked at the farthest edge of the faculty lot, we had barely stepped out of the car when Ms. Mullins came charging toward us.

Cameron *tsk*ed. "See, crime never pays."

"Listen, blondie," Brooke said, pointing a finger at him, "if you don't have anything nice to say—"

He stepped close and stared fixedly down at her, his eyes sparkling with humor. He meant to fluster her, and it worked.

"—then just . . . just don't say anything at all."

"Okay," he said softly.

Brooklyn turned from him slightly winded. Oh, this was getting so very, very good.

Ms. Mullins stopped short when she saw who we were with. After a brief recovery period, she eyed Jared up and down, did the same to Cameron, then waved her arms to herd us inside.

"You kids hurry in. There's some creepy reporter guy and a camera crew looking for you."

"Oh," I said in surprise. "I thought we were in trouble for parking here."

"I figured you might have to. That's why I came over."

Once again, Ms. Mullins saved the day. Man, I loved that woman. But before we made it to the door, creepy reporter guy found us anyway.

"Ms. McAlister!" he called, running with his microphone like they did on TV. He was short—well, for a man—and had dark slick hair plastered to his head. His cameraman, trying to keep up, slipped on the wet grass and almost fell. Which could have been costly. "Lorelei McAlister?"

"Crap," I said. I looked back at Jared and Cameron. "Go. Hurry before they get you on tape. Again."

The doors facing the faculty lot were always locked. Ms. Mullins tossed Cameron her keys, then turned back to the reporter rushing toward us, her arms raised to stop him.

"Gentlemen," she said with a fierce authoritative boom in her voice, "this is school property. I'm going to have to ask you to leave."

"I just need to ask Ms. McAlister some questions. I'm John Dell, Ms. McAlister, investigative reporter for the Tourist Channel."

I was a little surprised the Tourist Channel had investigative reporters.

Ms. Mullins stepped in front of him and almost got knocked in the face with a microphone. She couldn't have been more than an inch or two taller than me, but that didn't stop her for an instant. "I don't care if you're Walter Cronkite. This is school property and you don't have permission to be here." She glanced over her shoulder. "You girls go inside."

We obeyed immediately. As Ms. Mullins fended off the reporter, Principal Davis came bustling out the door Cameron was holding open for us.

He took in Cameron and Jared with surprise. "I see you two have kissed and made up."

"Not really," Cameron said, but Mr. Davis was already out the door and dealing with the intruders.

"Well, that was exciting," Brooklyn said as we rushed inside and headed for class.

"That guy's gonna be a problem," I said.

"Like we don't have enough of those already." Brooklyn kept an eye on Cameron, her insinuation clear.

"What?" he asked.

After Glitch caught up with us, we made plans to meet in the back hall between first and second hours. Brooke and I escorted Jared to Mrs. Geary's office, the school counselor, to iron out his schedule before we headed to our first class.

I was worried Ms. Mullins would bombard me with questions about creepy reporter guy, but she didn't bring it up once. She did, however, spring a pop quiz over the chapter I had neglected to read the night before. Grandma was going to kill me.

SOPHOMORE BLUES

"So, he said you were like forbidden fruit?" Brooklyn asked as we walked to meet the boys in the back hall.

Ms. Mullins gave us free time after the quiz, and I told Brooke everything Jared had said the night before. Well, the best parts anyway.

"He said I made his mouth water." The memory had me blushing with elation.

"Man, I want to be someone's forbidden fruit."

"Well, you are pretty fruity."

"True."

Glitch was talking to Jared when we strolled up to them, asking him something about becoming transparent, and I was amazed at all the attention directed our way. I was also a little pissed off. We had important stuff to talk about, and the last thing we needed was a bunch of spectators listening in on our every word. We were standing in a tiled alcove in the back hall that, unfortunately, amplified sound.

"Did you get your schedule?" I asked Jared. He was wearing a pair of Cameron's jeans—much to Cameron's chagrin—a red and black Riley High T-shirt, and an old bomber jacket Glitch never wore because the company had sent the wrong size. It practically swallowed him, but he was too lazy to send it back. It fit Jared perfectly.

"Yes. It seems I'm to be a sophomore." He handed me a folded paper. A tiny thrill spiked within me. He was a sophomore, like me. Yes! "I'm not certain it's a good idea," he continued. "I feel like I should be older."

"Well, you totally blend either way," Brooklyn said. "Cameron's a sophomore and you're both the same height . . . freaking-tall-foot-five."

"I suppose," he said, unconvinced.

Brooklyn seemed to be getting annoyed with all the stares too. One girl in particular had taken quite a fancy to Riley High's newest student. "Keep walking, freshman," she said, like being a freshman was something to be ashamed of.

"Do you feel out of place?" I asked Jared.

He lowered his head. "I do, but not for the reasons you think."

Cameron walked up then, his brows raised at Brooklyn. "That was rude. I'm impressed."

"Don't be." She craned her neck back and forth, but the girl had already started down the hall. "Sorry 'bout that!" she yelled after her.

Cameron shook his head. "All my hopes, dashed in a blinding moment of regret."

"Well, you were right," she said. "That was rude."

"You're rude to me all the time," Glitch said.

"You don't count."

He folded his arms over his chest. "I forgot I was pond scum. I'm like a minuscule one-celled organism in a multi-celled world."

"What are the reasons I think?" I asked Jared.

He placed his fingers under my chin and raised my face to his. I froze. One corner of his mouth tipped up in a devilish way as he nailed me to the floor with one steady look. The world quieted, and I wondered if he had stopped the spin of the Earth again, if he had stopped time.

"Listen, amoeba boy—," Brooklyn said behind me.

Nope.

"—it's just that being rude to you is different from being rude to a complete stranger." She placed her arm in Glitch's. "It's like that time you set your little brother's shorts on fire . . . while he was still wearing them. I mean, would you ever do that to a complete stranger?"

"I guess not," Glitch said.

"So, you feel better now?"

"No."

"You think I'm sorry I'm here," Jared said, his voice quiet and sure, "and that could not be further from the truth."

Sometimes I could see through his dark eyes straight into his soul. So old. So knowledgeable. And yet he seemed like a kid, like us. Charm radiated from every inch of his body, an innocent charm, like he was completely unaware he had it. I thought I saw silver flakes in his dark eyes. They sparkled as always when he smiled.

"You, you, you, you, and you."

I startled to attention as Mr. Davis barreled toward us.

"I need you five in my office now."

Concern made my heart beat faster. "All five of us?" I asked.

Mr. Davis's brows snapped together like he thought I was being smart. I wasn't. I was simply in denial.

He turned without comment and headed back toward his office. I glanced up at Jared. His smile had vanished. He watched Mr. Davis walk away, his expression guarded.

When we walked to his office, Mr. Davis was standing outside, talking to Sheriff Villanueva. A jolt of fear raced through me. This was it. This was the end. We were in so much trouble. I just wasn't completely sure why. I mean, what did we do wrong? Besides vandalize a car or two, shatter a few windows downtown.

Principal Davis turned toward us. "If you four will go in, the sheriff and I would like to talk to Lorelei alone."

Jared's hand was around my arm instantly while Cameron, Glitch, and Brooklyn shifted nervous eyes at one another.

"Sure, Mr. Davis," Brooklyn said at last, adding a light bounce to her step. As she walked past, she took hold of Jared's sleeve and dragged him, as nonchalantly as possible, inside.

Jared glanced over his shoulder, but I couldn't read his expression. I didn't think he was worried I would say anything. He seemed more concerned about me than himself.

"I guess you've made a new friend," Mr. Davis said.

I turned toward him.

"Anything else you care to tell me about Jared Kovach?"

I took in the two men. Sheriff Villanueva wasn't very tall, but I heard he'd been a Golden Gloves boxing champion. He had a strong presence, intense, though his kind features seemed to balance out his rough edges.

I shrugged. "I told you what I know."

"But you two have been hanging out more," he said. "Have you learned anything new?"

The sheriff's focus never wavered off my face. He was reading every move I made, every reaction I had to Mr. Davis's questions. I decided to cooperate fully. And a tad deceptively.

"Look," I said in a conspiratorial voice, "Jared's parents are having a really hard time right now. He's staying with us for a while, and we're doing everything in our power to keep him from becoming suicidal. I mean, he's been really upset. His parents are on the verge of divorce. They're about to lose their house in Santa Fe—"

"I thought he was from Los Angeles," Mr. Davis said.

Oops. "Well, right," I said, stuttering slightly, "I was getting to that. They lost their house in Los Angeles a while back, and now they're about to lose their house in Santa Fe too."

"They're going to lose two houses?"

"Yes," I said, praying that he believe me, "if his dad doesn't get a new job soon."

After a long pause, he said, "Okay, go on."

"Well, so anyway, he's staying with us until his parents decide what they're going to do. That's why he didn't show up back to school. He was hoping to be back with them permanently before the week was up."

The sheriff spoke up then. "Are you related?"

"No. Well, not exactly. His parents are very close to my grandparents."

"I thought you had just met him," Mr. Davis said.

"Yes. I did. But my grandfather has known his dad for years." Why was I saying these things? I was trying to keep my grandparents out of this mess, but one phone call and I was busted.

I'd gone crazy. It was true. Somewhere in the midst of all the chaos, I had lost my marbles.

"Why didn't you mention that the other day in my office?"

"Mr. Davis, I didn't feel comfortable talking about Jared or his family without his consent. I hope you can understand that. Jared's been really upset."

"Yes, you said that."

The sheriff passed a sideways glance to Mr. Davis before asking, "So, why don't you tell me what you know about a fight on Main Street and a vandalized Buick."

"A fight?"

"Yes, a fight. Between a tall dark-haired teenager and a tall blond one."

"Really? When was this?"

"On Tuesday, supposedly right after you left the Java Loft."

I gulped in air as I pretended to understand. "Wasn't that an earthquake?" I looked from one man to the other, my eyes wide and curious. I should totally become an actor. "Well, whatever it was, I missed the whole thing. Glitch and Brooklyn told me about it later that night. You can ask them."

"So, Jared Kovach could have been in a fight and you wouldn't have known about it?"

"Sheriff Villanueva, Jared was with his parents in Santa Fe. Remember, Mr. Davis?" I squinted at him questioningly. "I told you in your office yesterday, he was upset and wanted to be with them. He just got back late last night. He couldn't have had anything to do with a fight or an earthquake or whatever-the-heck else could've happened."

The sheriff surveyed me suspiciously. "Ms. McAlister, I have some rather credible eyewitnesses. And to be totally honest, both Kovach and Lusk look a little beaten and bruised."

You have no idea, I thought. Even though I didn't comment, I held my ground with an ultra-innocent expression.

After a moment, and a rather lengthy, annoyed sigh, he looked back at the principal. "This is getting us nowhere. Let's go back in."

When we entered Mr. Davis's office, I came to a screeching

halt just inside the threshold. My grandparents were there. In his office. Sitting. In his office. My heartbeat skyrocketed.

Grandpa stood.

"What are you guys doing here?" I asked him, shock forcing my voice into a breathy whisper.

"Bill," Principal Davis said, "if you would like to sit down, I'll explain what this is about."

Grandpa looked from the principal to the sheriff and back as we both sat down. "I'd appreciate that, Alan."

"But first, I'd like to ask Mr. Kovach a couple of questions." Mr. Davis paused to see if anyone would object.

I cast a worried glance at Jared. What would happen if Mr. Davis figured out who he really was? What he really was? What would he do? Then again, what could he do? Who on earth would believe him?

For some reason, being optimistic wasn't helping. My heart raced as I watched Mr. Davis.

Suddenly I felt Grandpa's hand cover mine. I looked at him and he winked. A reassuring smile lit his bright gray eyes, and I calmed almost instantly.

"Under date of birth on your registration form," Mr. Davis said, "you wrote 'not applicable.' Care to explain?"

My calm evaporated. He knew. Mr. Davis knew. I could tell by his expression, the knowing arch of his brows, the confident line of his pursed lips.

"Actually," Jared said with a disinterested shrug, "I didn't think I would be here long enough to have to explain."

"And why wouldn't you be?"

I cleared my throat. "Um, Mr. Davis, didn't I just explain that?"

"You did," he said, fixated on Jared.

The sheriff walked around the desk and leaned against it, looking at my grandfather. Then, in a strategy that caused panic to attack my insides, he repeated everything I'd just told him. Word for word. Syllable for tainted syllable. I cringed. Cowered. Tried to crawl into myself. My grandparents were right there, listening to every lie that had come out of my blasphemous mouth. Party over. I was going down and the landing would be hard.

Hysteria took hold as I sat stiff-backed in the chair beside my grandfather. I wondered if I would get time in the big house for lying to a sheriff.

"She said he's staying with you." The sheriff raised his brows at Grandpa. "Is this true, Bill?"

Without the slightest hesitation—without even a micro-second of pause—he answered, "Of course it is. Do you think my granddaughter would lie to you, Dewayne?"

"Well, no." He almost stuttered in disbelief.

"He's going to stay in the apartment behind the store as soon as we get it cleaned out. We'll both feel better with him close by, right, sweetheart?" He turned to Grandma in question.

She tossed him an exasperated glower. "I still think he should just use the empty room upstairs. That old apartment is drafty."

"Now, hon. We talked about this. He's a young man and he needs his privacy."

"I know. I just worry."

I sat dumbfounded. If either the principal or the sheriff had bothered looking my way, they would've realized just how much baloney they were being fed. Did I say I should become an actor? If anyone should be in Hollywood, it was my grandparents.

After rehinging my jaw, I turned to Jared and mouthed, *Did you do that?*

He shook his head, curiosity lining his face. I could have kissed my grandparents, showered them with love and affection and thanked them for all their wonderful wonderfulness. But that would draw unwanted attention from the authorities nearby.

And I'd have enough explaining to do when I got home as it was. For the moment, however, I chose not to think about it. I would face that obstacle when the time came.

Instead, I rejoiced in the fact that I had the coolest grandparents on planet Earth.

And I breathed.

NEWS FLASH

"I can't believe you got away with that."

I turned my attention to Brooklyn as we sat down at our usual lunch table, a slight dread crawling up the back of my neck. "Wasn't it cool?" I said, wondering if I would still think that when I got home.

"Grandma and Grandpa are like . . . like . . ."

"I know." I definitely had the picks of the litter. Even though I'd have to do some serious explaining later.

But all things considered, the day was progressing rather

well. We ditched the reporter, managed not to get arrested, and I found out that I would have two—count them, *two*—classes with one Mr. Jared Kovach. A smile crept across my face as I watched him wolf down his lunch. He had done the same at breakfast. Poor guy. Having never eaten in his life, he must have been starving.

"Our guardian angel has a certain myopic enthusiasm when it comes to food," Brooklyn said in observation.

Jared spoke up between bites. "I had no idea food would taste this good."

The rest of us stared down at our trays for a good long while, doubt and a bizarre sense of denial pinching our faces.

Glitch snapped out of it first.

"So," he said, "you only have those three laws? Are they similar to commandments? 'Cause we have, like, ten."

"Can you still do that transparent thing?" Brooklyn asked Jared, joining in on the inquisition. "Like when Cameron shot you in the chest repeatedly. Which was very rude, if you think about it."

"I would love to see the transparency thing too." Glitch waited expectantly for him to become transparent right there in the middle of the cafeteria.

"Wow," I said to him, pretending to be struck with wonder, "for someone who didn't believe me yesterday, you've sure come a long way."

"Oh, I believed you. Kind of. So can you?" he asked Jared again.

"I don't know. Part of me is human now, I think."

Cameron scoffed aloud.

Though I'd somehow hoped the rivalry between Jared and Cameron had softened, the tension seemed as strong as ever. They continued to shoot each other threatening looks, constantly bounced taunts back and forth. It grew more tiresome with each black scowl that passed between them.

Jared pasted on a humorless grin. "You disagree? That I'm part human now?" he asked.

Cameron leaned in, his voice menacing, as though begging Jared to throw the first punch. "Just gonna join the gang? Become one of us?"

Jared shrugged.

"News flash, Reaper. You're not human. You never will be. But you are a bitch. I guess that's something."

"Stop it, Cameron." I frowned at them both, unable to believe they were continuing with their ridiculous feud. Hadn't we gotten past all that?

"How do we know you won't change your mind?" Cameron asked. "Heck, you could kill her now and be back on the job before nightfall."

Jared stilled and regarded him a long while before responding. "It doesn't work like that."

"Really?"

"And this doesn't have anything to do with Lorelei."

Brooklyn decided to jump in. "Would you both just give it a rest?"

"If you fight," Glitch asked, excitement lighting his face, "are you gonna stop time again?"

I rolled my eyes. "Glitch, could you try to be a little helpful and put a stop to this?"

He almost laughed. "And get my ass kicked? Not likely."

With jaw clenched in frustration, I finally said, "If I have to, boys, I'll go for the shins again."

"Boys?" Cameron said.

I looked at him. "You two might want to consider that before starting World War Three in the food court."

After a moment, they both settled back in their chairs and focused on the trays before them instead of each other. But how long the truce would last, I didn't know. The shin thing would only get me so far.

Of course, not knowing how long the truce would last was only one of a million things I didn't know. I didn't know how long Jared would be with us, if the principal had recognized him, or even if the sheriff believed us.

And what would Jared do now? Would he really stay with us? I thought about my dream. Was that woman real? Was Jared really on a mission? Was he really created from light and darkness? Did he like the cream-colored sweater I was wearing? Would he like my hair better pulled back? Did he like skinny pasty asthmatic chicks or did he prefer girls with boobs?

"Well, hello there, Lorelei, Brooklyn." Fearless captain of the cheerleaders, aka the creature whose name shall not be spoken aloud, and Amber Gonzales, her second in command, walked up to us, interrupting in the process a very important moment of reflection. The Southern belles stood behind their brave leader, as disciples tended to do.

Tabitha and Amber—otherwise known as T and A—feigned a syrupy sweetness as they glanced between me and Brooklyn, waiting for a reply.

"Hi, Glitch," Tabitha said when she realized we weren't biting. Glitch threw them a bright smile. Ever since he fixed her laptop in three minutes flat, she'd been civil to him. "I just wanted to see how our newest student at Riley High was settling in."

Yeah, right. Annoyed, I looked past her to Ashlee and Sydnee Southern. Though they had their red and white cheerleading outfits on for the pep rally, they still seemed disheveled, distracted. They practically hid behind Tabitha and Amber, viewing Jared as though he were the Antichrist.

Interesting.

"You've met Tabitha," Glitch said politely to Jared.

"Hello again, Jared Kovach," Tabitha said. "I wanted to mention that it's spirit week and you showed up just in time." She flashed him a smile more plastic than Barbie's. Either that or my inferiority complex was rearing its ugly head.

Jared's mouth spread into a patient mask of benevolence.

"And," Amber said, practically drooling as she ogled him, "it's tradition for new arrivals to help with the pep rally."

"And this is Amber Gonzales," Glitch continued.

Clearly impressed, Amber's lashes fluttered like a lovesick butterfly's wings. Not that I could blame her, but as my grandmother would say, my feathers were ruffled.

Brooklyn quirked her lips in doubt. "Tradition?"

"It's a new tradition," Amber shot back.

"Clearly the deeper meaning of the word has escaped you."

I *tsk*ed Brooklyn. "Now, now," I said. "Let's not argue semantics. What exactly is he supposed to do?"

"You just show up, Jared Kovach. We'll do the rest."

I couldn't believe the open invitation oozing out of Tabitha's mouth. I forced myself to calm despite the annoyance sizzling inside me. I was jealous. It was pathetic. Tabitha and Amber were so much more in his league, and I was neon green with envy because of it.

A clunk sounded beside me as Ashlee dropped her phone. It landed under my chair. When she reached for it, her long sleeve rode up her arm and I saw one of the most bizarre things I'd ever seen . . . well, that day anyway. Her arm had been mutilated. In alarm, I grabbed for her wrist and pushed the sleeve past her elbow before she jerked it out of my grasp. I got a flash of fear when I touched her, but that was about it. Some prophet.

Without a word, she shot daggers at me and walked away with her twin in tow.

"What was that about?" Brooklyn asked under her breath. But I didn't want to say anything in front of team spirit.

"The gym at two," Tabitha said to Jared, finalizing her dastardly plan. "It'll be fun."

As they strolled away to wherever it was sugar-frosted flakes strolled to, Glitch just had to comment on Tabitha's name, as usual. "Tabitha Sind," he said with a smile of admiration. "You gotta respect a girl whose name is not only a complete sentence, but an intriguing one at that."

A plan formed as I watched Amber, Ashlee, and Sydnee follow Tabitha to their table. Their mother had basically abandoned them for an investment broker, but that was months ago. They had changed recently, become withdrawn and despondent. I couldn't help but wonder if they were being abused in some way. If so, we needed more info, more proof to go on besides the fact that they had a few hairs out of place. Ashlee had resorted to cutting herself, and I wanted to know why. If they were being mistreated, I could go to Grandma and Grandpa with hard evidence, hopefully enough to get them moved to a safe location. But I needed to know for certain who or what was causing their distress.

"Okay, guys," I said to Brooklyn and Glitch. "It's time to initiate surveillance. We need to find out what's going on with Ash and Syd. Who's up for tonight?"

"It's Friday night!" Glitch said in protest. "And I'm grounded."

"When are you not grounded? It's not as though that's ever stopped you."

"But we haven't had a decent night's sleep in days," he said, grasping for excuses.

"Oh yeah, like you were planning to go to bed early. I'm telling you, something is happening."

"Exactly. A football game. I have to be there."

"No," I said, "with the Southern twins. Did you see Ashlee's arm? Something is so wrong with them."

"Trust me," Cameron cut in, "there ain't a thing wrong with those two, unless you count the unusual and exquisite length of their legs."

Brooklyn turned a tight-lipped smile on him. "Thanks so much for that penis-driven observation."

"Anytime, moon pie," he said with a smirk. "Jealous?"

Glitch laughed humorlessly, his tone mocking.

She rolled her eyes. "As if."

Cameron leveled an amused smile on Glitch before refocusing on his fork. "Course, there is a ghost haunting them," he added as if in afterthought.

"A what?" I lunged closer to him. "What did you say?"

"A ghost," he said with a shrug, "ever since they moved into that new house."

"Are you serious? A real live ghost?"

"Ghosts aren't alive," he stated matter-of-factly.

Wow. I didn't know ghosts existed. 'Course, until yesterday, I didn't know for absolutely certain angels existed either. Or pretty much any supernatural being. I had faith and I knew in my heart, but seeing an angel in person was a different matter entirely. And I darned sure didn't know I was a prophet.

Brooklyn was unconvinced. "You're lying. That house can't be haunted. They just built it."

"Right," Jared said, jumping into the conversation, "but where did they build it?"

Cameron met his eyes and shook his head as though they were suddenly the best of friends and the rest of us were drooling idiots. "No one ever thinks about the land."

Jared shrugged his brows and nodded in agreement.

"So, land can have ghosts?" Brooklyn asked.

"Anything on earth can have ghosts. Land can be just as haunted as a house," Cameron said as he made a tepee with his utensils. "Even more so." He gestured toward the Southern twins with a nod of his head. When Glitch looked over at them, Cameron swiped his fork for stability. "They think it's their dead grandmother," he added.

"Is it?" I asked.

"No," Jared said, watching Cameron as he labored away. "It doesn't work that way."

An aggravated sigh pushed past my lips. "Someday, Jared Kovach, you'll have to explain exactly how it *does* work. But for now, we need to do something." I leaned in and spoke directly to him. "We have to help them."

He frowned in doubt, and I couldn't tell if it was directed at me or at the apple crisp dessert he was coveting. "What am I supposed to do?"

"Did you ever think that maybe that's why you're here? Maybe you're here to help people, to use your powers to champion the cause of those who are . . . well, championless."

"Lorelei," he said patiently, pushing his tray away, "I'm here because I broke the law. I'm just as carbon based as you are."

"You will never be as carbon based as I am. You're like Cameron, remember? Strong. Powerful. Nigh indestructible."

"Nigh?"

I sat back and crossed my arms. There had to be a reason for his presence on earth. Maybe that woman in my dream was real. Maybe she was trying to tell me something. This was too big, too miraculous to just be an accident. "Aren't you even curious?"

"Not especially," he said. Then he gestured toward Cameron's stainless-steel tepee with a nod, an evil grimace spreading across his face just as it collapsed rather loudly due to an inherent structural failure—utensils tended to slip on slippery surfaces.

Cameron cast him a frustrated frown, as though Jared had something to do with the downfall of his masterpiece, then began to rebuild it.

"Hey, man," Glitch said in sudden annoyance, "did you jack my fork?"

Then it hit me. "Fear the darkness."

"What?" Brooke asked.

I turned to her in wonder. "I just realized what Ashlee wrote on her arm. It said 'fear the darkness.'"

"She wrote on her arm?"

"Not exactly," I replied, blown away by the fact that Ashlee would mutilate herself. "It was carved into it. She cut into her own arm."

With a grimace, Brooklyn said, "That's disgusting. Crave attention much?"

"I don't think she did it for attention, Brooke. I think she's scared. Terrified. Do you know what it means?" I asked Jared and Cameron.

Cameron hunched his body, ducking his furrowed face in concentration, carefully linking prongs together, and said slowly, "It means Brooklyn thinks self-mutilation is disgusting."

I rolled my eyes. "Not that. Fear the darkness. What does it mean?"

He tipped a shoulder toward Jared. "Why don't you ask lover boy over there."

Jared cut him a razor-sharp warning.

"It seems Mr. Kovach has something of a reputation," Cameron continued.

"What kind of a reputation?" I asked.

"I don't have a reputation," Jared said, his voice even, threatening.

Cameron's face brightened with silent laughter. "Come on, Reaper. You can tell them."

Jared leaned forward. "Why don't you and I go discuss this outside."

"Shins," I warned. "And I am wearing steel-toed boots this time. Don't even mess with me."

But neither backed down. Crap. I knew the shin thing wouldn't last.

Cameron held his grin steady as he spoke. "See, messengers have to follow all kinds of orders, answer all kinds of prayers, all manner of requests. Including those that involve other supernatural beings."

"Like ghosts?" Brooklyn asked.

"Exactly. There are evil ghosts just like there are evil people. And any Joe Schmo can pray to have one evicted. You just have to believe, have faith in the Big Guy's word, and boom!" He made the umpire strikeout sign. "That pesky little poltergeist is outta here. And guess who sends them off to suffer in the fires of eternal Hell and damnation?"

He questioned me silently. I didn't move.

"That's right," he continued. "Your reaper, here. Azrael is somewhat of a specialist. And the ghost world doesn't think very highly of him. Right, Az?"

Jared sat stone still, hardly breathing. Personally, I found the whole idea rather fascinating. Who knew? But Jared seemed furious that Cameron was even talking about it. He cast a furtive look my way before refocusing on his hands folded on the table in front of him, his jaw tight.

"So, this ghost haunting the Southern belles, it knows Jared's here?"

"It knew it the moment he started stalking you."

"Cameron," I said, a gentle warning in my tone, "Jared wasn't stalking me. He was doing his job, remember? We talked about this."

Cameron shook his head with a soft chortle. "Please, Lorelei. Use some common sense, will you?"

"What?" I asked, rather offended.

"Angels, or messengers, or whatever the Hell politically correct term you want to call them are master manipulators of space and time."

"You should probably stop talking about now," Jared said.

"They can come and go in a blinding flash."

"Lusk—"

"He could have popped in, taken you, and popped back out before even I could have seen him. Or felt his presence on this plane. But he didn't. Why do you think that is?"

Jared shoved his chair back and stood. Without hesitation, Cameron did the same. Our table almost toppled over as they both did their best to intimidate each other. I shot up and did my darnedest to get between them. It was like trying to shove two cinder block walls apart.

With a hand on either chest, I hissed a harsh warning: "Do you really want to give Principal Davis a reason to come in here?" My gaze bounced back and forth. "Do you really want to give the sheriff a reason to be suspicious? He already believes you two were the cause of that little earthquake scenario. You'll just be giving him ammunition."

After a moment, Jared looked at me, his eyes dark with anger. "Keep a muzzle on your dog," he said, then turned to leave.

Not this time.

I grabbed his shirt and forced him to look at me again. "Is it true?" I asked. Was he really following me just to see me? To watch me?

He lowered his lashes and waited an interminable amount of time before answering. "Yes," he said, his voice deathly quiet.

Now for the sad part.

My soul took flight! My heart soared! A euphoric, deliriously giddy sensation washed over me with the knowledge that Jared was following me because he wanted to. Not because he had to, because it was his job. The realization sent a tingle rushing over my skin.

Jared glanced back at me then, and I tried to control my elation, a feat that proved impossible. Until I looked at him. Really looked. And reality sank in. "Why?" I asked, suddenly confused. "Why me?" Did he have any idea how gorgeous he was?

His lips thinned in frustration like I should already know the answer. He inched closer until his knee touched mine, his eyes, curious and intense, boring into me. "Because you move like fire rushing across a floor," he said, his voice hushed, velvety smooth, "like flames licking up a wall." The rest of the world crumbled away as he lifted my chin. "Your energy is liquid and hot. Even from a distance you burn, you scorch anyone who gets too close. You are wine on my tongue and honey in my veins, and I cannot get enough of you." He leaned forward and whispered into my ear. His warm breath sent shivers cascading over my body. "You intoxicate me, Lorelei McAlister. You will be my downfall."

"I'm not kidding, you guys need to sit down. Coach Chavez is headed this way."

My eyelids shuttered. We were standing just as we had been, with me in between the two cage fighters. I realized Brooklyn had been talking to us. Coach Chavez was on his way to our table.

"Sit down, hurry," I said to the boys, trying to snap back to reality. They obliged reluctantly.

"Hey, Coach," Glitch said, standing to head him off.

As they spoke, I sat in stunned silence, wondering what had just happened. Jared suddenly seemed way more interested in the pattern on the table than in me. Did I just have a vision? Or would that be considered wishful thinking?

"If you guys are finished, I suggest you clean up and go cool off outside," the coach said. He was a brawny man with thick black hair and a graying beard, and everyone liked him, including me. I didn't want to get on his bad side.

"Okay," Brooklyn answered, the forced nonchalance in her voice plain.

As we rose to clean our table, Cameron leaned in to me. "And, yeah, he can do things like that, too."

TEAM SPIRIT

"Where is he?" Brooklyn raised her brows in question as she scurried up the bleachers. The homecoming pep rally would start soon.

I was still in a state of dazed confusion. Cameron had seen it, the exchange between Jared and me, so it had to be real. But how had he done it?

"Uh-oh," Brooklyn said. "I'm sorry I missed it."

Oh, that was the other thing. Nobody but Cameron heard what Jared said to me. Not Brooklyn, not Glitch, not the weird chick at the next table drooling into her lunch tray. Nobody!

Could Jared have done something where only I could hear him? But Cameron heard him. Blondie got an earful, then snorted and strode out the door. Not that I cared. My feet weren't anywhere near the ground. Brooklyn said she'd been talking to Glitch, but honestly, how could anyone have missed such a speech?

"So?"

I blinked at Brooklyn. "So, what?"

"Where's lover boy?"

"Oh. Tabitha and Amber stole him," I said absently, referring to Jared's recent abduction by the sugar lumps.

"I wonder what they're up to."

"I wonder what it's like to have the intelligence of squirrel feces."

Brooklyn whistled. "Wow, I'm impressed. You go with that."

"I know it's wrong, but I just dislike them so much. Ever since they put toothpaste in my hair on the way back from camp, I've hated them."

"Right there with ya, babe. You know what I've noticed?"

"That deep down inside I'm really jealous of them, which makes me a lonely and pathetic loser?"

"Um, no."

"Oh," I said. "Then what?"

"I've noticed that ever since Jared saved your life, you haven't had to use your inhaler. Not once."

"Wow," I said. She was right. I hadn't even thought about it.

Brooklyn scanned the crowd. Glitch turned and waved from the front, where the football team sat. She waved back, then spotted Cameron sitting alone at the very top of the bleachers, apparently in the farthest corner he could find.

"You were right," she said. "That boy is just plain antisocial."

I turned and motioned for him to join us. He shook his head. I glared at him and waved again. Exhaling visibly in annoyance, he pushed himself off the bleachers and maneuvered through the crowd to where we sat.

"Happy?" he asked when he arrived.

I smiled. "Very."

The pep rally progressed with the usual antics and silly games. The pep band played and the crowd cheered. Each class tried to out-yell the other three for the honor of leaving school ten minutes early. The seniors usually won, their experience and impending release date—otherwise known as graduation—lending them a ruthlessness the other classes lacked from the get-go.

In one of the more amusing moments, volunteer tag teams from each class had to wrap a different teacher in toilet paper then race back to the finish line for the win. I laughed at the sight of Ms. Mullins being toilet-papered into a mummy.

But soon afterwards, I began to worry. The pep rally was coming to a close, and still no Jared.

"Where could he be?" I asked Brooklyn. "Do you think Principal Davis has him cornered somewhere? Or maybe the sheriff arrested him after all."

"I doubt it. Tabitha's up to something."

I watched absently as the cheerleaders acted out a final skit. Apparently, two members of team spirit weren't spirited enough. They stood back with their arms crossed, looking sad and despondent. So—in the crucial interest of school pride—the others escorted one of the two to a huge decorated box marked SPIRIT INFUSER.

They placed her inside and closed the lid. After a few seconds, the cheerleader jumped out of the box, full of life and an annoying, nails-on-a-chalkboard kind of joy.

"She's like a gerbil on Ritalin," Brooklyn said.

I beamed and continued to survey the crowd for Jared.

In the meantime, the cheerleaders—having had such great success with the first dispirited teammate—did the same with the second. Again, after the girl was placed in the box, she jumped out almost immediately, springing with happiness and energy.

"Hmmm," Tabitha said into the microphone. "Whatever's in that box sure causes a lot of excitement. What could it be?"

The cheerleaders lifted the lid, leaned in, and brought out a very embarrassed Jared Kovach.

I gasped aloud as the crowd cheered. Girls all around me screamed as Tabitha introduced the newest recruit to Riley High, like he was some kind of rock star. If they only knew.

In sympathy, Brooklyn wrapped an arm around my shoulders. "Just think," she said into my ear, "none of them have ever been called a flame licker by the guy."

"He didn't call me a flame licker."

"Right, sorry," she said absently, punching keys on her phone to check messages. So much for sympathy.

"Well, that was interesting," Brooklyn said as we strolled through the parking lot. Glitch had a team meeting before the big homecoming game, so the rest of us decided to hang at the Java Loft until then.

Despite the fact that we were all technically grounded, Brooklyn and I managed to get permission to go to the game. It was homecoming after all. The big game. The one event that we languished over all year.

Okay, we exaggerated a tad. But at least we got permission to go—with conditions, of course. We had to be home right after the game, missy. No ifs, ands, or buts. Later, when we inevitably got home late, we would simply explain that, first we had to wait for Glitch to help with team stuff, then Ms. Mullins wanted to talk to us about how well we did on the nine-weeks exam—emphasis on *well* and *nine-weeks exam*—then the parking lot was so full, we just sat there for-like-ever. We had no idea it would take us so long just to get out of a parking lot, Grandma.

I would look distressed and worried and on the verge of tears for missing the curfew that I would never dream of missing, ever in a million years. Grandpa would slide Grandma that *let's forgive her* look, *just this once*. Grandma would give in with a smile that held the tiniest of warnings. And life would return to normal.

Well, maybe not normal. Probably never normal again.

Anyway, all that should buy us just enough time to do some paranormal investigating.

I shook out of my thoughts, trying to remember what Brooklyn had commented about. Oh, right. The pep rally.

"Yeah, it was very interesting. Did you see how the cheerleaders were staring at Jared? It was bizarre."

Brooklyn's brows knitted together. "Lor, the entire student body was staring at Jared. He was kind of the main attraction."

"I know. But did you see Ashlee and Sydnee? They were totally freaked out."

After a quick shot at Jared from over her shoulder, Brooklyn said teasingly, "You were pretty freaked out when you first met him too."

I leaned in to her. "Yeah, but I was hot and bothered by him. They're just, like, bothered."

Brooke laughed.

Of course, Jared seemed bothered too. When we met up with him after the pep rally, Cameron smirked and said, "You're just going to fit right in, aren't you? Be a part of the in-crowd."

Jared ignored him, but he kept his head down as we walked to the parking lot. He seemed embarrassed, uncomfortable. The tension between him and Cameron hung thick and palpable in the air, and I wondered if they could ever be in the same room together without exhibiting homicidal tendencies.

I guess after his lunchroom confession, I wanted soft, knowing glances from Jared and winks full of affection. I also wanted promises of undying love and an endless supply of backrubs, but that could wait. Instead, all his energy was focused on postal boy. Cameron was totally stealing my bliss.

When we got to Cameron's pickup, he shoved the key into the lock cylinder. "So who prayed?" he asked without looking at anyone in particular.

I looked at him, confused, but Jared answered before I had a chance to ask who Cameron was talking to.

"Everyone prays eventually," he said as though they'd been talking the whole way.

Did I miss something?

"I just bet they do." Cameron scowled at him from over his shoulder. "You must enjoy that. Prayers of desperation. The suffering of others."

"Not especially."

Without warning, Cameron took hold of the jacket Glitch had loaned Jared and shoved him against the pickup.

Jared spread his palms apart and let him. Completely unafraid.

"You're a thief," Cameron said in a whispery hiss, "the worst of your kind. You come down to Earth and take what you want without considering the consequences, the chaos you leave in your wake. You hide behind shadows and legend and pretend to be noble."

While Jared's expression remained impassive, mine was not. I decided to put an end to this once and for all. So, like the idiot I tended to be in crisis situations, I tried to jump between them for, like, the millionth time, but Cameron turned on me, furious. His vehemence startled me and I stood there, unmoving, like a deer caught in the glow of headlights.

Jared's hand shot out and wrapped around my upper arm. He pulled me beside him protectively, his long fingers locking around my biceps, his expression no longer impassive. A hard warning glinted in his eyes. But Cameron grabbed me as well and tried to shove me out of the way.

It was the wrong thing to do.

The emotions coursing through Cameron's veins seeped into me, mixed with mine, churned and swirled. They encircled me like a vise, tightening around my chest. I gasped for air as breathing became almost impossible. For Jared as well. As though I were a conduit, I siphoned the turmoil out of Cameron and into Jared.

"Stop," Jared said as he pushed at Cameron, trying to catch his breath. I clutched on to Jared's jacket. "Lorelei, stop." This had never happened before. For some reason, I could feel Cameron's pain and I was passing it on to Jared. All the emotion. All the anguish. All the rage.

"So who prayed, hot shot?" Cameron continued, oblivious of what was happening, his anger leaching into me, his pain shooting through me and into Jared. "Some little brat from Timbuktu who wanted you to make sure her uncle arrived in time for her birthday party? God forbid that Barbie Vette show up late."

Jared grabbed Cameron's wrist with his free hand as Cameron pushed into him. The anguish was overwhelming. Cameron's agony had latched on to me with razor-sharp claws, slicing, suffocating.

"Cameron, stop," Jared said between gasps.

"Who?"

"Cameron, we can't breathe." His concern settled heavily on me. His fingers were still padlocked around my arm, and I could feel things I never thought possible. The world began to spin around me. I could feel consciousness slipping out from under my feet.

"Lorelei!" I heard Brooklyn shout as though from a great distance.

"Who prayed and changed history? Who made it possible for you to kill her?"

The darkness Cameron had kept buried for years consumed him. I could see it in his eyes, could feel its strangling hold envelop me, entwine its tentacles up my arm and around my throat.

And apparently it was doing the same to Jared. He had no other choice. I could feel it the second he made the decision, the moment he resolved to do what he was about to do. He had to show Cameron what happened.

With tremendous effort, he forced himself to concentrate despite the smothering fog. He placed a hand on Cameron's chest, nailed him with an intent look, focused all his energy. And just before he let the past devour us all, he whispered the truth.

"She did."

The past rushed up like a roiling sea beneath us, swallowing us whole. The world tumbled, spun out of control, then stopped. We were suddenly in a different place, a different time. Birds chirped and the sun peered through pine needles on the trees surrounding us, casting soft rays through the atmosphere to rest on the forest floor.

"Look, Cameron," a woman said.

Cameron looked to the side of the bicycle as his mother pointed to a bird running into the forest. We were in the past—I was in the past—and I was seeing the world through Cameron's eyes.

"That's a roadrunner."

He twisted back in his plastic yellow seat and watched as she pedaled up the mountainside, and she winked at him before turning back to the trail. I knew instantly who she was. I saw her as Cameron did. Beautiful. Young. Expression soft with unconditional love. Her blond hair gave in to the breeze, fluttering like butterflies around her backpack. He loved her hair. It smelled like apples.

She pulled over to look down the side of the canyon, being very careful not to get too close. The rich greens of the mountainside filled his vision on the right. The deep reds of the iron-rich canyon met him on his left.

"Isn't it lovely?" She turned and glanced over her shoulder at him. Her smile glistened in the sunlight, as bright as her aura and just as warming.

Then, for no explicable reason, she gasped and jumped back, falling with the bike to the ledge that overlooked the canyon wall. Harnessed in the safety seat, Cameron fell along with the bike into a bush. Its needlelike thorns punished him for invading its territory, but he didn't care. What had happened? Why did his mother jump like that?

With panic setting in, he tried to unfasten the safety belt, but his chubby fingers couldn't budge it. He craned his neck to look at her and managed to glimpse the top of her head. Her backpack had caught on the handlebars, dangling her over the edge. The back wheel had wedged on a fallen log, but her weight was rocking it loose.

He called out, tried to reach her.

"Cameron." Her voice quivered. She was scared and it broke my heart. "Cameron, honey, don't move. Whatever you do, don't move."

Refusing to listen to her, he pulled at his restraints.

"I've been bitten by a rattlesnake. I must have stepped on it."

No. She was wrong. She had to be. Rattlesnakes made noise. He hadn't heard anything.

The bike slipped, and she reached for a branch reflexively. But when the bike slipped a notch more, she relaxed her arms and forced herself to go still.

"Please," she whispered as she looked toward the heavens. "Please, I beg you."

He felt it coming before he saw it, the entity, the dark one. His lungs refused to expand. This one came for one reason and one reason only: It took people. He had seen it twice, and each time it left death in its wake. And sadness. A devastating sadness.

When it appeared, it knelt beside the bike and looked down at his mother. It was part fog and part flesh. She raised her eyes to it. This startled him. Could she see it? She had never seen them before.

"Are you sure?" it asked her.

No!

"Yes," she said. "I've never been more certain about anything in my life."

Without hesitation, it leaned over and touched the strap on the handlebars, releasing it.

His mother looked back at him, her eyes sad and desperate and full of love. In a blinding moment of panic, he pulled furiously at his restraints. He fought with every ounce of strength his three-year-old body had until she slipped quietly out of sight, falling into the canyon below.

The silence in the wake of his mother's death was deafening. He lay in the bushes for hours before a rescue team found him, letting the thorns punish him for not being strong enough, hating the thief for what it was.

He would never forget what it looked like. It was already gone, naturally, disappearing like the coward it was. But he would never forget it. And he would find a way to destroy it, to destroy them all, yes, but especially the dark one.

"Stop," Jared said, gasping for air.

Cameron blinked back to the present. He shoved Jared away from him, tears streaming down his face.

Jared released me, stumbled, and fell to his knees. I stood in shock, afraid to move, afraid to breathe. It felt so real, like I was there, like I loved her and knew her and died when she died.

"Lorelei." I realized Brooklyn was in my face, screaming at

me. I could barely hear her. "Lorelei, what's going on? What happened?"

My attention floated to Jared as he kneeled on a patch of grass, drawing in huge gulps of air. Then I felt the bile at the back of my throat and fought it with a hard swallow. With each heartbeat, Cameron's pain reverberated through my body.

A crowd had gathered. I saw faces around us, yelling like bloodthirsty spectators, encouraging Cameron and Jared to fight.

"Lorelei," Brooklyn said, quieter.

I reached up and squeezed her shoulder reassuringly; then she helped me to Jared, where I knelt beside him.

"You could have saved her," Cameron said, panting in turmoil and anger at what Jared had shown him. He slid down the side of his truck to sit on the pavement. "You just took her. If it had been anyone but you."

Cameron's sadness deepened to a mournful despair, but his hold on Jared seemed to ease. He could breathe almost normally again.

Jared turned to sit on the grass and surveyed Cameron from underneath his long lashes. "She called me by name," he said.

After a moment, Cameron's words sank in. I thought back to his memory. I looked through his eyes and glanced up at the entity enshrouded in darkness as it released the strap from the bike, as it sent Cameron's mother to her death. Then it looked right at me, eyes boring in to mine, but only for a microsecond before it vanished.

It was Jared.

I covered my mouth with both hands and sank to the ground, my heart breaking.

"So, that's your job?" Cameron said, wiping at the tears streaming down his face. "You give whatever people pray for?"

"No," Jared said between coughs. "There are rules."

Cameron laughed humorlessly. "Aren't there always."

"She did it for you."

"Ah, yes. Well, that makes it all better."

"You're still alive."

"And you're still a bitch."

The crowd wooed, waited to see what Jared would do.

I peeled my hands from my mouth and forced myself to focus on the more immediate risk, namely another Battlefield Earth. "Jared, please don't fight again," I said.

He turned to me, his dark eyes bright with emotion. I reached over and wiped a wetness from his cheek. His eyes had watered. He bent his head and buried it in a sleeve.

"I'm okay," he said after he wiped his face. "Is this over?"

Cameron sniffed, wiped his face again, his eyes slitted at Jared. "It will be when you're dead."

"But, Cameron," he said with a sigh, "I just got here."

"And I'm going to send you back."

"That's it." He stood and shrugged out of the jacket. Cameron followed suit. "Your mother sacrificed her life for you, and this is how you repay her? You sulk and pout and throw tantrums like a two-year-old?"

"You're pushing it, Reaper."

I scrambled to my feet as they faced off in the parking lot.

"Do you know what she'd say if she were here right now?" Jared asked.

Cameron stepped closer. "You're a bitch?"

"Exactly." He closed the distance, meeting him head-on, challenging him with the heavy set of his shoulders. "Only she'd be looking at you."

"What'd I miss?" Glitch ran up to the melee with an excited grin on his face until he saw who the crowd was watching. He looked over at me. "Again?"

"Again?" A strong masculine voice echoed around us as the

crowd parted and scattered immediately. "So there *was* a fight before," Principal Davis said as he approached us.

Brooklyn spoke up immediately. "They weren't fighting, Mr. Davis."

"They were never fighting," I said, jumping to their defense. "It's just an argument."

Mr. Davis said nothing, so I turned to him. He was staring wide-eyed at Jared's arms. At the tattoos. He paled and took a minuscule step backwards.

The instant Jared realized what Mr. Davis was looking at, he turned and searched the ground for the jacket. But it was much too late for that. Mr. Davis saw the one thing that would spark his memory of Jared from before. The same age. The same face.

Jared started to reach for the jacket, then realized how futile the effort would be. He inhaled deeply and turned to him, waiting for the principal's reaction.

"Mr. Davis," I said, trying to come up with some explanation. But what could I say? *Oh, yeah, Mr. Davis, we forgot to mention that this is the same guy who showed up the day your brother died and he's actually this messenger-slash-reaper guy for some otherworldly answering service and he came back here to spirit me off to Heaven and instead saved my life and changed history and now he's, like, stuck.*

I didn't think so.

But apparently it didn't matter. Before I could say anything, he turned and strode off. We were suddenly alone again.

"Are you two, like, bipolar or something?" Brooklyn stood, her resentment leaking out at Cameron and Jared. "'Cause they have medication for that." I realized she didn't really know what had just happened, what Jared had revealed. She barged up to Cameron, purpose in her every move. "You accepted, you butthead."

He turned to her, an unspoken question written on his face.

"Don't pretend to be clueless. You accepted. That beautiful woman asked you, and you accepted without hesitation."

I was awestruck. "You saw her? I thought I dreamed it."

"I think we all dreamed it," Glitch said.

Brooklyn's temper flared. She rose onto her toes to meet Cameron eye to eye, though she missed the mark by about a foot. "Don't make me angry," she said evenly. "You wouldn't like me when I'm angry."

I almost grinned. Somehow channeling the Incredible Hulk worked for her.

To my surprise, Cameron calmed instantly. He seemed almost mesmerized by Brooklyn. His hard features softened as he wiped his forehead on a sleeve.

Then he smiled. "Whatever you say, just don't bring out the water pistol again."

"Water pistol?" Glitch's jaw dropped. "That was a water pistol last night?" He seemed offended. "You protected us with a freaking water pistol?"

"Like I would carry a real gun." She rolled her eyes as if he were inane.

"Just what were you planning to do if your little scheme didn't work?" he asked, appalled. "Drown him?"

"Shut up, Blue-Spider," she said as she walked around to the other side of the pickup. "Least I had a plan."

Glitch walked to his car, mumbling to himself in disbelief.

I was still having trouble forming a coherent thought, having just had an out-of-body experience. I had visions all the time, but this was different somehow. More tangible.

"Lor," Brooklyn said slowly, seemingly aware of my coherent-thought problem, "why don't you and Jared go with Glitch. I'll go with bipolar boy and we'll meet up at your house."

Jared scooped up the jacket and turned to us. But he didn't

look at me. He averted his eyes and said, "Lorelei may not want to ride with me right now."

"Why not?" Her brows snapped together. "Lorelei?"

I found myself avoiding his gaze as well.

"Because she just found out what Jared really is." Cameron opened his door and climbed in before turning back to Brooke. "Did you happen to see who those children were afraid of last night?" he asked, referencing the dream we'd apparently shared. "Because it wasn't me." He started the truck then leveled a hard stare on her. "I'd just like that noted."

"Lor, what just happened?"

"Nothing. I'll explain later." I forced myself to look back at Jared. "Coming, Azrael?" I said, trying to lighten the mood.

He stepped reluctantly in my direction, then stopped. Just as Brooklyn was about to get into Cameron's truck, he said, "I didn't mean for that to happen. I had no idea you would be pulled in."

"I know."

"What?" Brooklyn asked.

"It's what I do, Lorelei. But more importantly, it was her decision."

And that was the truth of it. It was Cameron's mother's decision. Not Jared's. Not Cameron's. It was hers and hers alone. She sacrificed herself to save him, and Cameron would just have to deal with that fact. Then again, maybe that was the whole problem. Maybe he felt guilty that she gave her life for his and he couldn't accept it.

"So, what happened?" Brooklyn asked. "Did I miss it again? God, I always miss the good stuff." She turned and climbed into the truck.

Glitch honked impatiently, and I tossed him a silent warning. Then Jared said something that made my knees almost give beneath me.

"I saw you. Thirteen years ago. I saw you there in the forest, in the child Cameron's eyes. I saw you exactly as you are now."

I looked back at him. What did he mean? I shook my head. "I don't understand."

"I didn't know who you were. Because you were seeing through Cameron's eyes, I couldn't read anything. You weren't really there."

"You saw me watching . . . just now?"

"Yes, only thirteen years ago. Then, when I was sent here to take you, I remembered you instantly. I remembered the fire burning so bright around you, I could hardly look. I stopped time to study your face." He stepped closer and brushed his fingertips along my jaw. "You have an ancient soul, powerful and calm. The descendent of Arabeth. When I saw you again, I never wanted to take my eyes off you. I couldn't let you die. I couldn't let you leave, never to look upon you again."

He dipped his head and I twisted my fingers into his shirt as he bent to kiss me, my pulse skyrocketing. I raised my face to his, waiting, wanting more than I'd ever wanted in my life.

So, naturally, a split second before his mouth touched mine, Einstein honked again.

"Glitch!" I screamed, floored by his timing. I turned to him. He sat in his car, joy obvious in his expression. He'd done it on purpose. "I am so going to stab you in the heart!"

Jared chuckled. "Maybe we should talk about this later."

Disappointment flooded my entire being. "I guess," I said, vowing to make Glitch pay if it were the last thing I did on earth.

A BLINDING LIGHT

The cool silence of night in the Manzano Mountains coaxed me into a tranquil bliss. Fireflies hummed to the love songs of crickets. Gentle breezes swayed the leaves that clung to life after a festive, fertile summer, creating a soft, rhythmic lullaby. So when a loud crash splintered the evening air like a sonic boom, I nearly jumped out of my skin.

"Jeez, Glitch-head," Cameron said. "Could you be any louder?"

Glitch turned to him in frustration. "Did anyone ask you to come?"

"If you'll remember, moon pie over there insisted." He gestured toward Brooklyn as we hunkered behind a massive planter.

"Moon pie?" Brooklyn asked in a loud whisper, insulted by the reference.

"And you listen to everything she has to say?"

Cameron shrugged.

"I could be wrong here," Glitch said, his voice laced with sarcasm, "but I think you can take her."

"Glitch," I said as I inched closer, "what the bloody heck are you doing?"

"Yeah," Brooklyn said. "Can you pick locks or not?"

I looked to the side. "Oh man," I groaned. "You broke their garden gnome. We are so gonna be busted."

Glitch released a frustrated sigh. "Weren't you two supposed to stay hidden with Jared until I opened the door?"

"Well, you were taking so long. We were worried."

I almost laughed when he lowered his little lock-picking tools—otherwise known as a modified fingernail file and a paper clip—his annoyance with me obvious.

"Do you know where I should be right now?"

Here we go. "At the steak house?" I asked. "Enjoying a homecoming victory steak dinner, compliments of the Wolverine Booster Club?"

"Exactly! And why am I not there?"

Brooklyn raised her hand excitedly. "I know! I know! Because we begged you to use your infamous boy abilities to help us break into Ashlee and Sydnee's house while *they* are off enjoying a homecoming victory steak dinner, compliments of the Wolverine Booster Club."

Glitch turned without comment and continued working on the lock.

"I was right, huh?"

"Super right," I said. "You get extra-special bonus points."

"I have an idea." Everyone looked back at Cameron as he stood with arms crossed in bored contemplation. "Why don't we just let the reaper open the door. You know, since he's standing there looking annoyed."

We glanced up to see that Jared had already found a way into the house. He unlocked the door.

"Thanks," Glitch said.

"I've already unlocked it once. You locked it back."

"Oh, sorry."

"So what are we looking for?" A tad creeped out by the whole ghost thing, Brooklyn and I huddled together as we stepped into the massive three-story house.

"A presence," Jared said.

"I thought we were looking for a ghost." Glitch scoured the room with eyes wide.

"Same difference."

"Ghost, presence, apparition," Cameron added. "But I think this is something more. It's too strong. It might be a poltergeist."

"I feel it too," Jared said, nodding in agreement.

I was still checking out the digs. "Who the heck puts white carpet in a house?"

"And gold molding," Brooklyn said. "Could this house scream *my daddy's richer than your daddy* any gaudier?"

"So what's the difference?" Glitch asked.

"Well, wood molding," Brooklyn explained, "is much more subtle and adds a stunning touch to any room."

Glitch huffed his irritation at her. "I meant the ghost-versus-poltergeist thing."

"Oh, right," Brooklyn said.

I stifled a giggle.

"A presence is more like an energy," Cameron said, "left behind when someone dies. It's usually the result of a traumatic death." He took a vase off the mantel to examine it. "But a poltergeist," he continued, "is, well, a poltergeist. You've seen the movie. They're stronger and can be either really angry or just plain evil. What do you think of this?" He tossed the vase to Glitch, who caught it in unsteady hands then scowled at Cameron before reading the inscription.

He recoiled with a horrified expression and threw it back. "They keep their grandmother on the mantel?" he asked, gagging a little. "Who does that?"

Cameron laughed as he replaced the urn.

"I could live on this sofa." Brooklyn ran her hand along the buttery soft fabric.

I nodded in agreement before leaving the warm embrace of my best friend to inspect a painting across the great room. It looked like something from the Renaissance.

"Presence!" Glitch pointed to the upstairs landing then tumbled backwards over a coffee table. "Presence!"

"That was fast," Cameron said.

I looked up to see a darkness gathered near the ceiling, hovering, watching. A different kind of fear than I had ever known before took hold: a chilling, tingly, sweaty kind of fear. It wrapped cold tendrils around my ankles and crept up my spine to the back of my neck. This was way scarier than the movies. I wanted to run more than I'd ever wanted to run in my life. That whole fight-or-flight thing was leaning heavily toward the latter. Then, without warning, it swooped down at us.

More fear shot through me, pumping adrenaline by the gallons as I screamed and dropped onto an ornate rug. The darkness passed over me. I felt its energy reverberate like an electric wind, standing every hair on my body on end.

The presence retreated into the shadows as quickly as it had appeared. I scanned the room wide-eyed as Jared walked—no, strolled—to Glitch and offered him a hand, and I wondered if supreme beings were afraid of anything.

"Actually," he said to him matter-of-factly, "that was a poltergeist."

Cameron walked—no, strolled—over to Brooklyn as she huddled behind the sofa with a throw rug over her head. He fought a smile. "An angry poltergeist," he said in agreement. "And as ingenious as your disguise is, I'm fairly certain it knows you're here."

"Of course it knows," she said through gritted teeth, "with you standing there giving my position away to every poltergeist in the country."

He shrugged and turned to walk away.

"Where are you going?" she asked, her voice suddenly shrill.

He chuckled and stayed put by her side.

I rose cautiously to my feet, searching the corners of the vaulted ceiling, trying to control my panic. "It disappeared," I said, bewildered. Then reality sank in. "Wait, how exactly are we able to see it? I've never seen a ghost in my life."

"It must want to be seen," Cameron said, searching the ceilings as well. "Ghosts tend to make themselves scarce. You can thank your boyfriend for that little show. It's like an animal who puffs up when it feels threatened. This entity feels threatened with the reaper close by. It's making its presence known."

"Seriously?" I asked.

"Seriously. And just like a cornered animal, it will do anything to survive."

I was actually referring to the part about *your boyfriend*, but nobody needed to know that.

Jared stepped to me as I turned in a circle. "See it yet?"

"No," I said, trying to sound brave. I caught his scent, clean and earthy, and inched closer to him. "Can it hurt us?"

He lifted his shoulders. "Only if it wants to."

"Nice. You might have mentioned that."

"And ruin the surprise?" he asked, his expression playful. He had taken off the jacket in the car and his muscles were doing that flex-with-every-movement thing that mesmerized me into a trance.

"I think we should just get out of here," Glitch said as he walked to the fireplace to grab a poker, "and come back when we actually have a plan."

Before I could reply, I heard something from an alcove behind me. When I turned to investigate, I had to admit, the last few days had certainly been the most surreal of my existence. I'd been hit by a truck and brought back to life, seen the world freeze around me, gotten pulled back in time through someone else's eyes, and fallen in love with a supreme being.

But all things considered, the massive grand piano that had been upended and thrown at me as though polter-thing were playing fetch-the-Steinway with some massive ghost dog pretty much iced the cake. And tossed a cherry on top.

At least when the truck hit me, I didn't see it coming. Maybe once someone was supposed to die, that person couldn't escape it. Maybe no one could cheat death. Not for long anyway.

As the piano grew larger, Jared placed his fingers under my chin and turned my face toward his. He flashed a smile that could make grown women beg, and my heart faltered as a surge of longing enveloped me.

A warmth took hold, a strange euphoria. I had fallen in love with an angel, with a celestial being as old as time itself. How weird was that?

He pulled me into his arms—a place I had wanted to be for some time now—and let his eyes drift shut. When he lifted his face toward the heavens, a floodtide of energy cascaded over us. I could feel it, powerful and electric.

"Be still," he whispered to the universe. And the air thickened. The earth slowed. He opened his eyes as I wondered at the sparkling world around us.

"You can still do it," I said, transfixed.

He was enjoying my fascination.

And my fascination grew, because the piano, once solid, passed harmlessly through us. Hammers and strings flowed through my body. Keys and pedals floated past my eyes. I raised my hand and watched as an E-flat swept through my fingers.

"They fear my darkness," Jared said.

I glanced back at him. His eyes had become blazing pools of fire, as though an inferno were engulfing him from the inside out.

"They always fear the darkness." His mouth tilted up at one corner in a devilish grin. "But the light," he said as he lowered his head, "the light is so much worse."

I froze as his sculpted mouth descended onto mine.

A kiss, soft as a summer breeze.

A flash of light so bright, I could see it through my closed lids. Like a nuclear blast. Purging. Cleansing. Setting things right.

Then the world rushed back with hurricane force. I heard the piano crash against a wall, splintering into a thousand wooden shards. The house shook. The entity screamed.

And Jared's hand on my back pulled me closer, molded me to him. The kiss deepened. He slid his tongue along my mouth, and I parted my lips to let him enter. When his tongue slipped inside, a tingling sensation raced through me. It pooled deep in my abdomen, liquid and hot.

The entity's screams echoing off the walls kept rhythm with my pulse, with the blood and energy pulsating through my body, until the screams ebbed and faded into nothingness. A thick silence settled around us and I realized Jared's light had banished the entity. It was gone.

He pulled me tighter and walked me back to a wall, pushed me against it and pressed into me. His body, solid and strong, felt like molten steel against mine. His lungs labored as he explored my mouth with his tongue. I savored his taste, sweet like candy.

Bracing one hand against the wall, he tore away from the

kiss. But he didn't let me go. Instead, he placed his forehead on the wall beside me, panting, his muscles constricted as if in pain. "I'm sorry," he said, his voice husky and soft.

He was sorry? For what? I realized then that I was panting too. My legs were weak and I was sure I would have slid down the wall if he wasn't holding me.

"You're amazing," he whispered between raspy breaths.

I was amazing? Had he looked in the mirror lately?

"I'm blind!" Glitch held out his arms as he tried to navigate the room. "What the bloody heck was that?"

"Jared's light," I said proudly as I gave him my rapt attention. His lids were closed, his jaw clenched. I placed my fingertips on his mouth, cut to perfection, and he turned into them, kissed each one then brought up my palm and kissed it too, then my wrist, watching me from underneath his thick lashes. Each contact sent goose bumps spiraling over my arm.

"Well, it's freaking bright," Glitch said. "I think it burned the retinas out of my eyes."

Jared continued to stare at me for a long, breathtaking moment, then turned to Glitch. "I think you're wearing the late Grandma Southern."

Glitch stopped and patted himself. When the piano hit the wall, the urn must have tipped over and broke. He was covered in ash.

"Get her off me!" he screamed as he turned in circles and swiped at his shoulders. "Get her off me! Get her off me!"

Cameron laughed. He leapt casually over the back of the sofa and sat on an arm to watch. "You scream like a girl, man."

"She's everywhere," he said, his voice tinged with a sad, pathetic kind of despair. "I'll never get her out of my hair."

I couldn't help a bubble of laughter. He still had his eyes plastered shut as he shook his head. A fine cloud of ash surrounded him, reminding me of a character from Charlie Brown.

"Holy moly!" Brooklyn still had a throw rug over her head as she rushed toward the front window. "They're here! The Southerns are here!" She turned and surveyed the battlegrounds. "How are we going to explain this?"

"I ain't explaining diddly," Cameron said. "I'm outta here." He jumped off the sofa and walked to the patio door. Then he stopped and turned back to her. "Coming?"

Without hesitation, Brooklyn dropped the rug and scrambled after him.

I ducked down and maneuvered around a coffee table to look out the window. I could see two headlights meandering up the drive. Thank God we parked off the main road and walked up.

I glanced back at Jared. He'd followed me to the window.

"It's too late to go out the back," he said. "They'll be able to see us when they park in the garage."

"Glitch, for Heaven's sake, get down."

He was still swiping at poor Grandma Southern. "I can't see."

"Down, Glitch. Just let gravity do its thing."

"And yes," Jared said, "you can see. Try opening your eyes."

I had turned back to the window, but I heard Glitch say, "Oh yeah. Thanks."

Even as scared to death as I was, I laughed. He could be such a nerd. Which was probably why I loved him so much.

"So, what do we do?" I asked.

"We get the bloody hell outta here, that's what we do," Glitch said. He stood beside us.

"Actually," Jared said, "we wait. As soon as the garage door closes, we hightail it out the front and go down the mountain from here."

"Right," Glitch said. "That's what I meant."

I turned to look at Jared. His dark eyes were glistening as usual. His mouth formed a half smile, dimples emerging at each corner.

"On three," he said.

I snapped back to earth and waited for the count.

"One," he said, turning back to watch the garage door slide down. "Two." He took my hand into his and leaned down teasingly to whisper in my ear. In the quietest, most sensual voice, he said, "Three."

We jumped up and ran for the front entryway just as the door to the garage was opening.

"Wait!" Glitch whispered loudly. "Did you say three?"

"Come on," I called back to him.

We charged out the front door, raced over the manicured lawn, and fled into the forest as fast as our feet could carry us. Well, as fast as my feet could carry me. I had a sneaking suspicion Jared and Glitch could have run a bit faster. They were barely jogging.

But when we hit the forest, we got separated from Glitch. Jared yelled directions softly. "Down, Glitch. Just let gravity do its thing."

I almost laughed. Adrenaline and the taste of freedom—aka, getting away with breaking and entering and some fairly hefty acts of vandalism—rushed through me like a cool wind. We ran so fast, I couldn't believe I wasn't falling on my face. But Jared had a firm grip on my hand. He reined in when my feet slipped out from under me, grabbed my arm when I tripped, and kept me semi-vertical more than once.

Then he skidded to a halt and whisked me behind a tree, his movements sharp, calculated. Suddenly on full alert, he threw a glance over his shoulder, then crouched to the forest floor, pulling me with him. Something was wrong.

"What's going on?" I whispered.

He put a finger over his mouth and led me deeper into the woods. "Listen," he said after a moment.

"I think I got it all this time," a man's voice said.

I almost gasped aloud. Jared pulled me to his side as we peered through a thick bush at John Dell, investigative reporter for the Tourist Channel.

He leaned against a huge pine tree, cell phone in hand. "You won't believe it," he said, frowning at his cameraman, who could only stare at the house in disbelief, his camera hanging off his shoulder, forgotten. Their van had been pulled into a clearing behind them.

"It's her," he continued, "the prophet and one of the guys from the other day." He paused a beat. "Right, the dark one. You'll have to look for yourself. He has the markings of a messenger, but he's not one. He can't be. He looks mortal."

Fear crawled like spiders up my spine and burst over my skin, shuddering along the surface.

After another long pause, he said, "Oh, he'll cooperate. I have several fourth-degree felonies on tape to make sure of it. If he cares anything for the girl, he'll cooperate."

I clasped a hand over my mouth. He'd recorded the whole thing. They must have been able to see us through the huge front windows. We were so dead. What would they do to Jared? He would have to go into hiding. If the wrong people got ahold of that recording . . .

Creepy reporter guy closed the phone and turned to his stunned cameraman. "What'd I tell you? This is going to make my career. I knew I didn't sell my soul to that man for nothing." Then, as though he heard the thundering of my heart, the reporter's head whipped toward us.

Jared jerked me to the ground and covered my body with his. That's when I realized anger had engulfed him. He shook with it, his jaw clasped shut, teeth bared in fury.

"Who's there?" I heard the reporter say. Then footsteps crackled along the forest floor.

Jared closed his lids and inhaled deeply, as if trying to control his actions. Then he placed a hand over my eyes, leaned in, and whispered into my ear. "Whatever happens, don't look."

"Wait, why?" I whispered back.

But my question was drowned out by a soft growl from Jared, the deep sound prickling my skin with anxiety. When the reporter's footsteps reached the bush we were hiding behind, a whoosh of air pulsed over me, stirred my hair, and the weight of Jared's body was no longer pressing into mine. I opened my eyes in complete disobedience and found myself surrounded by a swirling, tangible darkness—thick, hot, and pitch black. It slid over my skin like static in the wake of a lightning storm, then seeped through the brush, a searching fog. It reminded me of the poltergeist, only darker and denser and pulsating with life.

I watched, mouth agape, as the fog slid along the forest floor. Was this what Cameron saw? Was Jared really the grim reaper? Would he leave now? Go back to where he came from?

Before my mind could make sense of what was happening, I turned and looked up into the eyes of John Dell. His mouth twisted into a sneer as he reached for me. I pushed his hand aside and scurried back, my eyes wide as Jared materialized behind him. An instant later, John Dell flew through the air. His body slammed into the side of the van as another technician looked out the open side door in surprise.

I scrambled to my knees to watch. Every move Jared made left a thick, lingering fog in his wake, like he was only part flesh, only part human. He graced the technician with a quick glance then touched his forehead. The man collapsed, falling face-first to the ground. Then Jared looked back at the cameraman. He'd dropped the camera and was inching away, placing one foot behind the other, arms raised in surrender. But Jared was in front of him at once, enshrouded in smoke and shadows. Another touch. Another fall. So quiet, it gave new definition to the word *eerie*.

My lungs, completely paralyzed, burned with their need for air. Were those men dead? Had Jared killed them?

A second later, a sharp crack resonated through the forest, and I looked over just in time to see John Dell fall to the ground, his head twisted at an odd angle, his neck clearly broken.

Jared stepped back as the man crumpled before him, and I slammed my eyes shut, suddenly afraid to look, to see what he was capable of. Then he growled again, like an animal, like an echoing thunder. The inhuman sound sent chills washing over me. I rose to my feet and took a wary step back. As though remembering I was there, he turned. The heat from his anger radiated toward me, hot and palpable. He took a step toward me, his head lowered, his chest heaving, his eyes bright like a predator preparing for its next kill.

And I ran. I gathered every ounce of strength I had and ran like I'd never run before. A blinding fear drove me forward. Twigs and branches lashed across my face as I slipped and stumbled down the mountainside. My heart pounded so hard, I could hear it pulsing in my ears. In the back of my mind, I knew I could never outrun him, but my feet didn't care. They pushed on, pumping, stumbling, catching, and pumping again. I actually fell twice, like those chicks in scary movies, the uneven terrain almost impossible to navigate. But I scrambled back up and started racing toward the road again.

Glitch's Subaru appeared like a haven below me. Just a few more yards. He hadn't caught me yet. Just a few more yards and I'd be safe. Or at least that's what I kept telling myself.

Then he was there. In front of me. Jared. No longer an apparition of smoke and fog, but solid, flesh and blood, regarding me with a mixture of worry and anger. I skidded to a halt and ended up falling back to keep from sliding into him. When he reached down, I tried to scramble out of his grasp.

"Lorelei," he said, "wait."

I scurried out of his reach with a frown, a warning for him not to come any closer. He seemed normal again. Normal. Like he hadn't just been something . . . not.

"Lorelei, I can explain."

Cameron was there in an instant, kneeling beside me. "What happened?"

"Guys!" Glitch came running down the mountain, yelling breathlessly. "Guys, there are three unconscious men up there." He stopped beside me and bent over, panting. "I swear. I think they're dead."

He'd stumbled upon the massacre. That meant he'd been close when Jared went postal. I glanced back at Jared, my eyes wide. "Would you have hurt him too?"

Jared looked down as though unable to face me.

"If you had seen him," I pushed, "would you have hurt him too?"

Cameron stilled, his muscles tense, his expression wary.

"What are you talking about, Lor?" Glitch asked, huffing from exertion beside me.

"Would you have killed him?" I asked again, my voice a mere whisper, afraid of what he might say.

Keeping his face averted, he said, "I didn't kill anyone."

But wasn't that what he did? Wasn't that his job? Maybe death came so naturally to him, he didn't think twice about it. Maybe, when his temper flared, he couldn't stop himself.

I shook so hard, my teeth rattled. Tears blurred my vision and I swiped at them angrily. Somewhere in the back of my mind, I knew I'd slipped into a state of shock. I'd just seen the deaths of three innocent men. Everything slowed, every sound echoed in my head, and a desperate sorrow swallowed me whole. I knew things I no longer wanted to know, saw things I no longer wanted to see.

When did it all become so serious? So real? Jared wasn't human. He didn't belong on this plane, just like Cameron said. He was trapped here because of me. And clearly, he could kill in a heartbeat if he wanted to. I hadn't taken that knowledge seriously before. Now I had no choice.

I heard voices but couldn't make sense of what anyone said. Then I felt Cameron pick me up and carry me down the rest of the mountain. Faintly, as if from a dream, I heard Jared call to me. But Cameron yelled over his shoulder.

"Go back to where you came from, Reaper," he said, his voice angry.

Then we were driving. The inside of the car felt like a funeral parlor. The inside of my heart felt even more dead, a hollow void where life had once thrived. I'd started crying and I wasn't entirely certain why. Glitch held me in the backseat and Brooklyn sat beside us, petting my hair, whispering promises that everything was going to be fine.

But she didn't see what I saw. I brought a supreme being onto this plane. A force so powerful, even other supernatural entities were afraid of him. A force that didn't play by our rules. Didn't believe in our set of moral standards. And I'd set him loose upon the human race.

Nothing would ever be fine again.

A DIFFERENT ANIMAL

A week later, the investigation into the injuries of three Tourist Channel employees outside a Riley's Switch residence raged on. Injuries. As in, no deaths. Everything the crew had recorded since their arrival had been erased, along with any evidence as to what they'd been doing outside a vandalized residence. None of the men could remember what happened. They could barely remember their own names. Cops questioned just about everyone in town and scoured the area for clues. The trail ran cold at every turn.

I knew it might look suspicious if I didn't go to school, but I just couldn't manage it. I felt like the world had dropped out from under me. Everything I had learned. Everything I had seen. And to top it off, Jared was gone. I had turned on him the minute he showed me his true self, practically ordered him away. He left because of me. He said he didn't kill anyone, and obviously he hadn't. But I wouldn't listen to him.

Still, that man's neck was broken. I heard it. I saw the unnatural angle of his head on his shoulders as he crumpled to the ground. And yet, according to police reports, there were no deaths. All three men were present and accounted for. I had accused Jared of the worst crime imaginable and sentenced him before he even had a chance to explain. I was no better than those people who had burned my ancestor, the prophet Arabeth, on the streets of her village. No trial. No chance to defend herself. Just a village teeming with fear and superstition. How was I any better?

With all the questions and doubt about what happened rolling around in my head, I missed a week of school. An entire week. I hadn't done that since I had pneumonia in the fifth grade. The homework Brooklyn brought me every day sat on my desk untouched. Just like the lunch Grandma and Grandpa had brought up earlier. They came in every so often to check on me. I knew they wanted answers, but I couldn't talk about it, not just yet. And even when I could, I'd have to come up with a whopper. The whole *I just don't feel good* would only last so long. I had no idea what I was going to tell them.

And to top it all off, I'd lost my necklace. Again. I had to have lost it either in the Southerns' house or in the forest outside it. Either way, I worried that, if found, it could trigger questions possibly leading to us.

"There she is," Glitch said as he and Brooklyn walked into my room carrying pizza and orange soda.

"Phew," Brooklyn said, "we were worried you might have gone out partying, it being Friday night and all."

I smiled and sat up. My bed was a rumpled mess, as were my pajamas and quite possibly my hair, but at least I'd managed a shower. "How was the game?"

Glitch shrugged and pulled a small table over to the bed. "We won. How was your day?"

The depression that had taken hold lurched inside me. I couldn't look at anything or do anything or say anything that didn't cause a deep sadness. Jared's absence had left a hole in my heart. My behavior toward him was reprehensible. After everything he'd done for me, I threw him to the wolves the first chance I got.

I took a deep breath and swallowed hard. "Should we invite him in?" I asked Brooklyn.

"I don't know. What do you think?"

"Well, you did bring Dr Pepper." I looked at the six-pack in her hands.

A sad smile spread across her face. She was sad for me and I felt so guilty because of it.

She walked to the window, opened it, and leaned out. "Hey, blondie. We got pizza. Can you leave your post for a little while?"

After a minute, Cameron crawled in from the fire escape. Brooklyn handed him a slice of pizza and a soda. He closed the window and sat on the seat there as Glitch sat at my desk and Brooklyn settled in at the foot of my bed.

Having them all with me, I suddenly felt famished. I inhaled two slices of pizza before slowing to a nibble on a third.

"I really didn't expect you to eat anything," Glitch said, disappointed. I attempted a small laugh. "Now I'm going to have to make popcorn to fill the void."

"Oh yeah," Brooklyn said, "we brought a movie." She reached over and took a DVD out of her purse. "It's your favorite."

I looked at it. "*Rocky Horror Picture Show* is not my favorite. It's your favorite."

"I know," she said. "But I figured you wouldn't enjoy whatever we got anyway, so at least I should have some fun."

What would I do without my very best friends? Wait a minute. What would I do? What if they suddenly died or moved or got deported? Can they deport Americans to foreign countries? What would I do?

Tears began to sting my eyes and I turned to grab my inhaler off my nightstand. After a quick spray, I sat breathing deep with my face averted until I could get my emotions under control.

"You don't have to hide from us," Cameron said.

I didn't turn back. "I know. This is just getting really embarrassing."

"Lor," Brooklyn said, "look at me."

I turned to her, my wet cheeks a dead giveaway.

She leaned in and covered my hands with hers. "I don't know what to do for you. How to help."

"You are helping," Cameron said, always the pragmatist.

A fresh supply of tears welled up behind my eyes, just waiting for someone to say the right thing, or the wrong thing, or pretty much anything.

I looked at Glitch. "Is this what it was like for you?"

He was caught off guard, and his lips pressed together. We had made a deal a long time ago not to talk about that spring break our second-grade year, but desperate times called for desperate measures. He glanced down at his pizza. "No. I was just . . . in shock or something. I don't know what happened. I barely remember it."

"Maybe Cameron can shed some light?" I looked over at him, my brows raised in question.

"I've never talked about it," Glitch said in surprise. "What makes you think Cameron had anything to do with it?"

"Just a guess. Am I wrong?" When neither of them answered,

I knew I was right. "Glitch, what happened? Was it anything like what's been happening here?"

"No, hon." He shook his head. "Not even close."

I looked at Cameron. "Did it have anything to do with an angel? With Jared?"

"No, Lorelei," he said. "It had to do with two very evil people."

"Cameron," Glitch whispered under his breath. He shifted in his chair, suddenly uncomfortable. I decided to drop it. If there was no connection, there was no reason to push for information. Not now, anyway.

"What did he look like?" Brooklyn asked out of the blue. I knew whom she meant without asking. I had told them about Jared, about how he had changed in the forest. I think I left them with the impression that he'd become a huge, green, one-eyed monster.

Even though he hadn't, I didn't know how to tell them what he did look like. "You'll never believe me," I said.

"Let me get this straight," Glitch said. "We've just witnessed things most humans are completely oblivious to. The stopping of time, that whole becoming-transparent-so-a-grand-piano-can-pass-through-you thing, the banishing of a pissed-off poltergeist, the mysterious memory swipe of three men in a forest . . . but no, you're right. We probably wouldn't believe you."

"Really, Lor," Brooklyn said. "How much more bizarre can this get?"

"Was he, like, all grotesque or something?" Glitch asked.

"No." I paused and thought back. "He was beautiful."

"Beautiful? I thought he was scary," Brooke said, clearly wondering what the big deal was.

"I didn't say he wasn't scary. I just said he was beautiful."

"Chicks actually call guys beautiful?" Cameron seemed appalled.

Brooklyn smirked.

"Okay," I said, "but you have to keep an open mind. That means you too, Glitch."

"We've been through this, remember? I'm totally open." He stretched his arms wide to prove it. "I'm an open book, an open door, an open sign that blinks in red and blue neon."

"Your fly's open too," Cameron said.

"Man." He turned and zipped up his pants before looking back. "Okay, I'm ready."

"*We're* ready," Brooklyn corrected. "We can take it. We're here for you. Lay it on us, baby."

"Okay, here goes." I hesitated a moment, praying they wouldn't have me committed afterwards. "He looked like . . . well . . . a grim reaper."

The room grew deathly quiet. All three of them sat staring at me. No movement. No expression. Maybe they didn't hear me.

Glitch, as usual, snapped out of it first. "Pizza, anyone?" He held the pizza box out.

"Glitch," I started, but Brooklyn interrupted me.

"That was kind of anticlimactic." She seemed disappointed.

For some reason, I was rather offended. "Have you ever seen a grim reaper?"

"I have," Cameron said, raising a hand. "But there's actually only the one."

I looked at him. "When you called him the reaper, I thought you were, you know, exaggerating. So there really is a grim reaper?"

With a shrug, he answered, "Not really. I don't know, kind of. That's just one of his names. And it's the one that fits him best, if you ask me."

"So," Brooklyn said, "did he have a scythe? You know, like in the movies?"

"That's funny," Glitch said. "Pizza, anyone?"

"Glitch," Brooklyn said, "stop trying to change the subject. But, seriously, did you see one?"

"He doesn't actually carry a scythe," Cameron said. "He kills just fine without one."

Something transcendent tightened around my throat when he said that. My second impression of Jared in reaper form was very similar. He didn't need any help doing his job. My first was just a general sense of *holy crap*.

"Though he does have a wicked sword I'd give my right arm for," Cameron continued.

"That's right." I pulled my knees to my chest. "He had a sword in my vision."

"But he was beautiful?" Brooke asked.

"He was," I said. "Stunning. Mesmerizing. He was like smoke and yet solid at the same time, and strong, like he could have crushed a truck if he'd wanted to."

"He could have," Cameron said, regarding his pizza absently. "Trust me." He took another bite.

Cameron really wasn't helping.

I surveyed the room to get a sense of my audience. Brooklyn sat deep in thought. Glitch seemed to be taking it okay. He was holding the pizza box in one hand and munching pizza out of the other, his eyes squinting as though trying to envision what Jared had looked like. Cameron, on the other hand, seemed completely oblivious, like he dealt with this sort of thing every day. I guess he did. I was beginning to understand what he might have been going through his whole life. He'd clearly been desensitized.

He finished his last bite of pizza and stood to look out the window.

"Cameron?" I said, wiping my hands on a napkin.

He glanced over his shoulder then back out the window.

"How did Jared just put those men to sleep?" I asked. "I mean, he just touched them and they collapsed."

A sigh slipped through his lips. "I don't know. I've never seen that." He reached up and wiped condensation off a pane with the sleeve of his denim jacket. "And the fact that you felt heat emanating off him has me pretty baffled as well."

"That's never happened before?" I asked.

He shook his head.

"Least he conveniently erased all the evidence of our breaking and entering gig," Glitch said.

"But are we absolutely positive he did?" Brooklyn asked, propping her elbows on her knees. "Those crime scene investigators were up there a long time. They don't usually investigate that intensely unless there's been a murder or a kidnapping or something. Who knows, the sheriff could be watching that recording as we speak."

She wasn't helping either. My insides were a jumble of nerves and thick, gooey sadness.

After a moment, and a couple of gulps of Dr Pepper, Cameron said all out-of-the-blue like, "Lor, there's a fact that you're going to have to come to terms with eventually."

I straightened, grabbed my ragged stuffed monkey, and scooted back against my headboard. "Okay."

He seemed hesitant, as though unsure of how to put into words what he wanted to say. When he did speak, it was with reverence, each word carefully chosen. "You need to understand that Jared is good, yes, he's light." He fixed his attention on me, and I knew I wasn't going to like the rest of what he had to say. "But he's also dark, Lor. He was created for a very specific purpose and has more power than his brothers. When a higher being says dark, what they're talking about is the absolute absence of light. The absence of good. Do you know what that means?"

When I shook my head, he continued. "The absence of good is a nice way of saying 'evil.' There's a part of him that's evil."

"But can't that be said about anyone?" I asked, jumping to Jared's defense. "Doesn't every being on earth have the capacity for evil?"

His brows slid together. "Not like this. Not to this degree. I'm not saying he has the capacity for evil, Lorelei. I'm saying he *is* evil. It's just as much a part of him as auburn hair and smoky gray eyes are to you. It's in him. In his genetic makeup. Inherent and pure."

"And so is good," I argued.

"True. But just so we're clear, supernatural beings aren't afraid of much. You have to be pretty powerful to scare Casper into pissing himself. The everyday poltergeist isn't afraid of angelic beings, Lor. Yet they're terrified of Jared."

I took a sip of soda, then rubbed my face on my monkey's tummy. "I think he's more good than evil," I said, standing my ground.

"You could be right." He leaned against the window frame. "I'm not saying he isn't."

"When I saw him in the forest," I said, trying to explain, "when he changed, I just . . . I kind of freaked out. I ran from him. He was so big and so angry and I thought he killed that man, so I ran."

"Lor," Brooklyn said, "that was totally the right thing to do."

"But when I thought about it later," I continued, "I realized he was protecting me."

Cameron disagreed. "You can't know that."

"Yes, I can. He pushed me to the ground, then changed and attacked them like he was protecting me. I was just so scared when I saw him. I'm such a girl," I said, utterly disappointed in myself.

Brooklyn scooted beside me and wrapped her arms around

my shoulders. "I wish I had been there with you. I'm so sorry you went through that alone."

I rested my head against hers.

"You've had a traumatic experience," Glitch said. "It's gonna take a while to get over it."

"I know, but I think it's more the loss. I just can't believe he's gone. I know how that sounds after everything that's happened. He's probably the last person I should miss, but—"

"He's not gone, shortstop," Cameron said.

My head snapped up. I watched him with way more hope than I wanted.

"He never left," he said reluctantly. "He's been here the whole time."

"Here? Like, *where* here?"

"Why do you think I've been staked out on your fire escape? He's close."

Now for the sad part.

My soul took flight! My heart soared! A euphoric, deliriously giddy sensation washed over me with the knowledge that Jared was still here. He didn't leave. He didn't go back to his day job.

"Do you know where he is?" Brooklyn asked.

"No, but I can feel him."

"What do you feel?" I asked, just wanting that small bit of knowledge to tide me over while I wondered if I would ever see him again.

He ground his teeth, hesitated, then said softly, "Pain."

I jumped up and ran to the window, searching the distance for any sign of him. "Is he hurt? Is he stranded somewhere?"

"No, not that kind of pain. Pain like yours. Deep. Desperate. It's disturbing. Between the two of you, I'm on the verge of committing suicide."

I put my hand on the window, wishing he would come back,

praying. But just the knowledge that he wasn't gone forever caused a flood of tears to sting the backs of my eyes.

"Please, don't cry."

"Holy sh—" Glitch fell out of his chair and Brooklyn yelped before plastering her hands over her mouth.

I closed my lids. His voice was like water on a scorched desert plain, welcome and nourishing.

"I'm sorry, Lorelei. I didn't mean to frighten you."

Without another thought, without the slightest hesitation, I turned and ran into his arms. He lifted me off the ground and held me for a long time, his embrace powerful, his body warm and enveloping.

"I'm so sorry."

"No," I said between hysterical laughs. "I'm sorry."

"You? You have no reason to be."

"After everything you did for me, after you saved my life over and over, I turned on you in a heartbeat."

"You didn't turn on me," he said with a release of air. "You were scared."

"Oh, my God," I said as I squeezed my arms around his neck and wrapped my legs around his waist. "You're back. I was so worried."

"I'm sorry."

"No, I'm sorry."

"Oh, for Heaven's sake," Brooklyn said, "stop apologizing. And, you," she said menacingly at Jared, "just where the bloody heck have you been?"

He buried his face against my neck. "I thought I should keep my distance for a while, you know, in case you never wanted to see me again."

"Please," Glitch said, "if shortstop and moon pie never wanted to see you again, you'd be the first to know."

I leaned back to look up at him. His jaw was darkened by days of stubble, his hair tangled, unkempt, his eyes bright with emotion. After a moment, his full mouth tilted into a lopsided grin and I couldn't help the sharp inhalation that slipped past my lips. He totally looked like a supermodel.

He glanced at Cameron and nodded once. "Cameron."

"Jared," Cameron said.

Their greeting was cool, but even that was better than the alternative: nine rounds in the McAlister house. Jared's dark eyes bored in to mine. I didn't wait this time. Life was too short. I leaned in and kissed him right on the mouth. The kiss deepened instantly, like we each needed to drink from the other. My lips parted and his tongue took instant advantage, tasting and exploring. The heat he exuded seeped into the fabric of my pj's. He sighed into my mouth and I breathed him in.

"This is awkward," I heard Glitch say.

Just then a knock sounded at the door. "Honey, can we come in?" It was my grandmother.

I broke off the kiss and jumped to the ground. Dizzy from the heavy panting, I glanced around to hide the evidence before realizing there was no evidence to hide. Okay, fine, I could do this. After a deep, calming breath, and a quick smile tossed to Jared, I stepped back, smoothed my pajamas, then said, "Come on in, Grandma."

She opened the door slowly and peeked around it. "You ate," she said, sounding pleased.

I glanced back at the empty pizza box. "Oh, yeah. I'm feeling much better."

With a pretense of pleasure, she offered me her ulterior-motive smile. I should've known she was up to something. "Good," she said, examining the room quickly, "then you kids won't mind coming downstairs for a bit."

"But—"

She closed the door before I could argue. Then, when I least expected it, she reopened it and said, "*All* of you."

"But—"

Nope. She was gone.

Man, that woman was quick when she wanted to be. But put her behind the wheel of a Buick . . .

"Um, maybe you should get dressed," Glitch suggested.

"Oh, yeah, you're probably right." I offered Jared a shy smile, only just realizing what I must look like, before scrounging up a clean pair of jeans and a plain black tee. "'Kay, be right out," I said, hurrying to the bathroom, suddenly unable to meet Jared's eyes. I swore on all things holy, if my hair looked bad, God and I were going to have a long talk in church this Sunday.

I changed quickly, brushed my teeth, and ran wet fingers through the mop on top of my head more commonly referred to as hair. It wasn't horrible, but there was always room for improvement. I let it fall down my back and offered up a silent prayer in the hopes that Jared liked redheads. Or dark auburn heads. Either way. He didn't seem to mind my coloring. So far, so good. A boy once broke up with me in the third grade because he said he didn't realize I had red hair until we went out onto the playground at recess. Our love had lasted twenty minutes. So as long as Jared and I stayed out of the sun, we should be good.

I stepped out to face the masses, though I zeroed in on Jared instantly. He was lounging against the wall, his arms crossed over his chest as he appraised me, appreciation lighting his face.

"Are we ready?" I asked, my voice more shaky than I'd hoped.

"I ain't going down there," Cameron said.

Brooklyn turned to him, mouth agape. "She said all of us, Cameron. Which means you too."

"The hell it does," he said, making for the fire escape.

She lunged forward and caught his T-shirt. "No way. If one of us faces the firing squad, all of us face the firing squad."

"Those are illegal now, right?" Glitch asked.

"Do you think this is about the Southerns' piano?" I asked, suddenly nervous. That thing must have cost a fortune. "We are so busted."

Jared's mouth formed a grim line. "I don't think anyone down there is worried about the Southerns' piano."

"Well, okay, I guess that's good." I raised my brows to Brooklyn, who nodded in halfhearted agreement, clearly worried now herself.

When we started downstairs, Jared wrapped a hand around mine as Brooklyn dragged Cameron by the hem of his shirt. Glitch brought up the rear. The stairs led to the kitchen, but I heard voices in the living room beyond that. And not just my grandparents'. Startled, I asked Jared over my shoulder, "What did you mean *anyone down there*? Who's here?"

"Lorelei." He pulled me to a stop just before we got to the living room door and stepped closer. "Whatever is said, whatever is done, I want you to remember who I am."

After a failed attempt at a smile, I asked, "Who are you?" I was so completely confused. Who was in my house? And what did this have to do with Jared?

He let out a long, withering sigh. "I'm the same guy you knew five minutes ago. I haven't changed."

I forced myself to think rationally. What did I really know about Jared? Every bit of information I received about him conflicted with some other bit, like trying to put together a puzzle where the pieces didn't quite fit. But I knew he'd saved my life. More than once. Wasn't that all that mattered?

Cameron stepped behind him and spoke over his shoulder. "Worried?" he asked with a confident smirk.

"What's going on?" I asked Jared in concern.

Cameron strolled past us and slid the pocket door that led to the living room. "Showtime," he said, a menacing grin on his face.

The door opened, and a room full of people stood and faced us, like a surprise party without the party.

SANCTUARY

Bright lights illuminated face after face, most of whose I recognized, including Sheriff Villanueva, I noted with a rush of panic. Compared to the Southerns' great room, ours was minuscule, but if I'd stopped to count, I knew I'd find at least fifty people in our living room, probably more.

I took a wary step back, but Brooklyn took my other hand and led me in. With her eyes on the sheriff, she said under her breath, "You were right. We are so busted." Then she looked up and screeched to a halt. "Mom! Dad! What are you doing here?"

Brooklyn's mom held out her arms to her. She was the most beautiful African-American woman I'd ever seen, petite like Brooke with the same delicate shape and soft brown skin. But her dad was tall and thin and almost as white as I was. He was super good-looking, though, so I understood the attraction.

Surveying the room, I saw Glitch's parents as well.

He spotted them at the same time and looked back and forth between the two in shock. "Dad, what's going on?"

"Cameron."

We all turned to see that even Cameron's dad was there. In that moment, Cameron's expression turned from cocky to almost embarrassment. "Dad, you shouldn't be here."

"Why?" he asked, stepping toward his son.

Cameron towered over him, as he did everyone else in the room except for Jared, the boys like two sides of the same coin, one dark and one light.

"Don't you think I've stayed away long enough?" he asked.

Cameron tensed as though suddenly annoyed. "Why now?" he asked under his breath. "You've never believed before. Why now?"

Mr. Lusk placed a supportive hand on his arm. "Son, I've always believed. Deep down, I've always known what you are. Pastor Bill called me and, well, clearly there are bigger things at stake than what even your mother could've imagined. It's time I got in the game instead of sitting on the sidelines." His mouth thinned into a solid line of regret. "I just wanted you to know I'm here for you." He glanced around. "For all you kids."

Cameron shoved his hands into his jeans pockets in discomfort. "Thanks, Dad."

I'd been so caught up in their discussion, I didn't realize until that moment that everyone in the room was gawking at Jared. Including my grandparents.

My grandfather snapped to attention. He offered Jared a

smile and held out his hand. "We're the Order of Sanctity, or, as we like to call ourselves now, the Sanctuary, and we're here to help in any way we can."

I blinked in confusion. The Sanctuary was the name of our church and most of these people attended on a regular basis. "Grandpa, what's going on?" But he continued to stare at the supreme being standing before him, his hand held in limbo. Did he actually know what Jared was? What he could do?

Jared scanned the room, stopping for a split second on each face before returning his attention to Grandpa. After sizing him up, he asked, "Do you know what I am?"

My grandmother's face lit up. She took Grandpa's outstretched hand and said, "You're a messenger. An angel."

Jared sighed as though disappointed, then raised one sleeve of his T-shirt, displaying the band of symbols tattooed around his biceps. "Archangel," he corrected.

My grandfather lifted the glasses dangling around his neck and stepped closer to examine the tattoo. He stilled. For a long moment he stood there, his face turning ashen in disbelief before taking a wary step back.

"You're—"

"I am Azrael," Jared said, matter-of-fact.

A uniform gasp echoed off the walls as every single face in the room froze. People started inching back, including my grandma's best friend, Betty Jo, putting as much distance between them and Jared as they possibly could. A few looked panic stricken. And two ran, the Mortons, a young couple who'd only recently moved to Riley's Switch. And they actually ran. They stumbled over themselves trying to get to the side door. Just as they were about to cross the threshold, every door in the house slammed shut in one thunderous clap. The couple stopped and looked back at Jared, their eyes so wide with fear I felt sorry for them, even as a shiver of fear rushed down my own spine.

The sheriff went for his gun in reflex. He caught himself, left the gun in the holster but kept his hand close.

Grandpa lifted his chin, steeled himself as though accepting his fate. "We ask you, Prince Azrael, to spare us."

"You're a prince?" Glitch asked, oblivious of the reaction of the room.

Jared ignored him, inspecting the sheriff for an uncomfortable moment, then answered my grandfather. "If you have to ask, then you know nothing of me."

"We know that you have as many names as your fallen brother Lucifer," Grandpa said, "some misconceptions created through superstition and ignorance, but most hard-earned." He inched closer. "We know that you've been absent from Heaven for so long, many of the beings there, the same ones that celebrate your conquests, also fear your return." Another step. "We know that you are the only celestial being ever created, *ever*, with the autonomy to take human life. None of your brethren, not even the other archangels, have that power. It is why you were created and it is yours alone." He took another step to emphasize his next statement. "And we know what you're here to do."

"We're not your enemies, Your Grace," Grandma said, her voice quivering almost as much as her hands. "We're your servants."

I hurried to her side and wrapped my arm around her waist, trying to assure her Jared would not hurt them, any of them. She hugged me to her before returning her attention to Jared.

He looked down at us, and I could see for the first time the nobility in his stance, the absolute power in the set of his shoulders. He took stock of me for what seemed like forever before asking Grandpa, "Why does she not know?"

The question surprised Grandpa. I could tell. But it surprised me as well. I raised my brows at my grandfather, growing tired of the riddles and the half truths that seemed to have permeated every corner of my life. Why did I not know what? What was all this about? Why was everyone here, and how did they know about Jared?

"We were going to tell her," Grandpa said, pinching the bridge of his nose with his thumb and forefinger, "everything, when she turned eighteen. But things have . . . accelerated."

"So, you're a prince?" Glitch repeated. Still oblivious.

"What good would it do, Reaper?" Cameron said, coming to stand dangerously close to Jared. "She doesn't need to know." He tilted his head toward Brooklyn. "None of them need to know."

Jared's head tilted in curiosity. "They have a right to know what they are."

"And what are they?" Cameron asked, closing the distance between them.

"Not again," Brooklyn said, but her parents had wrapped her in their arms and were pulling her out of harm's way. "Mom, Dad, it's okay. They do this crap all the time."

"Casey," Glitch's mom said, waving him toward her. She had soft brown hair and startlingly green eyes, her coloring so opposite that of her Native American husband's who beckoned Casey closer as well. "Casey, come here."

Glitch shrugged and threaded through the crowd to her. "Is he seriously a prince?" he asked in a hushed tone.

She clutched him to her, then turned back.

Jared answered Cameron, and as usual, his answer didn't actually answer anything. "They are taken."

"Calling the kettle black, now?" Cameron asked, his blue eyes glittering with a not-so-subtle warning. "Maybe your new friends need to know what they call you. The shadow prince. The sin-eater. The grim reaper." He leaned tauntingly close. "The Angel of De—"

In an instant, Jared pushed Cameron so hard, he flew across the room and slammed into the back wall. The house literally shook with the force, and everyone ducked, though they needn't have. Cameron landed well above their heads, then fell forward to land solidly on his hands and feet. I cringed. His body had left an indentation in our drywall. I wondered if it was just me, or if Jared really was growing stronger with every minute that passed. Not that Cameron cared.

Mr. Lusk had started forward, but a couple of the men held him back as Cameron coughed and fought for air. After a tense moment, he stood, squared his shoulders, then gave Jared a measured look, one that held such hatred, my insides groaned in response.

"Now we're talking," he said, thrilled that Jared had given him an excuse for another world war.

Just as both boys started toward each other, I rushed in between them and shouted as loud as I possibly could. "That is it!" I glared from one to the other as my grandmother gasped in horror. "I have absolutely had it!" I turned and poked Cameron in the chest. "Really? This again, really?" Then I gave my full attention to Jared. "And how old are you exactly?"

"Lor, honey," Grandma said, her voice soft with fear.

"I swear, if either of you lifts another finger toward the other, I will murder you both in your sleep."

Brooklyn broke free from her parents and marched over to Cameron. "This is going to hurt you a lot more than it hurts me." She reached up and took him by the ear.

"Ouch, holy crap," he said, bending to her will. And her razor-sharp nails.

She led him to the now-closed kitchen door, then turned back to Jared. He offered a surrendering nod, relinquishing his hold on the door. She opened it and sat Cameron at the table before sitting on the chair next to him.

Cameron rubbed his ear. "That hurt."

A few of us followed them into the kitchen. I sat beside

Brooke and motioned for Jared to sit next to me while my grand-parents, the sheriff, Glitch, and a few others gathered around. More filed in as room allowed, and I realized for the first time the parents of the creature whose name shall not be spoken aloud were there. They were so . . . blond.

"If we can now have a decent conversation," I said, issuing a silent warning to the boys, "I would like to find out from my grandparents exactly what is going on. And you," I added, look-ing directly at Jared, "aka, the Angel of Death—a blank I filled in days ago when Cameron first mentioned it—will stop trying to kill said Cameron every time he brings up your vast and varied nicknames." I couldn't blame Cameron for calling Jared the grim reaper. I'd done some research, and in many cultures the reaper and the Angel of Death were one and the same, inter-changeable entities that took the souls of humans for any num-ber of reasons. "And you," I continued, nailing Cameron with a baleful look, "will stop trying to pick a fight with the freaking Angel of Death. Really?" My brows shot up in disbelief. "The Angel of Death? You can't find a defensive lineman to pick on?"

Cameron shrugged, clearly ashamed. "They're all scared of me."

Well, that certainly fit the story Glitch had told us a few days earlier. But still. This was getting ridiculous. Cameron's dad tou-sled his hair, and I would've smiled if I weren't considering ritu-alistic murder.

"Now, Grandma, Grandpa," I said, contemplating each in turn, "what is going on? How do you know about Jared?"

"Maybe I should make some coffee," Grandma said, but Betty Jo beat her to it. As others set out food and drink for the masses— the Sanctuary liked nothing better than gathering and eating— Sheriff Villanueva and Mr. Lusk brought in more chairs.

"Grandpa?" I asked, begging him with my eyes. There were too many secrets. Too many unknowns. I just wanted to find my place in the world. And Jared's, because I really wanted him to stay. "How do you know what Jared is?"

"Sweetheart," he began, his mouth a grim line, "this all goes back to way before you were born."

"I'm listening."

"When your mother first met your father, she came home with such tales, we honestly thought she'd been brainwashed by some kind of religious cult."

Jared bowed his head as Grandpa spoke, listening intently. I couldn't tell what he was thinking, but after everything he'd told me, how could this be any worse? Or any more bizarre? I'd learned more in the last week than I'd ever known in my life. There really was an Angel of Death? Cameron was a Nephilim? I was supposedly descended from a line of mystical women? Really, how much more surreal could it get? I refocused on Grandpa.

"But they moved back here after they married and we were just thrilled to have them home. That's when your father introduced us to an ancient society of followers who believed that not only was there a war in the heavens between what we consider good and evil, but that it would spill out one day onto the surface of Earth. That because of the actions of one man, the one we refer to as the Antichrist, the battle would eventually be fought here, angels and mortals would join forces, and a prophet would be born to lead us to victory."

"It took your father a while to convince us," Grandma added. "But many things he said would come to fruition actually did. He explained he was the descendant of a powerful prophet by the name of Arabeth, and that before she died, she had predicted these battles. Each generation in the line waited for the next prophet to be born, for the girl made of fire to lead them."

"So, Mom and Dad knew what I was when I was born?" I asked in disbelief.

"Yes, honey," Grandma said. "We've been studying the teachings of the order for years. Reading ancients texts that predicted the rise of the Antichrist, your birth, the battle. The signs were all there that a prophet would be born, the exact phenomena Arabeth described. And that's when the archangel Jophiel visited your mother, Cameron."

Cameron's jaw tightened as the attention shifted toward him.

"That's when we knew for certain what was about to happen," Grandpa added. "She was very honored to have been chosen, and even more honored to have been your mother."

He offered a curt nod, and I was thrilled. A nod, curt or otherwise, was better than his signature glower. Maybe there was hope for him yet.

"When you were born," Grandpa said to me, "there was such celebration. Many more believers moved to Riley's Switch and the Sanctuary, or the Order of Sanctity as it's traditionally called, grew."

"And then," Grandma said, her face growing somber, "the unthinkable happened."

The parishioners stopped what they were doing to listen, each one sidling closer. To watch. To gauge my reaction.

"You started having visions when you were two," she continued. "And you saw the most amazing things, but you also saw things that terrified you, things you couldn't possibly have understood."

Grandpa took her hand. "When you were six, you kept having this one vision over and over. You said the afternoon sky was ripping open and that night was flooding in."

I gulped in remembrance. I'd been dreaming that very thing for years, of a tear in the sky and darkness flooding the earth.

"You remember, don't you?" Grandpa asked.

"Kind of." I shook my head. "But that wasn't real."

As though sensing my distress, or perhaps the distress that

was yet to come, Jared covered my hand with his. Both my grandparents watched as I laced our fingers together, but they didn't say anything. I did notice a few shaken faces in the crowd, but that couldn't be helped.

"Yes, pix," Grandpa said, "it was very real. What you saw was literally the gates of Hell being opened."

I straightened in my chair, and Jared tightened his grip.

"Someone, and we still don't know who, opened them."

Brooklyn's mother spoke then. "And we believe he had the power to summon demons."

I peeked at Jared, but he refused to meet my eyes, his jaw tight, waiting.

Grandpa nodded. "You saw it. You were six years old, and you saw the gates of Hell being opened. Your mom and dad rushed to where you led them. They tried to stop it, to stop him, but it was too late."

"We believe that by the time they arrived," Grandma continued, "hundreds of dark spirits had been unleashed upon the earth."

I sat stunned as I listened.

"Not demons, mind you," Grandpa said. "There's a difference. But whoever had the power to open the gates also had the power to summon a demon. And he did. He summoned the demon Malak-Tuke by name."

Something quaked inside me at the mention of that name. A name I didn't even recognize. I shook my head, an all-consuming dread spreading into every corner of my mind. "How can you know that?"

Grandpa frowned. "Because you told us."

That was impossible. I didn't remember anything of the sort.

"Why would anyone summon a demon?" Brooklyn asked, the disbelief plain on her face.

After a deep sigh, Grandpa said, "To be taken."

"Taken?" I glanced at Jared, then back to Grandpa. "What does that mean?"

"When someone is possessed by a demon, and that someone knows how to control it through spells and incantations, that person becomes very, very powerful. We believe he was purposely inviting Malak-Tuke, Lucifer's second in command, to possess him."

Brooklyn spoke as though from a dream. "Is that what happened to me?" She focused on Cameron, who clearly knew more than we did. "Jared said I was taken. Was I possessed?"

Brooklyn's mother scooped her hands into her own. "Not by a demon, honey," she said, rushing to reassure her. "You were possessed by a dark spirit."

"It's why we moved here in the first place," her father said. "The Sanctuary knew how to help you when we didn't."

"Oh, my god, I remember," she said, thinking back. "I remember being prayed over and"—her shimmering eyes found Grandpa—"and you freeing me."

A sad smile slid across Grandpa's face as Brooke's parents wrapped her in their arms.

"When you couldn't recall what happened afterwards," her dad said, "we didn't feel the need to tell you, to bring all that up again."

Brooke sobbed into her mom's jacket, then stopped suddenly, as though she'd had an epiphany. She glanced at Cameron and socked him on the arm.

He rubbed it, pretending it hurt, then said with a frown, "What'd I do?"

"That's why my aura's different, isn't it?"

"Her aura?" her mom asked.

Cameron shrugged. "Yeah, but it's not a bad different. It's just a different."

"Do you remember what it was like?" Glitch asked in awe.

She shook her head. "I don't. I can't remember a thing about it other than having bad dreams and being prayed over." She turned to my grandparents. "You saved me."

"No," Grandma said, "your mom and dad saved you. If they hadn't brought you here, you wouldn't have survived much longer. You were barely alive as it was."

"Unlike demons," her dad said, "dark spirits don't have much of an agenda other than causing pain and wreaking havoc."

She hugged them again as I stewed in a numb, soupy kind of silence. Brooke was possessed when she moved here? I couldn't help but wonder if she was saved before or after our throw down.

"We have maps," the sheriff said to Jared. "We think we know where the majority of the dark spirits went. They left quite a trail to follow."

Jared nodded. "I'll need them."

"Wait," I said, putting a stop to the strategic planning committee. "We can prepare for World War Three later. What happened to Mom and Dad?" I gave my grandparents the once-over, trying very hard not to be bitter. Had they known all this time? And they let me believe they'd just disappeared?

"We're not absolutely certain, honey," Betty Jo said when they didn't answer right away.

Was everyone in Riley's Switch in on this? I felt like a complete idiot.

"From what we've been able to piece together," she continued, "your father tried to close the gates while your mother tried to protect you from the dark spirits coming through. And then they were just gone."

"That's when it stopped," Grandma said. "Everything stopped. And as far as we can tell, you haven't had a vision since."

"Are you kidding?" Glitch scoffed. "She has visions all the time."

"What?" Grandma's surprise quickly turned to hope. Her face brightened with it. But she was wrong about me. Everyone was wrong. They had to be.

"I have visions," I admitted, vowing to stab Glitch later, "but they're stupid. They don't make sense."

Grandma and Grandpa smiled at each other. They were going to be so disappointed.

I took in Jared from underneath my lashes. He still had a death grip on my hand, and I knew this wasn't over. I sighed aloud and tried to fill in the blanks. "What about me?" I looked up at Grandpa. "I was taken too, wasn't I?"

His breath hitched, and he hesitated. Then, with his posture wilting, he whispered, "Yes."

My lids slammed shut. I knew it. Deep down inside, I knew I'd been taken just like Brooke, only I didn't remember being prayed over like she'd been. I didn't remember the release of freedom, the purity of being cleansed.

"We tried for a year," Grandma said, her face despondent, forlorn. "We did everything."

"It was like you'd absorbed it," Grandpa said. Then he stabbed me with a look of encouragement. "You were stronger than it, pix. It never controlled you. You always controlled it."

I took a mental inventory of everything I'd learned, including the gates of Hell opening, the impending battle, the possession. But still Jared clung to me, waiting, anticipating.

And then the truth dawned.

I closed my eyes, took a soft breath, then whispered, "It's still in me." When nobody argued, I opened my eyes and let reality sink in. "I'm still possessed."

Every gaze in the room suddenly had somewhere else to be. I stood and placed my free hand over my heart, fear suddenly gripping me to a blinding degree.

"I want it out," I said, losing the fragile hold I had on my sanity. "I want it out, now."

"It's too strong," Jared said, speaking at last, his voice airy with regret. "If we exorcise it now, it will kill you. It will fracture your soul and leave you for dead. If your grandparents had succeeded, you would not be here today. And they probably wouldn't be either."

"But they got one out of Brooke. I don't . . ." Then it hit me. The looks of despair. The air of hopelessness. I focused on what Brooke's mom had said and stared at everyone aghast. "The man who opened the gates of Hell had the power to summon demons." I swallowed hard. "It's a demon. I was possessed by a demon."

Again, no one argued.

I stumbled back, remembering the vision I'd had of Jared, the one in which he'd been fighting a demon. A huge beast with razorlike talons and sharp, shimmering teeth. "The man summoned Lucifer's second in command to be taken by him, but he took me instead."

"I'm so sorry, honey," Grandpa said, his voice cracking with sorrow, "we tried everything."

But I barely heard him. The idea of having something so heinous inside me, so incredibly evil, reminded me of the nightmares I used to have of being covered in bugs. No matter what I did, I couldn't get them all off.

"And now you know all there is to know," Jared said, regret thickening his voice. "You know my trespasses. If you had died, Lorelei, if you had gone to Heaven, you would have been freed. But I brought you back. I broke the law. And now you are the one who has to pay the price."

I stood and tried to leave, suddenly unable to breathe in the cramped, crowded space, but Jared stood as well and placed a hand on the back of my chair, blocking my path.

"I told you she didn't need to know," Cameron said under his breath. "It's not always better knowing the truth."

I placed a hand on Jared's chest. "I just need some air."

"Lorelei," Brooke said, her eyes saucers of shock and fear, "we can figure this out."

Her concern crushed me. What could they do? What could any of them do?

I ducked under Jared's arm. He didn't stop me.

"Wait," Glitch said. "You're not alone, Lor. We're in this together."

I looked back at him. "Not this time." When I got to the door leading to the store, it wouldn't budge. I felt a surge of energy, as though Jared had released it, then slid it open.

"Lorelei," Grandma said, but when I turned back to her, she wilted under my pleading stare. Clearly, she had no healing balm for demon possession.

"Don't just let her go," Glitch said, jumping to his feet. "Why did you release the door?"

"I didn't," I heard Jared say.

With hurt and despair pushing me forward, I strode through the store to the front door. As I shoved it open, I heard Cameron arguing with Jared. "Just let her be alone for a while," he said to him.

For once we were on the same page.

THE DEVIL INSIDE

How could I not know? All this time, all these years, and I knew nothing of supernatural beings, of prophecies and secret meetings going on right under my nose. How could I not know that Brooke had been possessed? That I was still possessed? From what I'd gathered, if a dark spirit possessed someone, it could be exorcised. But if a demon possessed someone, the odds were apparently in its favor. Which sucked.

I'd planned to walk around the store and go into the woods to think, to breathe, but I made it as far as our dirt parking lot when I began replaying the past in my mind. I remembered seeing it, the gate, like a bolt of lightning that had been split down the center, hovering in the afternoon sky while night seeped out of it. Only it wasn't night. The oily thick blackness that leaked into the bright sky was in fact hundreds of dark spirits escaping onto our plane.

I sank to my knees as the memory took hold, as I saw it from my six-year-old eyes. The bright edges of the gate, the rip in the fabric of reality. I didn't know what it was. I remembered being utterly confused by what I was seeing and the look of panic on my parents' faces when I described it. My father, so handsome and strong with his red hair and scraggly stubble. And my mother, so absolutely beautiful. She had long cinnamon hair. I would play with it for hours, brushing it, braiding it.

While Dad would grill his famous hot dogs or whistle a tune as he watered the grass, she would read fairy tales to me. Only they weren't fairy tales. I realized now my parents were preparing me, telling me story after story of the legends that had been passed down for centuries, cultivated through the lineage of the prophet Arabeth. Stories of heroes and champions. And they believed I would join the ranks of such adventurers. As though it were that simple. As though I were capable.

I recoiled inside myself as my parents' last day on earth materialized in my mind. With a burst of light, I saw us by the ruins of the ancient Pueblo missions outside Riley's Switch. My father stood reading from a book as a gale-force wind tossed him to his knees, his strength minuscule in comparison.

"He'll do it, pix," Mom said as she held me tight behind a clump of bushes. "He'll close the gates, don't worry."

But I was completely focused on the dark shadows that darted past us, each one nothing more than a blur before it disappeared over the hills, slithering along the ground like a vaporous snake.

Mom began chanting something, but I didn't understand the words. She closed her eyes, clutching me to her as her hair whipped around her head in a frenzy. Then everything stopped. The wind. The noise. Mom lifted her head and looked back for a split second. An instant later, we ran. She stumbled to her feet, her hold like a vise around my waist, and headed for the car.

She spoke words of encouragement, but I knew they were just as much of a lie as the calm was. I'd looked over her shoulder. I saw what she'd seen. The splinter in the sky was now circular, the clouds around it swirling like an angry tornado. With a loud crack, the wind picked us up and threw us to the side.

Mom lost her footing and we crashed to the ground. But she didn't give up. Crawling on her knees, she fought the windstorm with all her strength. We were almost to the car, her hand straining for the door handle when she stopped. I heard soft gasps as she disentangled my limbs and tried to literally shove me under the car. I remembered the tears staining her cheeks, her hair falling over her face, her eyes wide with uncertainty. The last word she uttered was a mere whisper.

"Hide," she said a microsecond before she was ripped away.

I'd been clutching on to her shirt and was jerked forward with the force. I stumbled and fell, the space where she once stood so completely empty.

The winds howled around me when I crawled to my knees and looked up to search for her. But a beast stood before me instead. A monster as tall as a tree. He studied me, waiting, and my hands curled into fists. My teeth welded together as I fought the sting of my hair whipping into my eyes.

Then the strangest thing happened: He dematerialized. He became fog and I breathed him in, his essence hot and acidic. It burned my throat as I swallowed him, scorched my lungs as I inhaled until he was no longer and we were one.

"No!"

We turned and saw a man running toward us. A most curious sight, we thought.

"No!" he yelled over the wind, skidding to a stop beside us, falling to his knees. "No, I summoned you, dammit! Not her."

He was screaming in our face and we didn't like it. We looked over, found a stick, and decided to stab him. Part of us was surprised at how easily the stick penetrated the material of his shirt and sank into his abdomen. The other part was pleased. The dark spirits no longer rushed past us. If they got close, they would turn suddenly and head in a different direction, like fish in an aquarium. We watched as the gate in the sky closed. We watched as the wind died down and the countryside settled into complacency. We watched as the man staggered away from us, his eyes wide with fear.

And then we lay down and slept.

I covered my face with both hands as the memory faded. I wasn't crying. I'd dug in my heels, set my jaw, and held that girl-ish reaction at bay—and yet my lashes were still saturated, salty tears still ran in rivulets down my cheeks and dripped off my chin as I peeked through my fingers and stared wide-eyed at the gravel beneath my knees.

I sat in stunned stillness. Trying to accept what had happened as reality. Failing. Grasping the edges of reason. Losing my grip. Clawing. Ripping. Sinking.

"The boss wants a word."

A word. I frowned.

"Now."

My line of sight slid down to land on an expensive pair of men's shoes planted a foot apart in front of me. It traveled slowly up dark pants; a light blue shirt, half-tucked; sleeves rolled up to the elbows; and a red tie. The same red tie he wore that night in the forest.

John Dell scowled at me. "I'm sick of this place and I'm sick of you. Get in the van." He pointed to the official Tourist Channel van parked a few feet away, sliding door open, like a mouth waiting to swallow me.

I blinked back to him. "Go to heck," I whispered, my voice breathy and tired. It seemed all I could manage. I felt more drained now than I had when Brooke and I decided to stay up for two days straight. If there were ever a time for an energy drink, now would be it.

Before I could even think about standing up, my head whipped around and a blinding pain exploded in it. I spun and fell to the ground as the world tumbled beneath me. After taking a moment to orient myself, I struggled onto my hands and knees, then watched in awe as blood dripped from my head onto the powdery earth below.

And quite frankly, I'd had just about enough of it.

I crawled onto one knee and turned on him. Slipping into my best glower, I lowered my voice, controlled the tone and inflection of every word, every syllable, striving to make myself sound menacing, as I had only days earlier with Glitch. "Do you have any idea what I'm capable of?"

His eyes widened a fraction of an inch before he caught himself and narrowed them on me in suspicion. "Besides painting your nails?"

He'd hit me with the butt of a knife he had wrapped within his meaty grasp. The knife looked old. Ceremonial. Which couldn't be good.

"Please," I scoffed. "Why do you think the boss wants me? Wait, he didn't tell you, did he?" When the man hesitated, I continued. "How do you think I survived a two-ton truck slamming into me, you idiot?" I started to stand, but the world tilted to the left, so I stayed put and continued the menacing bit. This could actually work if one of two things proved true: I had some really cool superpower I'd never known about or John Dell had an unnatural fear of short pixie chicks with unruly hair.

"Oh, my god," I heard a feminine voice say. It was accompanied by the rhythmic click of heels coming from the sidewalk in front of the store. "Did you fall again?"

No way. Surely the creature whose name shall not be spoken aloud had better things to do on a Friday night than watch me bleed into the dirt.

"Do you even know how to walk?"

I looked past Mr. McCreepy, slammed my eyes shut to stop the spin of the earth, then focused on one of the dumbest people I'd ever known. The guy had a knife, for heaven's sake.

"I'm looking for my parents. Oh, wait, aren't you that reporter?" She flipped a strand of long blond hair over her shoulder and flashed him her twenty-dollar smile. "You know, I've done some acting."

"Tabitha, wait," I muttered, trying to shut her up. Partly to save her and partly because the high-pitched whine in her voice was making my head throb even worse.

Too late. Mr. McCreepy pulled her in front of him and put the knife to her throat. From this angle, her head was so freaking big.

"Oh, my gosh," she said.

"Get in the van," he repeated.

"O-okay."

"Not you," he said to Tabitha, annoyed, then fixed a warning glower on me. "Now."

With the world tossing me to and fro, I felt absolutely useless. And I was pretty certain by that point I did not, in fact, have a latent superpower. Surely, he wouldn't actually hurt her. I couldn't give up my advantage now. I almost had him convinced I was nigh indestructible.

With a smirk, I decided to call his bluff. "Go ahead, kill her."

Before I even had time to blink, the knife sliced across her throat. I looked on in disbelief as blood cascaded out of her neck and down her chest to saturate the pretty white blouse she wore. She grabbed her throat with both hands, her eyes wide with shock as the most disturbing gurgling sound bubbled out of her. Dell let go. She slid down his body to land before me, the blood coursing through her fingers unheeded.

I closed my eyes, blocking out the scene, the gush of dark red. When I reopened them, we were . . . back.

"Now," Dell said as he held Tabitha against him, the knife at her throat, anger apparent in his volatile expression.

I jumped in surprise, looked around, then swayed a little with the movement. We were back. How on earth? Maybe I really was a prophet. I'd just seen the future, and it did not look good for Tabi. Which was too bad, really.

No, I thought, my hopes dwindling. I couldn't let him kill her. I would probably feel guilty about it later. I looked up at him and suggested an alternative: "You're right. We could get in the van, or we could just wait a minute."

He tightened his hold. "Wait? For what?"

"For him."

I pointed past him as Jared stepped up, and again before I could even blink, he'd grasped the man's head between his two large hands and twisted, breaking the man's neck. I gasped as a sharp crack echoed against the building. Dell's head sat contorted in an unnatural angle, his stare empty as he crumpled to the ground, and it was exactly what I'd seen in the forest. Every movement. Every sound. Jared hadn't killed him then. I'd merely seen the man's future, probably when he tried to grab me and I shoved his hand away. I saw the agony of his last seconds on earth.

Tabitha stumbled to the side as everyone ran out of the store toward us. She caught herself—which, in those heels, was impressive—and flew into Jared's arms. "You saved me!"

Oh, for heaven's sake. I was possessed, my head was pounding, and now I had to watch my archnemesis slobber all over my man? Brooke and Glitch got to me first, Glitch literally sliding across the dirt lot to my side. "Are you okay?"

Before I could answer, I heard a woman's scream.

"Tabitha!"

Tabitha's mom came running out of the store, her face frozen in shock. But not for the reason I'd thought. She and Tabitha's dad pulled her off Jared. "Your Grace," she said, bowing her head repeatedly in reverence, "we're so sorry. She doesn't know."

Jared disentangled himself from her and, ignoring them, kneeled beside me.

"Mom, that man had a knife to my throat."

"Tabitha, you can't just grab people like that," her mother scolded as the sheriff checked Dell for a pulse.

"Mom! Are you even listening? Wait, did you call him Your Grace?" She glanced back at Jared, and I could almost see cartoon hearts bursting out of her eyes. "He's royalty?"

"Lorelei," Jared said, and without waiting for a response, he scooped me into his arms and lifted me off the ground. I caught a glimpse of Grandma and Grandpa as they hovered around us, Grandma's hands plastered over her mouth and Grandpa's brows kneading in worry. But I felt safe, so utterly and completely safe, that I let the tilting and the swirling stop, nestled farther into Jared's hold, and tumbled into oblivion.

"No."

"But, Jared—"

"No," he said again, refusing even to consider what I'd asked.

With a sigh, I turned to my grandparents, who were standing on the other side of the hospital bed. "Grandpa, make him listen."

He worked his jaw in discomfort. "I'm not sure that's a good idea. Prince Azrael is right." He and Grandma had yet to take to Jared. They tensed every time he got near me, cringed every time he touched me. And when he wasn't looking, I caught a glint of fear in their eyes. It saddened me. But, ever the hopeful soldier, I ignored their misgivings and hoped Jared would grow on them.

In Jared's defense, he kept a reverent distance from me in their presence. "We don't really call ourselves princes," he said.

"Oh," Grandma said, her voice tinged with uncertainty. "I just thought Archangels were considered the princes of Heaven."

"True, but we're not actually *called* the princes of Heaven."

"Are you called jerks?"

Brooklyn backhanded Cameron on the shoulder as Jared said simply, "No."

"Maybe not to your face," Glitch said. "So, what does it feel like?"

He'd been asking me the same question all morning. Over and over. Kind of like what I'd been doing to Jared.

"Glitch," Brooklyn said from atop her perch on the end of the bed, "if you ask her that one more time, I will stab you in the head."

"No, you won't." He turned back to me. "But really, what's it feel like?"

He wanted to know what it felt like to be possessed. To have a demon living inside me. "I don't know, Glitch. I don't feel any different today than I did yesterday, except for the fact that now I know. Please, Jared."

"No." He said it with the same inflection, the same gentle tone he'd been using since I started the conversation. Apparently, he was not as easily swayed by my obnoxious repetitive behavior as my grandparents were.

"But it's not in you. It's in me. And I trust you completely."

"Lorelei McAlister," he said, his voice soft with understanding, "we can't risk your life by trying to exorcise it. Like I said before, you've somehow absorbed it. It's there, but it's lying dormant. I've never seen anything like this. Most humans don't live a month with a demon inside them."

Wonderful. "Brooke got to be exorcised." I crossed my arms and stuck out my tongue at her. "She gets to have all the fun."

She laughed with me and tickled the bottom of my foot through the blankets.

"The reaper's right," Cameron said. He was standing at the foot of the bed, hood up, hands stuffed into pockets. I had a feeling Brooklyn had dragged him there, and Glitch seemed none too happy about it, if the parade of glares he continually cast Cameron's way were any indication. "It would fracture your soul. Even if you survived, you would never be the same again."

Brooke turned back to him. "My soul isn't fractured, and Lorelei's strong. I think she could handle it." She winked in support.

Cameron hunched his shoulders and lowered his head. "Actually, it is."

"What?" She raised her brows in question.

My grandparents looked at him askance as well. For all of their knowledge, even they couldn't see what Cameron could.

After taking a draught again, he said, "Your soul. It's fractured."

She scooted around to him. "What do you mean?"

"That's why it's so different. So amazing."

"Amazing how?" she asked, her suspicion growing.

He offered a one-shouldered shrug. "I don't know. I've just never seen anything like it. It's broken. There's a crack down the middle and while the aura all around you is normal, a light projects out of the fissure, so bright that when you stand just right, you're blinding."

"So," Glitch said, his head bowed in thought, "you've been checking out her crack?"

After a tense moment of silence, we burst out laughing. Well, most of us. Apparently Glitch wasn't trying to be funny. He glared at Cameron accusingly. Naturally, Cameron glared back. Someday I would find out what had happened between the two of them, but for now, the uneasy truce between the two supernatural beings in the room was enough to tide me over.

Grandma had filled me in on the events since last night. Apparently, Jared was being hailed as the town hero after saving Tabitha's life and thwarting an attempted kidnapping. She told me that, in fact, most of the townspeople did not know about the Sanctuary or the ancient society, which made sense because my grandfather never mentioned it in his sermons. It really was a secret, made up of believers from all over the world, about fifty of whom lived in Riley's Switch.

My grandparents already had men fixing up the apartment behind the house for Jared, and I could tell they were getting used to his presence. My grandmother wasn't nearly so jittery, and she'd even joked with him a couple of times. But she still insisted on calling him Your Grace.

So all this was going on while I lay waiting to be discharged from our urgent-care facility after staying all night for observation. I'd suffered a concussion at the hands of Mr. McCreepy. I almost felt bad that he'd died, but Jared said his soul no longer belonged to him anyway. He'd sold it long ago. The sheriff's report confirmed everything, and I was beginning to see the bright side of having him in our secret club. The fact that he was in on the whole thing, even in Mr. Davis's office that day, freaked me out. The guy could act.

Mr. Davis, on the other hand, was going to be a problem. He

had not been shown the secret handshake and was apparently growing more suspicious by the moment. We would have to walk on eggshells around him for a while.

I sobered and asked Jared the other thing that I couldn't let go of: "Do you know what happened to my parents?"

He shook his head. "I'm sorry."

"That's okay." I couldn't help but be disappointed.

With a knowing smile, he added, "But I do know that if your parents were pulled into the lower dimension, Lorelei, if that's what happened, even the gates of Hell cannot hold the righteous. They would not be there still. There are rules, remember?"

I took a deep breath, determination guiding me. "That may be true, but I have to know, Jared. I have to find them." A quick glance toward my grandparents revealed the emergence of hope in their eyes. They were thinking the same thing. Surely, with the help of an archangel, we could find my parents, their daughter and son-in-law.

After placing a hand on his forearm, I asked, "Will you help me find them?"

He lowered his head. "I will do everything I can, everything in my power, but I can't make any promises."

"No, that's okay. I understand." I couldn't help the zing of excitement that rushed down my spine. We had a chance, and it was more than we had yesterday.

But Jared's expression turned grave. "Now that you know what I've done, perhaps my aid will allow you a small amount of generosity. It's still early, but someday I will ask if you can forgive me my trespasses."

I rolled onto my side, astonished that he would even say such a thing. "How can I forgive you when you haven't done anything wrong?"

"Lorelei," he said, releasing a slow, controlled breath, "I have kept you a prisoner on this plane. When you realize that, when that time comes, I will ask again."

"I'm pretty grateful for that part as well," Grandpa said, relaxing his guard just a little. He took Grandma's hand into his own. "Maybe where you come from what you did was wrong, but around these parts, we call that a miracle."

I couldn't have agreed more.

"So what now?" Brooklyn asked.

What now, indeed. I knew one thing for certain: I would never give up on my parents. They had risked everything trying to protect me, to protect the world. I would find them, no matter what it took.

"That woman in our dreams," Glitch said, "she said you now had a mission. Is it to find the dark spirits? Is that what this is about?"

"That is a good place to start," Jared said.

Cameron nodded in agreement. "And we need to find the man who opened the gates in the first place. If he has the power to summon demons, there's no telling what else he's capable of. Or what he's done in the last ten years."

"Do you think that's who's after Lorelei?" Grandma asked. "The man that reporter referred to as his boss?"

"It's possible," Jared said.

"Well, that's disturbing on a thousand different levels," Brooke said.

Once again, I couldn't have agreed more, only I'd lost myself in the dark depths of Jared's eyes. I tended to do that when he looked at me. Or when he looked at anything near me. Or pretty much whenever his eyes were open. He'd shaved, but a shadow darkened his jaw nonetheless. His mussed hair fell over his brow, the tips getting caught in his ridiculously long lashes when he blinked. His sculpted mouth was the most delicious thing I'd ever seen, and I wanted so very much to kiss it. But that would've been a tad rude with Grandma and Grandpa right there. Especially considering their distrust of him.

"I've been thinking," Brooklyn said as I gawked at the god sitting next to me, "if you two get all lovey-dovey and decide to elope to Las Vegas where Jared uses his powers to clean up at the poker tables and you guys buy a mansion in the Manzano Mountains with twenty-seven rooms and decide—because you're rich and all—to buy a new computer, can I have your iMac then?"

"Brooke," I said, cringing as Grandpa cleared his throat and suddenly had a window to inspect. Not Grandma, though. She didn't budge an inch, her gaze unblinking as she waited for my answer. "Um, no, you're not getting my iMac."

"Dang."

"iPrecious stays with me. I have to write all this stuff down. I *am* a prophet, after all. I think that's what prophets do."

Jared grinned. "Are you sure you're okay?"

I let my eyes drift shut and stilled the thoughts swirling in my head. The truck hitting me. Jared saving me. The fights, the ancient society, the visions. I pushed it all away and focused on the warmth of Jared as he sat beside me. With one final thought trying to surface—the demon inside—I forced it down with a hard swallow and whispered, "We're fine."

Turn the page for a sneak peek at the sequel

to *Death and the Girl Next Door*

death, doom, and detention

Coming March 2013

DORMANT

"This class is never going to end."

My best friend, Brooklyn, draped her upper body across her desk in a dramatic reenactment of Desdemona's death in *Othello*. She buried her face in a tangle of arms and long, black hair for effect. It was quite moving. And while I appreciated her freedom to express her misgivings about the most boring class since multicelled organisms first crawled onto dry land, I wondered about her timing.

"*Miss* Prather," our government teacher, Mr. Gonzales, said, his voice like a sharp crack of thunder in the silence of study time. "Is there something you'd like to share with the class?"

Brooklyn jerked upright in surprise. She glanced around, her eyes wide as our classmates snickered, either politely into their hands or, more rudely, outright.

She blinked toward Mr. Gonzales and asked, "Did I say that out loud?"

The class erupted with laughter as Mr. G's mouth formed a long narrow line across his face. Miraculously, the bell rang, and Brooklyn couldn't scramble out of her seat fast enough. She practically sprinted from the room. I followed at a slower pace, smiling meekly as I walked past Mr. G's desk.

Brooklyn stood waiting for me in the hall, her face still frozen in surprise.

"That was funny," I said, tugging her alongside me. She fell in line as we wound through the crush of students, fighting our way to P.E. I wasn't sure why. I didn't particularly enjoy having my many faults and numerous shortcomings put on display for all to see, so why I would fight to get there was beyond me.

"No, really." She tucked an arm through mine. "I didn't mean to say that out loud."

I couldn't help but laugh despite the weight on my chest. "Which is why that was funny." I hadn't felt good all day and was praying for some bizarre yet harmless disaster to close the school down early. Like a butterfly infestation.

"You don't get it," she said. "This is exactly what I've been talking about. Everything is weird all of a sudden. People are acting strange and the world has dark, fuzzy edges."

Before I could suggest a visit to the school nurse, an arm snaked around my neck from behind and I felt something poke my temple. A quick sideways glance told me it was a hand shaped to resemble a gun. "Give me all your money," Glitch said through gritted teeth.

I shook him off and grinned at him from over my shoulder. "Brooke feels fuzzy."

He bounced around until he was facing us, walking backward with his backpack slung over his shoulder, his brows drawn in concern. "Fuzzy? Really?"

"I didn't say I *felt* fuzzy. I said the world has fuzzy edges."

He looked around to test her theory then back to us before shrugging. How he managed to walk backward in this crowd was kind of awe-inspiring. If I'd tried that, I would soon resemble a pancake covered with lots of footprints.

Glitch, a connoisseur of computers, skipping and coasting through school with less than stellar grades, was best friend number two. We'd grown up together. He was half Native American and half Irish American and had the dark skin and green eyes to prove it.

He shook his head. "I don't think it's so much fuzzy as nauseatingly yellow, a color that is supposed to calm us, I'm sure. But did you hear?" he asked, suddenly excited. "Joss Duffy and Cruz de los Santos got in a fight during third."

Brooklyn pulled me to a stop, her expression animated. "What did I tell you? Joss and Cruz are best friends. Everything is turned upside down."

As much as I hated to admit it, she was right. I'd felt it too. A quake. A disturbance in the atmosphere. Everyone seemed to have a short fuse lately. The slightest infraction seemed to set people off. We'd been warned about an impending war. Was this how it would begin?

With a sigh, I started for P.E. again. Maybe we were reading too much into it. Or maybe the moon was full. People did crazy things when the moon was full. I didn't want everything to be turned upside down. I'd had enough of upside down when my parents disappeared ten years ago. When I was hit by a truck a couple of months back and almost died. And worse, when I was possessed by Satan's second in command.

Some days I was almost okay with the fact that, when I was

six years old, a demon slipped inside my body, nestled between my ribs, curled around my spine. Other days that fact caused me no small amount of distress. On those days I walked with head down and eyes hooded as my vertebrae fused in the heat of uncertainty and my bones writhed in sour revulsion.

Today was one of those days.

I'd awoken in a panic to the sensation of being crushed, unable to escape an invisible force, unable to breathe. The remnants of the nightmare still ricocheted against the walls of my mind, squeezing my lungs until air became a precious but fleeting commodity. Which could explain the panic attack.

And the dream was always the same. In it, I would float back to that day so long ago and inhale the beast all over again, his taste acidic, his flesh choking and abrasive. Since I was only six at the time, one would think it was a small demon, possibly a minion, a lower-level employee. Like a janitor. But I'd seen him that day. How his shoulders, as black as a starless sky, spanned the horizon. How his head reached the tops of the trees. Small was not an accurate description.

And now, thanks to my need to regenerate, I could relive that memory over and over. Yay, me. On the bright side, I'd ditched that other recurring dream I'd been having since I was five. The one where bugs scurried under my sheets and up my legs. That thing was messed up.

Still, if not for upside down, Jared would never have come to Riley's Switch. We may only be a tiny speck on the map of New Mexico, hidden among juniper trees and sage bushes in the middle of nowhere, but we were important enough to warrant a guardianship in the form of the Angel of Death. That was something.

"And Cameron has been acting strange, too," Brooke continued, mentioning the fifth member of our posse, as Glitch called our group of misfits. But I hadn't seen him in a couple of days, which was odd.

"That's because Cameron has a crush on you," I said without thinking. I cringed when Glitch turned away.

"No, seriously," she said, oblivious. "He keeps asking if I'm okay. If you're okay. If Glitch is okay."

Glitch whirled back around and glared, but Brooke missed it once again.

"We need to practice," she said, pulling a compact mirror out of her backpack. "Try again, only harder."

She handed it to me as Glitch glowered at her, suddenly in a sour mood. "Really? Here?"

"Yes, really, here. She has to be ready."

Along with all the other magnificent oddities in my life, I'd apparently been born some kind of prophet. I had visions. Or, well, normally I had visions. I hadn't had one in weeks, and Brooklyn was convinced I just needed to practice. She'd read that a shiny surface helped psychics see into the future or the past, hence crystal balls. But according to her research, mirrors worked just as well. Hence her compact.

"I have to get to History," Glitch said, his shoulders tense. "Mr. Burke threatened to skin me alive if I'm tardy again, though I don't think he actually has the authority to do that."

"Later," I said, opening the compact. That boy had issues of late.

As we exited the main building and headed for the gym, I looked down into the mirror. Brooke dragged me along so I wouldn't stumble. I concentrated as best I could, trying not to focus on the fact that my gray eyes seemed darker than usual and my auburn hair seemed curlier. Curlier! I leaned in for a closer look. Oh, the gods were a cruel and humorless lot. Because that's what I needed. More curls.

"Does my hair seem curlier to you?"

"Curlier than an ironing board, yes. Curlier than a French poodle, no. Now concentrate."

Concentrate. Fine. But even at their height, my prophetic visions weren't terribly useful. And I normally had to be touching someone to have them. I had to either be touching the person I was prophesying about or had to have touched him at some point in the recent past.

But Brooke was bound and determined to expand my skills, to widen my periphery so I could have visions on the fly. So far, our attempts had yielded exactly squat. Unless I was touching said fly, nothing happened.

Kind of like now.

After a solid twelve seconds, I gave up. "You know, it would help if I knew what to concentrate on."

Brooke patted my arm absently, staring into her phone. "Concentrate on concentrating."

For the love of Starbucks, what the heck did that mean?

I lifted the mirror again. Shook it a little to make sure it was working. Held it at arm's length. Squinted. Just as I was about to give up entirely, a vision, dark and alluring, materialized behind me. I sucked in a soft breath at the sight, even though, admittedly, there was nothing prophetic about it. Wearing the sexiest grin I'd ever seen, Riley's Switch's own supernatural being in the form of Mr. Jared Kovach walked up behind me.

I stopped and turned. He was wearing his requisite jeans that fit low on his hips and a gray T-shirt with a brown bomber jacket thrown over his shoulder. The cloudy day had splashed color across the sky behind him. A hint of orange, pink, and purple served as a backdrop to his powerful set of his shoulders, the lean hills and valleys of his arms. Somehow I didn't think that a coincidence.

I tried to subdue the jolt my heart I received every time I looked at him. The wind molded the T-shirt to the expanse of his chest, revealing the fact that he was cut to simple perfection. And he had this way of moving, this animal grace, that could mesmerize even the stoutest of minds.

"How was your last class?" he asked, stopping in front of me. His voice, deep and smooth like butterscotch, caused a fluttering in my chest, a rush of heat to my face. How could any being, supernatural or otherwise, be so perfect?

"Pretty boring," I said, clearing my throat to recover. "But it did have an interesting twist at the end." I grinned at Brooklyn.

"That's good," he said.

I nodded and glanced at his arms. The bands of symbols that lined his biceps were visible beneath the edges of his sleeves. The designs were ancient and meaningful, symbols that stated his name, rank, and serial number in a celestial language. Or that was my impression. I loved looking at them. Thick dark lines that twisted into curves and angles. A single line of them wrapping around each arm. They looked like Native American pictography combined with something alien, something otherworldly.

"Not good," Brooklyn said, tapping on her phone. "It was awful. I'll meet you in P.E. Keep practicing."

She wandered off, still gazing at her phone, as Jared asked, "Practicing?"

I snapped the compact closed and stuffed it into a pocket. "The whole vision thing. Brooke swears I just need to practice."

"Ah." The humor in his liquid brown eyes was infectious.

Jared had come to Riley's Switch a couple of months ago to do a job. That job was to pop in, take me a few minutes before I was slated to die anyway, then pop back out again. But he'd disobeyed his orders. He'd saved me instead, thus breaking one of the three rules that celestial beings are bound by. Even the powerful Angel of Death. As a result, he was stuck on Earth. Stuck helping me. According to prophecy, I was supposed to stop an impending war between humans and demons before it ever started, but how I was supposed to manage that, nobody knew. Least of all me.

I pointed over my shoulder and started to turn. "I guess I'll get to class now."

He nodded and looked into the forest behind the school. "Are you okay?"

"Me?" I stopped, surprised. "I'm great." When he looked back at me, his eyes full of doubt, I said, "Well, I'm better than I was a minute ago."

One corner of his full mouth lifted in a delicious smile that melted my knees. "So am I."

A person would have to be blind not to notice all the attention Jared drew every time he made an appearance. And I couldn't help but notice that when he bent to kiss my cheek, more than one girl at Riley High stopped dead in her tracks.

He put his fingers under my chin and lifted my face to his. "I'll be close."

Ever since Jared had arrived in Riley's Switch, he'd been kind of undercover as a student. Partly because we didn't really know what else to do with him without drawing unwanted attention, but mostly because he wanted to stay close to me, to keep me safe. I liked to pretend it was because he liked me, but I had a sneaking suspicion it was more because of my status as a supposed war stopper. I tried not to think about that part of the prophecy that had been handed down for centuries. My stomach clenched painfully every time I did.

So instead, I focused on the dark brown depths of Jared's eyes, shimmering beneath his thick black lashes.

Oh, yeah. That felt better.

Sadly, P.E. was going to require effort. We were ordered to run the Path, which was a footpath in the forest behind the gym. Fun for some, life-threatening for others. I was about as coordinated and sure-footed as spaghetti. This was not going to end well.

"How are you supposed to practice if we keep having to work in all of our classes?" Brooklyn asked as we jogged along the forest track, dodging tree branches and navigating the occasional rut. We'd had a dry winter and leaves crunched under our feet.

"It's crazy, right?" I said, teasing, my huffing breaths only slightly wheezy. "To expect such a thing from an establishment of learning." I checked the pocket in my hoodie to make sure I'd remembered my inhaler. Nothing screamed *unattractive* like a face bluing from lack of oxygen.

"Exactly."

I had a feeling Brooklyn reveled in my prophetic status. She talked about it all the time and urged me to practice. To concentrate. To concentrate harder, darn it. Of course, she'd seen almost as much as I had when Jared came to town. She now knew there were things that went bump in the night. They were real and they were scary and they'd almost gotten us killed, so I couldn't really blame her obsession. Though I could complain about it every single chance I got.

As Brooke went on about her new plan of action, one that would surely strengthen my visions, I saw a dark shadow dart past to my right. I stopped and a girl behind us slammed into me.

"Watch it, McAlister," she said, pushing past me. I stumbled and caught myself against a tree trunk.

Brooke jumped to my defense, squaring her shoulders and jamming her hands onto her hips. "You watch it, Tabitha."

"Please," she said as three other girls ran past. "Like you could take me on your best day."

Tabitha, also known as head cheerleader and my archenemy, just happened to be about seven feet tall to Brooke's five. She smirked at us before continuing her trek through the forest, her blond head bobbing through the trees.

Brooke offered a hand for me to steady myself as I brushed leaves off my shorts. "How rude."

"When is she not rude?" It was a sad twist of fate that Tabitha had P.E. with me, the person she most despised and most loved to harass. "But I did stop in the middle of the path."

"Why? Did you have a vision?" she asked hopefully.

"Kind of. I saw something."

When I pointed deeper into the forest, we both leaned forward and squinted for a better look. Two girls walked past, clearly having given up on the whole jogging thing. I could hardly blame them.

"Well," Brooke said, "I don't see anything, but the way this day has been going, maybe we should get back to the gym, just to be safe."

But I had seen something. An outline. A shape that resembled a head peering from behind a tree about thirty yards away. I stepped closer as something farther down the tree trunk moved. I focused as a ray of light glinted off a silver blade.

I froze.

"Don't you think?" Brooke asked.

I eased my hand around her arm and stepped back onto the path. She caught on instantly and looked into the forest again.

In a hushed whisper, she said, "I still don't see anything."

"I do." When the shape emerged from behind the tree, hunched down like it was going to attack, Brooke gasped, finally seeing it. I squeezed her arm tighter and whispered, "Run."